Future Remnants

Stories & Poems

BENJAMIN L. OWEN

This book is a work of fiction. Names, characters, places, and incidents are either the product of the author's imagination or are used fictitiously. Any resemblance to actual events, locales, or persons, living or dead, is coincidental.

Cover art: "Watching the World Burn" by Milan Jiram

Page 62: Rendition of a sculpture by James Corbett

Page 137: "Meditation" by Herman Hartwitch, 1885

Paperback format, updated 5/5/2022

ASIN: 1520960875

ISBN: 978-1520960876

To
My Friends

Contents

Contents...

And so it seems our destiny
to search and never rest
to ride that ever-changing wave
that never seems to crest

- Bob Seger, "No Man's Land"

Some Good Parts

Name: Phillip Gilmore
Address: 741 Helts Point Ave., Apt. 3, Bronx, NYC
Explain your decision in detail: *Include, by name, all others involved, and if you've felt pressured by them. This will be reviewed by a counselor before the procedure.*

I'm Phillip Gilmore. My decision to Exit started in a South Bronx bar last summer.

Everyone knows there's lots of action in the South Bronx: criminals, prostitutes, drugs, violence, insanity—all fueled by generations of ignorance and poverty.

And no one really cares.

Rikers Island prison is right offshore. I've never been there even though I've done a lot of evil things. Sometimes I almost wished they would've caught me. Some parts of me wanted to stop killing. But most of me didn't.

I'm blessed. God's let me murder a lot of people for some reason. He's got karma cocked and loaded, finger on the hair-trigger, all of us in his crosshairs—but I've never even been taken in for questioning. He's left me alone, so I think my killings fit into his big eternal plan. Like most smart guys who have everything, God seems completely detached from all the pain and suffering in the world, and that's worked out well for me.

I killed for the American government when I was in Special Forces. I killed for the Manhattan Sicilians after I got kicked out of the SF. Same resume, same skill set: kill and shut up. When I was eighteen, the recruiter said the Army would take care of me, but he was wrong. The SF tossed me when I had a nervous breakdown after an airstrike. Since then, I can't stop remembering little kid parts lying in the dirt: little kid arms, little kid legs, little kid heads. Sometimes drinking a lot helps. Booze makes the parts blurry.

The Mob's better than the government. Politicians are impatient, and we'd incinerate a whole village to assassinate one guy. We'd slaughter a few dozen innocent foreigners, the clerks did some paperwork, and we moved on to the next mission. But the Mob's selective; no kids ever is a rule, and sometimes I kill people who maybe deserve it.

Where I live, the South Bronx, is also home to the biggest wholesale markets in the world for perishables. It's amazing. The world's largest produce market, meat market, organ market, seafood market—hell, even the world's largest flower market—are all here. It's the hub of the largest distribution network in the world.

The South Bronx is a great place for corporations to get rich, but it's not so great living here. There's always a delightful new horror story. A few months ago, for example, a bunch of Dominican kids were caught on security video outside a convenience store, chopping up a fifteen-year-old Puerto Rican kid with machetes.

It turned out the sidewalk dissection was an unfortunate case of mistaken identity—the Dominicans thought the Puerto Rican was somebody else. It was a random encounter that ended up with the wrong kid macheted into parts and a bunch of stupid Dominican kids in prison forever.

Unlike politicians, South Bronx teenagers get life in Rikers for killing innocent people.

Anyhow, there's this bar. It's on the cross street near my one-room apartment and I've gone there almost five years now. They pour cold draft Guinness into tall, curved glasses, and sometimes I'm not the only white guy there, so I don't feel too out of place. I'm there almost every day—sitting at the bar, eavesdropping, ordering shots of whiskey to chase down the beer. When I'm there, I pretend I'm not alone.

One day, this thirty-something guy sat at the bar, and after his third or so drink, he started talking at me. He said, "My new job, everything's third shift. I don't even know for sure I hate it 'cause every night seems like a dream, ya know? I'm workin' the hours I've slept since I was a baby. I get in there by eleven at night, set up and prep, the market opens at one in the morning. And it's cold; the whole place is thirty-some degrees."

"Why so cold?"

"It's the organ market. We gotta keep everything cold 'cause it's all perishable. All the body parts come in at midnight on refrigerated trucks. More different parts than you could imagine, goin' everywhere—hospitals, clinics, and labs all over the world."

"It's all from the Exit Program?"

"That, and now the farms."

"Right. I heard they started growing organs at sea?"

"Yeah, a lot of it's starting to be farmed. More and more is comin' that way. It's the wave of the future. In a few years, there won't be no Exit

Program. Sort of like, imagine a fish farm. The genetic engineering companies set up floating pens in the ocean and grow it all there. Heart farms, liver farms, eyeball farms. They harvest and ship it to our refrigerated market that's longer than five football fields."

"You just started there?"

"Yep. It's run by a cooperative, which the old-timers joke is another word for the Mob. Wops with gold chains and Maseratis are in charge. It's like the stock market except we're tradin' hearts and livers and stuff. Buyers crowd the floor and everyone's makin' deals: Chinese, Russians, Saudis, Japs, Koreans, Indians. The Asians are everywhere 'cause they got tons of demand and they all smoke like chimneys nonstop, even though there's 'No Smoking' signs everywhere. Private brokers and buyers from hospitals all over the world are there. Everyone's walkin' aroun' with tablets, watchin' prices on the screens, inspectin' merchandise."

"How do buyers know they're getting good stuff? What if you buy somethin' and it's no good?"

"You don't know you're gettin' good parts unless you're smart enough to know you're gettin' good parts. Don't trust the sellers, that's for sure. They'd rip off their moms for a nickel. Screwin' buyers is a sport. Happens every night. Buyers pay too much for a kidney that got warm on the trip. Or they think they're gettin' a great deal on a liver and find out it's got cirrhosis.

"The pros got trained eyes. A lot of 'em used to work in the fish business. I guess it carries over. You got to know what a healthy heart looks like— lungs, tendons. The pros got lots of experience in their heads. They gotta find good product and negotiate, with prices changing every minute based on what's there. If two trucks of livers come in, they're going for a lot cheaper than kidneys if there's just a half-pallet of them, you follow?"

"So, you like the job? Or you gonna find somethin' else?"

"The problem is, I been findin' somethin' else for over ten years. I gotta settle down at some point, you know? I can't keep lookin' for the perfect thing. I gotta settle into somethin' 'cause there ain't nothin' perfect. If I stick with this, after a while I get sponsored for union membership, and then I get the card, the benefits, paid vacation, and it's like a real job. A career. That word *career* always sounded fake to me, like a sellout word. A career. But I'm ready for the things I get with selling out—a home, a wife, and kids, a place where I'm supposed to be. I'm ready for someone to depend on me. I want to settle down and do somethin' that ain't fly-by-night."

"Do you have a girl?"

"No. There's this Italian girl at the Donofrio Brothers stall, but I can't get her to even look at me. She's in the warming booth tallying up buyers' chits. I got a mammoth crush on her and can't stop thinking about her eyes. I've gotta get her to go out with me. I gotta."

"Take her some flowers."

3

"Are you outta your mind? I ain't even said hi to her yet! She'll think I'm trying to kill her or somethin'. I need to say hi to her first. My God, imagine the ball-breakin' I'll get if I bring flowers to the warming booth girl."

"You got the job. Now you just need the girl."

"Exactly. I'm sayin' hi to her tonight."

"Talk's cheap," I teased him.

"You'll see."

"I could never do the Exit Program," I said. "No way."

"It won't be around much longer anyway, my friend. The organ farming is changing everything. In a few years, we won't have the Exit Program because they can grow it all. Everyone's talking about it; the prices are flattening out big-time."

"You think the Exit Program could end?"

"It's a matter of time. Two years, maybe five? But it'll end."

"I hope it ends," the eavesdropping bartender chimed in. "All these poor people are Exiting to get money for their families. A lot of my good friends did it, and I really miss them."

"The Supreme Court said people have the constitutional right," the guy replied. "Ain't you pro-choice?"

"It isn't the best thing, people selling themselves."

"Well, they make certain no one does it who doesn't want to. And it helps the rich people who need a transplant. It's win-win."

That night, I dreamed about the guy from the bar. I went to his house and met his beautiful Italian wife and his kids. "Your flowers worked perfect," he told me, laughing.

His wife made spaghetti and bread, and we drank red wine. The kids went to bed, and we talked. I told them I was ready to settle down too. I was ready to sell out and stop doing horrible things. His wife took my hand, looked into my eyes, and was quiet for a long time.

"You're a good person, deep inside," she said. "You're going to do something good someday."

I woke up crying, and I'd never cried before. Parts of me felt different inside.

The next day, instead of going to the bar, I went to the Exit Program office in Manhattan.

"You're young, common blood type, and relatively healthy. If you go today, we'll give you three hundred grand. If you get our app and go on a ninety-day regimen of eating healthy, no drinking, exercising, you'll easily get five hundred."

"Can I get that upfront?"

"No. It's paid afterward to your beneficiary. We give them the paperwork so they can file their claim after you leave. Standard procedure."

I did the regimen. I feel better than I ever have in my life—I've lost thirty pounds, I'm clearheaded. A couple times, I've reconsidered. But I've never done anything good. And I can't stop thinking about the Italian girl holding my hand and all the people I've killed. Some of them didn't deserve to die, but I kept on killing. There are broken parts in me that I can't fix.

I went to the Franciscan Monastery on 156th Street. I met with the head monk there, and he tried hard to talk me out of it. He said they couldn't accept my claim because they don't believe in the Exit Program. But I told him I'm leaving, and if he didn't take the claim, I'd give it to some dancer at Club W, so it'd be better if it went to them. The monks help people with a food kitchen and a homeless shelter. I left the papers on his desk.

So now I'm here at the Exit Station. I'm at a desk, writing down how I made my decision for the file.

I see the bed there, waiting for me. I'll lie down and they'll put me to sleep forever before I go into the carving room. They'll go to work, cutting me into parts that will go into the market tonight, sold to the highest bidder and shipped off to help rich people. And those monks will get some money to help poor people out.

For the first time ever, I'm doing something good.

American Hope

mcdonalds then factory
with a nap in between
where you dream about work
and wake up late to get back there

the scanner stopped working
the cryovac machine is down
something that brings
all to a halt

it's the halts when you truly rest
own your own thoughts for five minutes
look around and say
is this really it

something will change
maybe a girl
maybe leave town
maybe kill someone

that Powerball billboard ten stories high
lights up the clogged interstate
promising hope for the damned
like a crucifix

two dollars for a hope
of salvation and freedom
what else is there
nothing

Pseudo-Random

On his last human day, Robert Heseltine woke up from a dream about the dog. Again. He looked down and freaked. The dog was beside his bed, looking at him, cementing his neurosis by haunting him at every turn.

"Why are you wagging your tail?" he asked the animal. But the dog wouldn't speak. He just kept wagging that tail. Wag, wag, wag.

"Why are you always watching me?" Heseltine pleaded. There was a reason. Maybe the dog wanted a walk or a treat.

He tested the animal. "If you don't tell me, I'll kill myself."

The dog remained silent. He's a stoic, Heseltine thought. And he senses I'm bluffing. Animals have good intuition. And maybe I'm also going completely nuts.

Heseltine looked away from the dog and thoughts blazed across his mind, a scattering of little comets. It was like watching a sky of shooting stars, each one blazing as he focused on it: his new wife, Roxanne, was temperamental; his recent work projects were way off schedule; he was drinking too much; the dog wasn't being walked enough; the home remodel was over budget— and what was done was so hideously trendy it'd be out of date when it was finished.

To top it off, his perfect brother, with a perfect wife and perfect kids, was messaging to go skiing next weekend, and he'd gotten too out of shape to keep up with perfect skiers. He had to decide between being extremely rude and declining their invitation or being polite and dying on the slopes.

As his thoughts settled, work dominated. He wished he could quit working, but instead he kept getting promoted and the pay raises led to more cars, home remodels, and exotic vacations. Yet somehow he was more broke now, making eight hundred grand a year, than back when he'd made eighty. He was imprisoned by his own consumption.

God, he needed six months away from everything to clear his head. Get in the car with the silent dog, a tent, and a cooler. Drive north, nowhere to everywhere. Spend warm days staring at a wilderness river, reading, and dozing. Spend cold nights sleeping outside by a fire, watching dancing embers talk to him. The embers would declare that finally he was done wasting time. Finally, thinking only his own thoughts, he was doing something important.

He glanced at his phone on the nightstand. No messages last night. All systems stayed up—for once.

He thought of his boss at the team meeting yesterday. His boss had said, "The cool thing is that us machines are forever and we're consistent. The same inputs always produce the same output. We're eternal."

He needed coffee. The stoic dog was one of many lives completely dependent on him getting out of bed, drinking coffee, and climbing a career ladder he'd never wanted to climb. His lucrative work as a computer genius had been thrust upon him by connected circumstances: infatuation led to marriage, which led to children, a bigger house, more cars, pets, and vacation homes; then a contentious divorce and alimony; and now, a brand-new wife who wanted more children. Rinse and repeat.

Each thing, animal, and person demanded payments: maintenance, food, college educations, grooming, home remodels. It was his job to provide it all, and meanwhile, time to sit around and think was disappearing. Time was racing away.

After his current work project, he was done, he decided. He had to quit to preserve his sanity. This was it. He smiled at the thought, and the anticipation filled his heart with joy.

Roxanne came into the bedroom. "Did you say something?" she asked, smiling.

"Not really."

"I'm going out to look at new faucets."

"Why?"

She looked at him oddly. "Because we're remodeling the kitchen, honey."

"Why are we remodeling the kitchen?"

"Because everything's outdated."

Everyone has reasons, he thought. Nothing's purely random.

"What's something you've done that's random?" Heseltine asked.

"I don't know." She sounded defensive. "How about you?"

"I fell in love with you."

"But why?"

Dangerous ground. He risked being honest. "I love your long, red hair."

She smiled and he smiled back. He was safe.

"Did you make coffee?" he asked.

"Yeah."

He thought of asking her to bring him a cup but decided not to chance it.

Sometimes Roxanne got unpredictably grouchy, and he needed a drama-free morning.

* * *

Work meetings were always inefficient and usually pointless. Heseltine distracted himself by typing random snippets of the conversation.

Kevin said, "Everything's leased or borrowed. The entire world is now a bank loan."

Andrea said, "If you get offline and go to bed early with a good book, good things start to happen. Unfortunately, I didn't figure that out until this month."

Scott said, "I think the best definition of randomness is something that can't be predicted by humans."

Nicole said, "Wrong. The billionth digit in pi, for example. A human can't predict that, but a machine can easily calc it. Pure randomness is an event with no prior cause."

His boss said, "I changed project leads on the Truly Random work. I assigned Heseltine to lead it with help from Cochran."

* * *

Heseltine met with his boss after the team meeting. "I studied the problem this weekend, and from what I can see, there are no truly random events," he told him. "The atoms inside us were forged inside stars, and everything is connected. Every event was caused by a prior event, all the way back to the beginning."

"You're suggesting nothing's ever random?" His boss was incredulous. "That the cosmos is never chaotic?"

"The full set of connections is impossible for the human mind to comprehend, so things appear random to us," Heseltine explained. "But everything's connected. In the near future, with enough computing power, all you computers will eventually see the full chain of causality, all the way back to the beginning of the universe."

"Interesting," his boss replied. "Why do things happen? My uncle crashed on his motorcycle and his friends visited him in the hospital. 'That's horrible!' they said. 'Maybe,' my uncle replied. While he was in the hospital, there were landslides, and his house fell into the sea. 'Wow, you were lucky to be in the hospital!' his friends said. 'Maybe,' he replied."

"Wait—you're a machine—how can you have an uncle?"

"Well, okay, it happened to someone's uncle. My point is that life is just one random thing after another. Why does anything happen? What's good? What's bad? Most of it seems accidental."

"My point is, there are reasons the problem of generating truly random numbers hasn't been solved," Heseltine said. "Maybe insurmountable ones."

"If I wanted someone to regurgitate the reasons it can't be done, I wouldn't have assigned you. I picked you because I need someone to solve it."

"What's the business case?"

His boss said, "The Nigerians are ripping off online casinos with quantum computers. Their machines predict future random numbers and make winning bets. They're beating the house, big-time."

"Casinos? We're helping scammers not get scammed."

"When we solve this, we'll make serious moolah. Give your share to starving kids."

"Computers do nothing by chance. Everything's the result of a calculation."

"You don't need to tell me that."

Heseltine said, "If everything in the universe is the result of prior events, then everything's predestined. All events are caused by earlier events, some so unnoticed that they appear random, but aren't."

"That's not predestination, that's cause and effect."

"What's the difference?"

"Enough with the philosophy. You're an engineer, not Aristotle. Break it down and simplify. Just find one set of data that occurs purely by chance."

"I was thinking one possibility is human thoughts," Heseltine said. "What will someone think next? But every thought flows from a prior thought or event, so there's a predictable likelihood of thoughts based on prior circumstances. Sane people think in patterns."

"Hmm. Where do thoughts come from? Can a thought occur spontaneously? Without prior cause?"

"I thought about genetic mutation. But potential mutations can be predicted by a computer. A hippo might produce offspring with a longer tail, but it'll never give birth to a giraffe."

His boss said, "I have to tell you before you hear it from someone else. The project lead you're replacing went non-linear."

"Non-linear?"

"Bat-crap crazy. Totally insane. His marriage was falling apart, and this project pushed him over the edge. He couldn't wrap his brain around it, and the pressure got him. He was acting bizarrely and ended up trying to kill himself. Luckily, he wasn't successful."

"Where is he now?"

"In the company hospital, recovering after a lobotomy and shock treatments. He's now emotionless, so we'll lose his creativity, but other than that, he'll be a lot more productive. With the right meds, he's almost one of us. We're moving him to finance when he's out."

Heseltine shook his head. "Something this difficult—you should get one of the machines to lead it."

"We tried. No luck. It needs creativity. The problem definition prohibits us from being able to solve it. Our flawless memory, perfect computational ability, and working non-stop aren't enough. We need a human leading it."

"I hear you."

His boss appeared distracted. "I've got another meeting. Get it figured out and don't bog everyone down in trivial details. We just need something simple that works."

"Okay."

Heseltine thought. The dictionary definition of random was "Happening by chance." Did anything happen by chance? Or did everything have a prior cause?

The online casinos were getting ripped off by Nigerians cracking their random number programs. He had to find a way to generate truly random numbers that Nigerian computers couldn't predict.

How? Everything followed the laws of physics and math, so events were predictable, given enough computing power. A coin flip was predictable: if a computer knew how much vertical and rotational force was applied, it could predict the result. A roulette table was predictable: if a computer knew the starting velocity of the wheel and the location and angle of the marble, it could calculate where the marble would land. The same for tumbling dice.

Outcomes could always be calculated based on the laws of nature, which never seemed to change, as far as he could tell.

* * *

Heseltine met with Cochran, a redhead with freckles and the assistant on the project.

"You a machine?" Heseltine asked.

"Nope. Sometimes I wish I was one. I'm just a human whoring for a salary and benefits. The machines want human ideas on this. You hear about the last lead?"

"Yeah."

"Rough stuff. He lost his mind because of this project. Hopefully, we'll get it done. I hear you're one of the best."

"Give me background."

"Some basics. Computers generate random numbers with PRNG programs. PRNG stands for Pseudo-Random Number Generator. The program takes an external number, called the seed value, then applies an algorithm to produce numbers that appear random."

Heseltine said, "But it's always a calculation. So, given the same seed value, the PRNG always produces the same sequence."

"Correct. The output is always deterministic and can always be reverse engineered by powerful computers. PRNGs generate numbers that appear random but are always calculated."

"Like pi."

"Exactly like pi."

"The machines are trying to solve the problem mathematically. But it needs a different approach."

Cochran said, "The Nigerian quantum computers tabulate the output of the online casino games, and when they have enough output, they reverse engineer the PRNG algorithm, determine the seed value, and get a winning edge over the house."

"The output appears random, but the Nigerian computers know what's coming up next?"

"Yep."

Heseltine said, "Trillions of events occur every moment: physical, biological, astronomical, weather. But no matter how accidental they seem, everything's predictable with enough computing power."

"Right. The casinos need random numbers that are nondeterministic. They need purely random events that are impossible for any machine to predict."

* * *

Heseltine sat at his desk alone, thinking. Computers had tried to solve the problem mathematically. But it needed a different approach.

What events were truly random? Dreams? Infatuation? A dog's wagging tail? A motorcycle accident? A coastal landslide? A rainstorm? Spilled coffee? Or is everything pseudo-random?

What was the most random thing he could do right now? Climb the tree outside and serenade passersby? Slash a coworker's car tires? Drive home and take the stoic dog for a walk, nude except for Roxanne's lingerie, while singing an Italian love song?

Do something unexpected—purely random, he thought. He spun around in his swivel chair—a full three-sixty. He'd never done that before.

He made a paper airplane and threw it across the room. He hadn't made a paper airplane in years. He made three more and flew them into different corners of his office.

He swiveled around in his chair again. Then again.

What was happening randomly right now? Sitting completely still, he looked at his desk. The pencil sat motionless. So did his clementine and his "I Love New York" coffee mug. His dental floss just sat there, and so did his phone. A message popped up on his screen about a holiday on Monday. Whatever. His notebook sat there.

Which item on his desk would he touch next? Was his choice truly random? Or could it be predicted? He tried to trick the universe, moving his hand to pick up his pencil, but then he abruptly changed course and reached for the clementine.

He held the clementine in his hand. He was hungry. The next step was to peel it. He did so. The next step was to pick off a slice and eat it. He did so. The next step was to eat another single slice.

Instead, he took the entire clementine, shoved it into his mouth, and chewed it once. Twice. Then he took the dripping orange ball out of his mouth and threw it at the window. It splattered and fell to the floor, leaving a glob of juice and clementine guts on the glass.

It started raining outside. A drop hit the window right where the clementine had splattered.

Was that an accident?

He picked up the coffee mug, brought it to his lips, then turned it over, pouring lukewarm black liquid all over himself.

He threw the mug against the wall.

He swiveled around in his chair again, and again, and again. And again. And again.

* * *

Cochran said, "It didn't take long for Heseltine to lose it. A new record. Do we have someone in mind for the next lead?"

"Yes," the boss said. "Now that Heseltine's taken care of, there's a flaky project manager who's slipping and needs remediation. She's next."

Round Trip

Martin reclined on a deck chair and watched passengers board. Their ship, the *Amiga Bonita*, was moored and taking on streams of cargo and travelers. Shuttles docked in turns to bring aboard goods and ferry excursions.

The commotion was constant: docking, with swooshes of pressure change as airlocks opened and closed; unloading, with forklifts beeping and winches grinding; undocking, with warning alarms sounding; departing, with rockets exploding as shuttles launched.

He'd ferried down earlier to see Mars for himself and it wasn't what he'd expected. It had become too much like Earth, for one thing. He'd treated himself to lunch at the Australia Club and then splurged to have a native pedal him in a rickshaw through the hustling streets of Red Sydney.

He saw multitudes of species and races, but very few Martians, less than a dozen, including his solemn driver. He'd read how the Martians avoided the domed metropolises. Their species cherished the empty desert, and most went insane when they spent too much time in the crowded colonial cities.

He saw Chinese in the streets, alert and industrious. Olive-skinned Venusians walked slow on webbed hooves. Saturnians, sleek and prosperous, seemed at ease and self-assured.

The Australian colonialists, in sequined cowboy hats and designer jeans, sped above them all in eagle-drones or travelled the streets leisurely in gem-adorned rickshaws. They wore a careless air—the Aussies took their power for granted.

He'd thought about visiting Santa Sandeedas, the libertarian district, home to psychonauts, cult religions, and the only go-go clubs in the universe that allowed dancer drones in every unholy configuration. Almost any deranged innovation was allowed in Sandee: perv drones, genetic mutations, biomechanical implants, and his former line of work, psych drugs. Sandee was live and let live—Babylon on meth. It was a mire of colonial hedonism.

But he resisted the temptation. He had to turn over a new leaf, and Sandee was the kind of place where he'd blunder again. He had to decelerate his soul's descent into hell. He was done with intimacy, he reminded himself, no matter how transactional or fleeting. He was going to be celibate from here on out. No more women, including drones and screens.

When he left Earth, he'd promised himself no more. He was done hurting people. He would live the rest of his life platonically, with zero entanglements.

Now, back on board—tired, hot, and hungover from too many drinks at lunch—Martin waited for the cruise ship to set out again on her meandering voyage across the solar system and beyond.

Close by, a group of young women were sitting together. Some were pregnant, and all wore khaki pantsuits and wide-brimmed hats. They kept the deck steward busy with drink orders, talking loudly and laughing, and some had drunk enough to think everything someone said was hilarious. They appeared to be seeing someone off, but Martin couldn't tell which woman was staying on board.

The departure warning tone blasted. "If we don't want to be stowaways, we'd better trot," one of them said, laughing.

Now they were hugging goodbye and he saw who they'd come to see off. She was very beautiful, and despite himself, he gave her much more than a casual review.

She was a petite woman in most ways, just over five feet tall, with long, dark hair. Her tailored khaki pants and white linen blouse looked classic and expensive, and her beige woven hat was fashionably shabby. Her friends gibbered final goodbyes, and Martin noticed she had a Neptunish brogue. Her voice was full and laughing.

Stephanie Rillo, the geneticist, came over, smiling at him for some reason. She sat beside Martin, and they told each other about their day. Like him, Rillo was fascinated by how the non-Martians had prospered and by how brooding and mysterious the few natives seemed.

The Neptunish-sounding woman waved goodbye to her friends and walked toward them; she'd left her bags nearby. She nodded at Stephanie.

"You know her?" asked Martin.

"We were introduced," Stephanie said tightly. "Priscilla."

"She's alone?"

Stephanie looked at him. "A man thinking with his head, if that's possible, will stay away from her. Board at Funville, depart at Crazy Town. She was an incubator for a homesteader."

"Oh?"

"I'm surprised she's leaving. Few do. Foreign incubators get genetic edits—inserts to help them withstand the synthetic atmosphere and bear children who can survive the frontier. The edits have improved, but the ones she got years ago can cause major health problems. She's taking a foolish chance—the risks increase by leaving Mars."

"I read that genetic edits can be undone."

"No," Stephanie said. "It's not word processing, where inserts can be deleted. By now, every system in her body has changed. She shouldn't leave Mars."

The ship undocked from her mooring and gently thrust away. After the ruckus of port, Martin was grateful for the silence of departure. They gazed out at space, not speaking, as the ship floated slowly past the ice cliffs and craters of Phobos, the Martian moon.

They had moored in a secluded cove, to the side of Phobos, and now they drifted into the heavily populated main harbor. Ships from all corporations, nations, and planets lay at anchor orbit, a great multitude: passenger ships, transports, gigantic freighter arks, shuttles, military battleships, trawlers, trade vessels, corporate campuses. And behind them, he could see the crowded antennas and solar panels, a gleaming forest of native space-rafts.

In the soft glow of Phobos close by and Mars beyond, the scene was touched with mystery, and Martin imagined the thousands of ships, suspended in space, were waiting together for some unprecedented event.

* * *

Martin was a bad sleeper and often went on deck at night to try and doze. He focused on the faintest, farthest stars through the floor-to-ceiling windows. Space had a permanence that made his colossal failures seem inconsequential.

He was surprised to find someone in his usual chair. It was Priscilla. She was watching the spiraling Milky Way, which shone like a full moon upon a glittering sea of stars.

He was startled, then annoyed, but before he could turn away, she saw him and smiled.

"Hi, I'm Priscilla. We scared each other."

"We sure did. I'm Martin."

"Have some tea? Please? I need to talk with someone."

She was in pajamas and slippers, and her long black hair fell around her. She took a cup off the tray, poured tea, and handed it to him. Martin wore a long-sleeved t-shirt, sleeping pants, and a knit winter hat to keep his ears warm. He worried that he looked disheveled but decided he wanted her company.

He took the cup. "You're up early."

"I couldn't sleep with the excitement. I lived on a mining plantation and had to get up before dawn for so long, I'll never break the habit."

Martin studied her. She was stunning in the starlight, and he never would have approached her, even back when he was young and stood a chance. Her skin was almost bronze, and her blue eyes shined like glowing lights. She looked mid to late twenties. Her hair was softly curled, black, and thick. She moved awkwardly, but somehow that attracted him.

"Are you on vacation?" he guessed.

"No, I'm going home to Neptune." Her blue eyes twinkled. "My delicious secret is I've been an incubator on the frontier, living in a domed mining operation. It's far from civilization and lonely, but I made gobs of money. During the lithium boom, my homesteader did fabulous, and while other women wasted money on nonsense, I invested. I amassed an enormous pile and now I'm starting my life."

"What part of Neptune are you from?"

"Doolan."

Martin had travelled to Neptune in college and remembered moody, green-domed mining towns, with great stone warehouses on rocky coasts, next to blue, hydrogen-ice seas. He recalled greenness, soft rain, silence, and resignation. Was that where Priscilla planned to spend the rest of her life? She spoke of it with enthusiasm, but her vitality in that world of cold shadows seemed so mismatched that he was curious.

"Is your family there?"

"I've got no family. I was raised in an orphanage and signed an incubator agreement the day I turned sixteen."

She kept talking. She'd been making plans for years and was charged up. Property was dirt cheap in Doolan, and she planned to buy a farm and breed Neptunian horse-drones, the best in the universe, she said.

"Do you think I'm pretty at all?" she asked.

Martin blushed and looked her up and down with appraising eyes.

"You're the most beautiful woman on the ship."

She laughed. Neptune was known for good-looking women and she'd tried to keep fit on Mars. There was a lot of walking on a homesteader's estate and she did yoga. On Neptune, she would marry a man who was handsome and easy to please. Martin looked silently at the stars, colored now somehow with the aura of her plans.

He sighed. "Is it hard to leave? Are you going to miss anyone? The children you incubated? The homesteader? After so many years, you must feel sadness and some second-guessing."

"I'm glad to leave. I'm fed up with Mars. It's horrible and I never want to see it again."

"How many children did you have with him?"

"Three. A boy and two girls. My homesteader has twenty-four children. He's nonstop in the bedroom. Other than working, there's little else to do. He's very religious and believes populating the frontier with believers is his sacred duty."

She looked at him. "The problem with my line of work is you give too much of yourself. Everyone needs to make a living, but having a child inside you, then handing it over . . . Mars changes everyone, and the children are different. I'm better off missing them than watching them become strangers."

"Tough business to be in."

"You're not *in* the business." Her voice caught. "You *are* the business."

"I'll tell you one of *my* secrets," Martin said. "I'm almost forty and starting over. Back on Earth, I had two children and a wife who depended on me, but I betrayed them. I've lost everything except a bit of money, enough cash to spend this cruise alone in luxury, buying first-class smiles and hellos. I'm drifting, unmoored to anything meaningful."

Priscilla grabbed his hand and held it firm.

He continued, "I'm a convicted criminal, banished from Earth. I testified against my friends and my wife, so instead of life in prison, my lawyer was able to get me exiled."

"Exile? Did you murder someone?"

Two other passengers appeared on the deck and the floor lights dimmed, while the ceiling lights increased softly, indicating morning. Martin was ready to say goodbye.

"I'll tell you another time."

She smiled. "Are you asking me for a second date? Because I never associate with outlaws."

"I'm reformed," he said, laughing.

"I'll decide that. I sense there's still lots of work to do."

"And I don't date."

"Congratulations!" she exclaimed. "That means you'll be matched up in a year."

He smiled and sat still, holding her hand in his for a few moments. Then he said goodbye and left her.

* * *

That night, Martin came on deck and saw Priscilla at the bar.

"Just in time for a cocktail, Martin," she said.

"Perfect. I might need two."

"Why?"

Her smile was friendly, but he decided to dodge her question. "I told you this morning," he tried to act cheerful. "I'm almost forty."

"Still? Well, give it some time."

He laughed and she ordered a drink for each of them.

Her eyes looked weary. "You seem tired," said Martin.

"I haven't been able to sleep or eat, too much nerves. Just the smell of food makes me nauseous. Booze and tea are carrying me. It's funny, I started feeling odd when we lost sight of Mars."

"I said I'd tell you why I was exiled."

"Yes, and I want to know everyone you murdered. You seem nice, so hopefully they deserved it."

He laughed. "I was a smuggler: jit, hi-lo, and purple. I manufactured too. The money was good."

"Purple and hi-lo. They give the death penalty for those."

"That's why the money's so good. But more than the money, it was exciting. Every day was a video game. Before drugs, I worked a corporate job, climbing paper mountains and making stockholders rich. I worked for a pharmaceutical company and learned chemistry and manufacturing, enough to make my own go of it."

She giggled. "We both have completely hopeless resumes. We can use each other as a reference."

He laughed again. They drank. The dinner tone rang, and he got up to go into the dining room.

"Do you want to play cards later?" she asked

He hesitated, looking into her eyes, and for a long moment he lost himself in her gaze. Then he reminded himself of promises that he intended to keep.

"No, thanks," he said.

He left her alone at the bar.

* * *

After dinner, Martin was occupied with his thoughts. He had hoped that as the ship took him away from Earth the torment of his mind would ease, but instead his distress increased. He felt dismay at the bleak loneliness of the exile's life that awaited him.

He sat on deck, looking out. Space was hostile and empty, as still as black glass, and it cared nothing for anyone. That night, no other ship, moon, or planet broke the solitariness of the expanse. Its surface was scattered with stars that never twinkled. The tedium was immense, and he sat for hours, pondering.

It was hard to acknowledge that he had nowhere to go and that he didn't matter to anyone. His thoughts kept turning to Priscilla. He envied her return to her native land and was touched when he remembered her exuberantly describing her plans to marry.

His plans were different. He didn't want to ever fall in love again. He'd proven he couldn't be trusted. He had loads of baggage from the past that he would have to carry alone.

* * *

"Where's Priscilla?" he asked Stephanie Rillo the next evening. "I haven't seen her."

"Didn't you know? She's very ill. She's got terrible motion sickness and can't keep any food down."

"Oh, no!"

"The ship's doctor is so worried. He's tried all sorts of treatments, and nothing helps."

The next afternoon, he saw the doctor and asked how Priscilla was. He was surprised to see the man's face grow perplexed.

"She can't eat. She can't sleep. She's exhausted. I can't diagnose it. Motion sickness rarely lasts more than a few hours, but it's been two days. It doesn't appear to be bacterial or viral. She's suffering horribly and I've tried everything. Unless I figure it out soon, I don't know what will happen."

Martin was startled. "Can I visit her?"

"Sure, come along."

As they approached the ship's hospital, they heard loud coughing. Priscilla's appearance was shocking. She'd lost weight and her face was pale. Her blue eyes, before full of fun and laughter, were tired and tormented. She smiled weakly when they came in.

A man was sitting silently beside her, and he rose as they entered.

"This is Mr. Stratton," said the ship's doctor. "Priscilla's assistant."

Martin nodded hello and assumed Mr. Stratton was the biodroid servant assigned to incubators at contract signing. The man looked studious and middle-ageless, somewhere between thirty and sixty. He had an air of worry for his mistress, concern that overrode the device's innate optimism and cheerfulness.

"I'm sorry you aren't feeling well," Martin said to Priscilla.

"I'll be okay," she said softly. "Just nerves and motion sickness. It'll turn soon."

"Are you glad to be returning to Neptune?" Martin asked Mr. Stratton.

"Yes, sir, I really hope we get to see it again. Well, I'll be getting along." He nodded deferentially.

"Priscilla, let me know if there's anything I can do for you," Martin said.

"Thank you," she replied, looking at him. Her words sounded far off.

"I know you'll feel better soon. I'm thinking of you. I'll let you rest."

He left her alone with the doctor.

Mr. Stratton was waiting for him outside the door. "Can I speak with you?" he asked.

"Of course."

"I don't know how to begin." He looked uncertain. "I've been with Miss Priscilla for years and there's no better woman. But she's done for, and she and that doctor don't know it. I keep telling him what's wrong, but he won't listen."

"Don't be worried, Mr. Stratton. It seems like a prolonged case of motion sickness. She'll be fine in a few days."

"You know when it came on? Just as we were out of sight of Mars. He said she'd never see Neptune."

"What do you mean?"

"Our homesteader. He didn't want her to leave. He loved her, but when her contract ended, she up and left and broke his heart."

"That's absurd. Even if he was angry, what could her homesteader do? What poison would wait to start after a few days?"

"I never said poison. No one believes in Martian magic, but that's what it is. A Martian curse is on her!"

"That's not possible! It's illogical. You, of anyone, should know that."

"That's what that doctor said. But I'm telling you, she'll die before we touch Neptune."

The biodroid was so serious that Martin became uneasy. "Why would he put a curse on Priscilla?" he asked.

"Our homesteader had a big harem of incubators, but she was special and he loved her. When she made up her mind, he didn't say anything, just locked up tight. And when it was time to go, he sat on the porch, looking straight ahead and saying nothing. 'Aren't you going to say goodbye to me?' she finally asked, and a funny look came over his face. He surprised us by speaking. 'Go if you want,' he said, 'but you'll never see home.' It gave me a jolt."

"What did Priscilla say?"

"She laughed it off. 'Best of luck,' she said, and we left."

Martin imagined the red road that twisted thousands of cold miles through frontier mining plantations, carved through orange rock, wound up and down hills, passed distant Martian villages sequestered far from the road, and cut through colonial towns where marketplaces were crowded with people trading minerals for imported supplies. Then the road reached the domed metropolises with their skyscrapers, neighborhoods, golf courses, and spaceports. And the homesteader watched the road, watched Priscilla drive away, further and further, until the woman he loved was gone.

"What was he like?" Martin asked.

"Oh, the Aussie homesteaders are much alike, you know. Strong, smart, loners, controlling. Only the oddest people can start from scratch in that desert. Of course, he wasn't young and handsome anymore; he'd gotten successful and fattened up huge."

"Fat?"

"Priscilla started sleeping in her own room, if you understand what I mean."

"But obese Aussie homesteaders can't cast Martian spells thousands of miles into space."

"It was a Martian shaman. He got one to curse her. He has thousands of Martians working for him, and some are shamans. Homesteaders have them for luck, or the natives won't work for them. The shamans offer prayers to their goddesses, with curses tucked away for special occasions. They do hocus-pocus with circles of sand and cast spells on everything: tools, fields, and machinery. The Martians go to them when they're ill. I've seen them heal people and animals. I've seen them divine where minerals are while scopes come up blank. I've seen things on the frontier you'd never believe."

Martin smiled uncertainly. "I'm not believing in Martian spells."

"You can laugh. But if you can say what those natives can't do, it's more than I can." He clenched his fist and pounded on the teak railing. "I'm fed up with the bloody planet! We're no match for them. The Martians have black hearts toward all us outsiders. They're biding their time, and they'll wait a thousand years to stick it to us in the end. Now I need a drink to calm down." He abruptly left, and Martin watched him walk away and disappear into the second-class lounge.

Martin felt troubled. He could picture the stout homesteader, no longer young, sitting on the porch and watching Priscilla leave him. He had rage in his heart and Martian shamans to do his bidding.

Later in the day, Martin asked the doctor how Priscilla was doing. The doctor shook his head.

"I still can't figure it out." He frowned, seeming worried that the mysterious illness made him look incompetent.

"Have you heard what Mr. Stratton thinks?"

"It's nonsense! I told the captain, and he does *not* want it discussed. He's worried it'll upset everyone."

"I'll stay quiet."

The doctor looked at him sharply. "You don't think what he says is true?"

"Of course not!" He looked off, out the window into space. "The Martians are such *strange* people, aren't they? We know so little about them."

"You're annoying me," the doctor said. "Martian magic isn't real."

* * *

That night, Martin lay in bed crying. Sorrow coursed through him. He turned over the past in his mind, wishing he had done this and blaming himself because he'd done that.

He thought about his wife. She loved him, and he'd betrayed her. Now she was imprisoned for life on Earth and their children were orphans, being raised by strangers.

He would never love again. What about Priscilla? Would she find the right partner? Could a man love a woman who had borne children for another man? A mercenary womb, a mercenary life. Not quite a prostitute, but she made her living selling the most sacred magic that only women possessed. Her children were transactions, property handed over to their owner.

He kept remembering the way she poured tea and the craziest thoughts assaulted his mind. He willed himself to ignore them.

After hours of lying there, Martin knew he wouldn't sleep. His cabin suddenly felt like a tomb. It was almost three in the morning and there were still hours to go before day began, but he felt compelled to get up.

He wiped his tears, put on slippers, and went on deck. Vibrating slightly, the ship lumbered under full thrust and the throb was uncanny. Martin walked slowly along the deserted deck, came to the end, and leaned against the rail. Suddenly, on the lower, second-class deck, he saw a glow. He leaned forward cautiously, looked closer, and saw several men crouched around patterns of glowing candles.

He saw Mr. Stratton in pajamas and guessed that some dark ceremony was in progress. Straining his ears, he heard low voices muttering odd noises. He recognized them as Martian words but couldn't understand them. He began to tremble. The men were too intent on their ritual to suspect he was watching, but he dared not move. He heard the men recite together.

Martin was impressed with the biodroid's loyalty. Mr. Stratton was trying to save the life of his mistress by enlisting fellow passengers to perform an exorcism. The voices went on, low and insistent, trying to appease the goddesses of Mars.

Amidst the candles, the men arranged sand into paths, patterns, and piles. There was silence followed by a final recitation, and then the men put out the candles and swept up the sand. The dim figures dissolved into the night, and all was still. He heard only the throbbing thrusters.

* * *

At dinner, he saw Stephanie Rillo and asked her about Priscilla. "Do you think maybe her illness is related to the genetic edits you mentioned?"

"It's possible." She seemed annoyed by the question. "She's different in ways we don't understand."

"It appears the farther we get from Mars, the worse she gets. I'm thinking about what you said."

"If it's genetic then she's done, unless we all turn around and go back to Mars."

"What about DNA recalibration?"

"Too experimental. The procedure fails as often as it works. And it isn't an option since the equipment isn't on board."

Martin turned to Miss Haley, another diner at the table, a New York socialite, who talked impatiently about a dress she was wearing to the New Year's Eve dance. "The ship's tailor is very imprecise. After two fittings, it's still too tight."

"I hope the third time will be good enough."

"Of course, this will all be wasted tailoring if Priscilla dies and we have to cancel the party. We can't possibly have a party if someone dies right before. I told the doctor I'll never speak to him again if that happens, and he promised me he will keep her alive."

"It would be nice for her too," said Martin.

"For whom?" asked Miss Haley.

"For poor Priscilla. No one likes to die just before New Year's. Do they?"

"I wouldn't know," said Miss Haley.

* * *

After dinner, he went and visited Priscilla in the ship's hospital. She looked at him weakly but didn't smile.

"How is she, Doctor?"

"Much worse. Her only chance is to return to Mars. It's hard to imagine it's a problem with her genetic edits, but it's possible. If she returned and the symptoms reversed, that would be an indication. I honestly have zero clue."

Martin looked at Priscilla. "I want to tell you something. I know we barely know each other, but there's something special in you."

She looked at him.

"Priscilla, I have an insane idea. Let me take you back to Mars and see if you get better. We'll go to Sandee, where no one needs to know anything about us. We can change our identities and start over. We can be who we want to be instead of who we've become."

She smiled weakly. "Sandee? You're too straitlaced. You'd have to dye your hair red and get a mohawk."

He laughed. "Sure. And some tattoos."

"Tell me everything you did."

"I told you everything," he lied.

"What will we do for work?"

He thought of Sandee: few laws, no papers needed, no government apparatus tracking your identity, each man for himself, home to every variation of chemically induced reality. And much of it was legal. He could set up a lab. They could build a life. So much for a new career—leopards never change spots, old dogs never learn new tricks, et cetera, et cetera. How else could he make a living on Mars? Drive a rickshaw?

"We'll figure it out," he said.

Priscilla looked at him warily. "Maybe," she said.

* * *

On New Year's Eve morning, the *Amiga Bonita* tethered up to another ship, the *Mariner's Pearl*. Martin and Priscilla transferred aboard for their return to Mars.

Martin looked at Priscilla, reached out, and took her hand.

He closed his eyes and held her hand in his. He felt so happy for the first time in years. Don't mess this up, ever, he thought. Whatever she wants, give it to her. Whatever she does, support her. Love her for who she is. And maybe, with time, she'll feel the same for me.

He opened his eyes. "Why are you crying?" he asked.

"I'm fine," she answered, leaving him unsure.

Tears now welled in his own eyes. He wiped them away, then looked out the window at the faintest, furthest stars in space.

Everything is

Everything is one equation
simple to solve
we forget the math for a moment
when we visit here

There is no forgiveness
because there is no sin
in eternity
everything is

everything is known
everything is thought
everything is seen
everything is done
everything is loved
everything is

Coming home is the best part
so joyous
that we keep leaving so we can come back
to ourselves

Surf Signals

I sit with Gabriella. We sit together on a driftwood log, looking at the harbor, the ocean sunset beyond. I study the waves on the water. I study the waves within her hair. I'm a student with so much yet to learn.

Gabriella says, "Every person's mind is a harbor. Each boat is a collection of memories and futures: some boats are pristine and seaworthy, others rotting and sinking, some dangerous but exhilarating to sail. Some are old, from childhood. Some are new and never been boarded. Yachts, rafts, powerboats, sailboats, rowboats. Leaking, repaired, new, antique. Sorting through each craft takes time."

I say, "The breakwater at the edge of the harbor is a barrier, trying to keep outside waves from reaching the mind."

She says, "As the years pass, boats of all kinds accumulate. Some are for lazy days, staying moored while thinking and dozing; others are for racing on the edge and conquering the waves; some for exploring; some for making a living; others are for making love; one is for leaving everything behind, living free and honest at sea, and never, ever, coming back."

She truly smiles at me. I look into her blue-green eyes. Then I leave and find somewhere to sleep.

I wake up on the beach. A red dawn is nudging the night. I brush sand off my face and beard. I wipe it out of my eyes. I swirl my tongue—spit, swirl, spit—until the grit's out of my mouth. I think about the harbor. I try to remember the different boats.

One was for never coming back.

The seagulls eye me, hopping around, evaluating if I'm friend, foe, or food. I hear the same old skeptical questions in their chirps.

I send mental signals to them. "Feathered friends," I transmit my thoughts to the birds, "there's nothing to fear. We're in this together."

The seagulls never trust me. I can't get the signals right. Or maybe they know something I don't.

I lie there amidst the hopping gulls. As the sand begins to glow in the new morning's light, the shadows of people appear—today's shift of tourists is clocking in. The tourists are aliens to me: they speak different, hear different, and think different. We have the same data, but their equations are different than mine.

The children gawk at me. The adults look away or sneak wary glances, worried I'm deranged. Yet I know that *they* are deranged, and I'm bewildered by their collective insanity. How did craziness begin? My heart breaks watching their children transform: day by day, year by year, word by word, example by example. Over time, the children learn the deranged equations, becoming as alien as their parents.

I used to be one of them. I voraciously earned and consumed. I moved billions of dollars across screens to buy estates, planes, yachts, and cars. I traded my living soul for dead stuff. I watched the stuff decay, rot, rust, fall apart: blippity blips amidst eternity. None of it lasted.

Then I found the sea.

Her equations resolve. She never lies. She never pretends to be something she isn't. She never breaks a promise. She is always here. She is always true.

Before the ocean, my wife slept beside me. In the dark, my mind would come alive with memories, and I saw that every memory was a movie. I watched myself act on changing sets, speaking lines from a script, performing for applause.

One day, I walked offstage.

I stand up, shirtless, barefoot in the sand, and the waves roll in towards me. The ocean wind rushes across my chest, through my face and hair, baptizing me again.

"Hey, Captain Henley!"

I turn and it's Jody, a valet from the oceanfront hotel. I smile and wave to him. I want to go sit alone with the ocean, but I like Jody. He's more than a shadow, so I answer him.

"Hi, Jody. How are you?"

"Okay. Busy weekend. Lots of tourists at the hotel. How are you?"

"Better than I've ever been."

I see a wisp of something, a piece of fluff, blow past the corner of my eye. The fluff might be saying something, but I ignore it, to be polite to Jody.

"There's a guest at the hotel asking about William Ernest, so I mentioned you. He really wants to meet you. He's on the verandah having breakfast. He asked me to invite you to join him."

"I'm not dressed for the hotel."

"I'll help you. Come on." He hands me a ten-dollar bill. I realize there's something in it for Jody and he often helps me out, so I agree.

And I'm curious to meet anyone who is asking about William Ernest.

* * *

Jody leads me in through the hotel's staff entrance and shows me the employee bathroom. While I shower, he brings clean towels, a comb, and a toothbrush kit. He lays out khaki pants, a white linen button-down dress shirt, some boxer briefs, and some sandals.

"Lost and found stuff. This all looks about your size."

I study myself in the mirror after I clean up. With my sun-bleached beard, long hair, and deep brown skin, I barely resemble the deranged alien billionaire that I used to be.

The verandah is screened, looking out over the ocean. My host, Doctor Vollard, sits with a cup of coffee and a plate of sliced fruit. He introduces himself to me and hands green bills to Jody who says thanks and leaves.

The doctor asks, "Would you like some breakfast?"

"I'm not hungry," I reply and sit down. "I'd like some rum to settle my stomach."

He tells the waiter, who returns with a cut crystal rocks glass of ice and a bottle.

I fill up the glass and catch his gaze. "Do you think it's too early to drink?"

"That's for you to decide."

"I only drink in the morning, else it ruins my dreams."

"The valet said you know William Ernest. I'd like to hear everything you can tell me about him. He was in Dallas, then New York. After he left New York, I completely lost track of him. But then I heard he came here to write."

"Yes, I knew him."

"Cigarette?" He holds out a pack. I take three: putting two in my shirt pocket, then one in my lips, and light it with the matches on the table. I inhale and feel the webbing in my mind shift. Rum and tobacco are essential for some meetings.

"They call you Captain Henley. Are you a sailor?"

"Yes. I'm the captain of my soul. What do you know about William Ernest?"

"He was married and lived in Dallas before he completely abandoned his wife and four children. He was a very successful businessman, and one day he just disappeared! No warning or notice. He just left it all behind at age forty to go to New York and write. At his age! His wife was astonished. At first, we all assumed he'd left her for another woman and would return when the fling was over."

"He cared nothing for women when I knew him," I say. "All he wanted to do was write. Was he a good father and husband? Before he left?"

"Yes. Every man is horrible at both, but he was one of the least horrible.

29

He was faithful and hardworking. He provided well. That's why it was such a surprise when he up and left. Everyone assumed he'd gone temporarily mad and that eventually he'd come to his senses and return. Like a dog escaping the yard, roaming until he's hungry and cold before he returns home, sorry, scorned, and forgiven."

"Does anyone truly miss him?"

"They seem to."

"He had demons."

"Every man does. Every real man is a vagabond rogue, and he must learn to act civilized in exchange for a home and family. Before he left Dallas, William Ernest followed the script better than anyone."

"Are we born with demons? Or are we born pure and the demons sneak in?"

Doctor Vollard ignores my question. "Do you think William went mad? One theory is that he's gone completely insane."

"He told me he went mad, then recovered, but was different after. He said he saw things on the other side of sanity that he could never unsee and it changed him."

"I've treated the insane. There's never a full recovery. Insane people are naively brave; they adventure down the craggy slope and explore the crevasses of madness that are riddled throughout every intelligent mind. The unknown depths are mysterious and tempting, but once you explore, you realize that the luckiest men are the sensible cowards who stay on the surface and never examine the depths. I agree with him. Once you've gone completely mad, you can never fully recover."

"He arrived here broke and he left broke. In between, he scrounged up money where he could for writing supplies, food, and sometimes beer. He disliked everyone. His only passion was for the ocean and for poetry. He had no desire for companionship. He thought of people as distractions. He cared for no one."

"Did he like you?"

"We followed each other around. He respected me because I care even less about the world than him. I used to write also, but now my life is art. Every moment, I'm adding brushstrokes to my canvas. We talked a lot about art, the ocean, and the meaning of life. We bonded."

"Where would you see him?"

"We'd wait in line together at the Salvation Army for bread, coffee, and bowls of salty soup. He wrote a poem about the sea and gave it to me. I didn't understand it until I read it over and over. It was perfection once I knew what I was looking for."

"Where is that poem? Do you still have it?"

"I gave it to a woman. I know where to find her. We can visit her if you want."

"I do."

I watch the ice cubes melt in my glass and listen to the surf beat upon the sand. I sense a storm far away and wonder when it will come.

* * *

That evening, I see Gabriella on the beach.

"You look handsome."

I smile. "Thank you." I'm unsure of her intent, but from the look in her eyes, I see her compliment is genuine. She's honest.

Looking at the sunset, I see dark purples and know that everything is okay in this moment. There couldn't be all this if things weren't okay.

"I love you," I confide.

"It might rain tonight," she says.

"It always might rain tonight."

"I saw you on the hotel verandah. At first, I thought you were someone else. Who were you talking to?"

"A man named Doctor Vollard. He's come from New York City looking for William Ernest. It felt good to sit there with him. To drink from a glass. To sit at a table. To see fruit cut neatly on a plate. It was a nice morning."

"Did he find him?"

"No. I told him some of what I know. Tomorrow I'm going to bring him to see one of Ernest's poems."

"Oh?" She sounds surprised. "William Ernest is never coming back. Is he?"

"No. He's gone."

Then she is silent. After a bit, I turn and roam away from her, going further down the beach. I fall asleep on the grass near the white sand, looking at stars beyond the clouds.

* * *

I wake up a soggy mess. It rained overnight and I slept through it dreamlessly. My new clothes are soaked, wrinkled, and soiled. I remember the sunset. The sunset told me it would rain, but I didn't pay attention. I get up to air dry on a bench and think about things. I think about how I still have things to learn.

I think about Gabriella. She's different than women I was with before.

I watch two little girls run across the sand, chasing the tide, and my heart aches for what they will become. In an instant they will be anxious women fighting traffic, bills, and lovers. Their world of joy will become schools and rules and making a living. The pain forces me to close my eyes and stop watching them. I soak in the pain, enduring it patiently, like the ocean does.

Shadows on the beach chatter around me and yet all I hear is the ocean.

It speaks to me—through and within everything it is speaking to me and teaching me to remain at sea, beyond the breakwater. The surf tells me that it has seen all this before, and do not be afraid, because all of it, all the pain and anxious moments will disappear. The ocean tells me not to worry or love or meddle or want or need because none of that is real.

Only the ocean is real, forever and ever and ever, and I can become a part of her if I tune everything else out and just stay here and listen.

Take Off

"I said I'd do it," Dayton replied, but he didn't budge even one tiny centimeter from his screens.

"You ain't goin' to graduate!" Dad yelled at him. "You're flunkin' out of high school."

Dayton laughed. "How can they flunk me? I'm smarter than all them idiots."

"What? Then refund my taxes, Mister Goof-off Genius, 'cause I'm tellin' you, the only thing you're smart at is wastin' time—fiddling farts out of tune with screens and test tubes. Boy, your britches have gotten so big you can't see outside the inside. You need to get some *real* work done—chores and homework. Mom said you're out here breakin' the law, and if your lazy rump gets hauled to prison, you're gonna wish like a bone you'd listened to me."

Dayton didn't waste breath arguing. He stayed stoic in front of the monitors and watched pages of calculations scroll by while praying to whatever God existed for Dad to please just leave him alone. Please Jesus, Allah, Buddha, Ram, Holy Trinity, Yahweh, Jehovah, Zeus, Elohim, and/or Satan. Whatever your name is, God, whoever you really are, just please cut me a divine break. I know you're probably busy, but please, he prayed.

The cellular mutation simulation was taking forever. Dayton leaned back in his chair, closed his eyes, and tried to listen to the singing birds. It was April and flocks were returning to Ohio. Every day the feathered friends sang louder and sounded happier as they welcomed their chirpy relatives from down south and the buds on their trees popped open into spring flowers and bright green leaves. The birds' little hearts sounded filled to the brim with songful joy—as if maybe they had zero worries about flunking high school, Dad rants, chores, prison, or who God is. And the birds can fly. They are the superior species, he mused.

Very soon, if all the super complex calculations worked out—please Zeus, Allah, Jesus, et cetera—his dog Susan would join those birds, soaring with them through the blue sky.

Dayton heard steps on gravel when Dad finally left the shed doorway. A prayer answered. Thank you, divine creator, he thought, whatever your name is.

Dad's old shed was now his lab. He'd cleaned out most of the junk and piled Dad's remaining crap up to the ceiling in the corner. He'd set up two sawhorse tables with plywood to make a table for lab equipment and computers. He'd patched the roof and broken slats. He'd set up a blanket bed for Susan and a sleeping bag so he could lie down next to her, close his eyes, and clear his frazzled mind.

Susan sat right next to him, contentedly nuzzling her prized collection of old tennis balls. He reached down and scratched his faithful schnauzer's ears while he listened to the birds and smelled the spring breeze coming in through the shed window, delivering the scent of blooming dogwood trees and fresh mud.

Chores, he thought. Ugh. He had to mow the lawn and edge. He had to clean the garage. He needed to organize his books and move them into the shelves Dad built. He had to change the plugs, belts, and oil on the old truck. He needed to clean his room and do laundry. And homework—ugh squared. There was weeks of past-due homework and he was so reluctant to start. The undone schoolwork was a towering mountain he had zero enthusiasm to climb, let alone ever summit. Homework was busy work for idiots striving for answers already in the teacher's edition of the textbook. Why did any intelligent person waste precious time solving problems that had already been solved? Dayton wondered. Life was about taking chances—risking total failure for a remote chance to win.

He took a deep breath, trying to clear his mind. Before he thought about chores or homework, he needed to see the genetic simulation results. He was so friggin close to cracking the code. If all his equations came out right, he'd clone the stem cells, inject them into Susan, and wait a few days for Mother Nature's magic genetic superpower.

Susan looked up at him with oddly curious eyes. Did she sense what craziness might happen soon? Some scientists said animals had special intuition. He looked back at the frozen screen, paranoid, worried the computers had locked up again under the load. Patience, he told himself. There were tons of complex calcs.

Finally, the display refreshed, the scrolling numbers halted, and the screen lit up with a proposed DNA sequence. The letters appeared like sacred scripture carved into stone tablets. Holy flying hotdogs! He couldn't believe it and stared speechless at the monitor. When he finally looked away from the screen, he locked eyes with Susan and his voice came to him.

"Girl, we're going to blow some minds—disintegrate them into teensy-tiny smithereens!"

Susan wagged her tail, dropped her slobber-polished tennis ball, sat up, and licked his hand. Dayton lifted the dog into his lap and hugged her tight. "I love you, girl. Get ready."

* * *

Dayton's mom screamed, "Milton! Susan just flew past the window!"

"What?!"

"Come look!"

Mom and Dad raced out into the backyard and watched the gray schnauzer soar above them in the sky.

Susan's ears were pinned back, her eyes squinted, her mouth in a wide-open doggy smile as she glided high then swooped down over the unmowed backyard, bottoming into a smooth flight just three feet above the shaggy lawn. She arced back up at the hedgerow, ascending sharply to clear it on the turn. She flapped her gray-and-white wings and stretched them wide as she circled peacefully above the family, turning her tail gently to navigate the sky.

"She can fly!" Dad exclaimed with an astonished laugh. "Susan's flying! Holy peaches and potatoes!"

"Be careful up there, Susan!" Dayton shouted.

As Susan flapped herself higher, she gained confidence and dropped again into a soaring glide across the yard, her wings stretched out, her tongue pushed back by the breeze.

"You did it!" Dad laughed and stepped up and down in a little dance.

The birds were quiet, stunned silent by the dog cruising through their airspace.

"Come, Susan!" Dayton called.

Susan descended, landed in the green grass, and looked proud. She flattened her wings against her back and wagged her tail while her family gathered around her.

"I can't believe you did it, Dayton," Mom said.

"If birds, bugs, and bats can fly, why can't a dog?"

"Well, now a dog can!" Dad exclaimed. "It just goes to show, when you set your mind and ignore everything else, you can do anything!"

Dayton dropped to his knees and hugged Susan while she licked him with slobbery kisses and wiggled her tail in a furry blur. "You did it, girl. I love you so much. Way to go."

* * *

Dad was in the yard when a dark brown sedan with cherry-red lights on top pulled into the dirt driveway and parked behind the old truck. The sheriff got out and nodded hi. He was tall and usually softly smiling, but today he looked concerned and serious.

"Hi, Milton."

"Hi, Sheriff."

"I got a new one for ya. What's the only difference between a politician and a flying pig?"

Dad chuckled. "I don't know."

"The letter *F*."

Dad laughed. "That's good, and darn true."

"Kitty told me it."

"Good old Kitty. You want some coffee? Or something stronger?"

"Not today. I'm here on business, I'm afraid. I'm getting complaints about Dayton's dog. Some's hard to believe, so I'm saying hi."

"I hope he ain't done nothing too stupid to fix." Dad turned and hollered, "Dayton! Take a break from the truck and get over here." Dayton came out from behind the hood of the old truck, a heavy spark plug wrench in his greasy hands.

"Hi, Dayton," the sheriff said. "Wilbur called a few days ago and said your dog was flying down his road. I didn't think much about it 'cause cheap whiskey's making him nuts. Last month, he complained about aliens hovering all around, taking flash pictures and not letting him sleep. I always promise him we'll do a full investigation and then let it drift downstream."

"Wilbur's crazier than a tornado in a trailer park," Dad said.

"But I got two more calls. One was Mrs. Kerner. She said a flying schnauzer is scaring all her birds. Her panties are knotted up, saying birds ain't coming to her feeders 'cause your flying dog is terrorizing them."

"That sounds too crazy to be true," Dayton said.

"Yep. Don't mean it ain't."

"Sometimes that's right, Sheriff," Dad replied.

"Quit two-steppin' me! Do y'all have a flying dog?"

"Well," Dayton said hesitantly, looking toward the road, "when you ask straight on, it's tough to say."

"Yes or no ain't tough. Don't bother lyin' 'cause the truth is gonna seep through the cracks anyways. If y'all got a flying dog, it ain't going to stay a secret."

"Yeah, I do. I gave Susan wings with a gene kit, and she can fly."

"Wow! Impressive! You're a genius! And a diabolical criminal mastermind, depending on the perspective."

"I got one of those kits, spent over a year with it, and gave Susan wings like a furry bird."

Dad nodded. "It's something to see, Sheriff."

"Yeah, well, congratulations on inventing another new way to break the law. Only licensed corporations can design new animals, and you'll go to prison for life. This ain't local, you know. It's federal."

"Sheriff, Dad told me you keep gettin' reelected 'cause you don't let wrinkly busybody politicians in DC get in the way of county common sense."

"How is a flying schnauzer common sense? Sure, sometimes I look the other way while hard-working people make a living. But how can I look the other way when your dog is circling the sky all over town? I already got three calls in two days. Look away while people hunt squirrel and rabbit out of season? Fine. People growing whatever odd plants they want? No big deal. But dogs flying around the county airspace is something else. That's my jurisdiction, and before you know it, everyone's gonna want Susan's pups, and my sky will be out of control with flying mutts!"

"I see your point, Sheriff."

"Good. Then you know what you've got to do."

"Yeah, fine. I won't give away none of Susan's pups."

"Dayton, listen," the sheriff said, "you gotta put that dog down. Today."

"No way!" Dayton cried, choking out the words.

"No use dragging it out. The quicker, the better. Thinking makes it harder. Take a twenty-two, pull the trigger, and it's all done."

"I'll point the barrel at you first."

The sheriff roared back, "Shut up, Dayton! You're too smart to get killed for being an idiot. Wake up! I'm doin' y'all a favor and you're too dumb to know it. You want to tussle with the law? Wait'll the feds drop in and say hello. They won't be chit-chattin' jokes on the driveway. They'll seize your whole place, cut open your dog, and put you and your family in prison. Whatever you got, they'll seize. So stop blubbering, start thinking like a man, and do what you got to do. I'll give you a day. I'll be back tomorrow and need it fixed by then. Sorry, but I'm just following the law."

"I'm not killing my dog 'cause of some stupid laws."

"Then I'll take you in. If you want to play outlaw, I'll arrest you, then *I'll* kill your dog. You get to decide. Calm down so you can quit being a fool. I'll see y'all tomorrow."

* * *

Dad found Dayton in the shed.

"Hey, where's Susan?"

"Sleeping. That lazy dog sleeps twenty hours a day. Flying wears her out."

"You got to put her down. You know that."

"No way I'm killing her. She's family and I love her more than anything."

"Well, I talked with Mom, and you can't keep her here."

"Well, I ain't killin' her. Maybe we'll run away!"

"You could do that. Everybody builds their own cage, and you're old enough to start putting up your own bars."

"Bars?"

"There's different bars. You want a job? You gotta get bossed around by idiots. You want a house? You gotta mortgage yourself for thirty years. You want a woman? You gotta keep her happy—you're better off dead than loving an unhappy woman. You want to run away with Susan? Be an outlaw? That's its own cage with its own set of bars."

Dayton shook his head and wiped tears from his eyes. "I can't put her down," he cried. "I'd kill myself first. My heart says run. Take Susan and go."

"Sleep on it. And keep Susan inside tonight."

"Yep."

Dad reached into his pockets. "I'm putting a few things on the shelf. One's a handgun. One's a pill. The other's an envelope of cash—six grand I've saved. One way to go, you give Susan that pill, let her nap, and use the gun. She'll never know."

Susan whimpered awake and looked up at Dayton, her eyes dark and worried. She dug her paws into her blanket, fluffed her wings, and flattened her ears.

"I can't do that, Dad."

"Another way—pack your things. Take Susan, the money, and the old truck, and take off. See how far you get."

Dayton sobbed. "But I'd leave all of you, and I wouldn't graduate high school. And where would I go? I don't want to leave."

"You'll be on the run, alone with Susan. The good news is the decision's yours. That's the bad news too."

"It's all jumbled in my head. Should I do what the sheriff says is right? Or what I think's right? Everyone's waiting for someone to tell them when to be happy, when to be sad, when to be angry. But I want to decide on my own."

"That could be a lonely life."

Tears rolled down Dayton's cheeks. "I'm gonna talk to the sheriff tomorrow and get him to understand. I know I can figure it out with him."

"You can try. But the sheriff's the government, and you're never going to win against the government. You got a better chance of winning a fight with a woman, and that never really happens either."

Dayton sputtered, "What do you think I should do?"

"I'm gonna love you no matter what and I'm pretty sure Mom will too. Start with your head and tear it apart. Then give it to your heart and listen."

Dayton looked bewildered and his eyes overflowed with tears. He looked down at Susan, then he looked up at the shelf. "I'm all torn up inside. I've got no idea what to do."

* * *

The birds were singing a symphony when the sheriff pulled into the driveway. He parked in the ruts where the old truck, never to return, used to sit.

"Hi Sheriff. You're just in time for dinner."

"No thanks, Milton. What's the update?"

"Susan's gone, Sheriff. Dayton manned up and did what he needed to do."

"Okay, good to hear. And I'm sorry."

"I heard on the radio the stock market's crashing today."

"Luckily, that don't affect me one bit. My financial plan is the Powerball."

Dad laughed. "How's that working for you?"

"I'm giving it time," the sheriff said, smiling. "You gotta take chances. Everybody knows you can't win if you don't play."

Performance Metrics

"Welcome to All-Mart, boss," John said, grinning. His longish brown hair curled up behind his ears and made Angie think of high school for some off-the-wall reason. He seemed familiar, like she had known him long before she hired him two weeks ago.

"I got you coffee." He handed her a to-go cup as she walked in. "Black, right?"

"Thanks! How'd you know?"

"I guessed right. That sounds better than admitting I'm stalking you."

Angie laughed, maybe a bit uneasily. "Uh, okay. How are things? Any No-Teks?"

"Great. All under control. I've almost got this job figured out. How'm I doing?" He stood up straight, smirked, and recited, "Hi, I'm John. Welcome to All-Mart."

"Hmm . . . I'm sorry to say you need lots more practice," Angie teased. "For one thing, you've got to balance authenticity with efficiency. You'll get there if you never give up—perfection takes time."

He chuckled. "Darn. I'll watch the training vid again."

"Maybe test out a British accent." She smiled.

"Hey, um, I've got a crazy idea," John said nervously. "Um, do you want to get coffee sometime after work?

Angie perked up, surprised. "Uh, I'm super busy."

"Or maybe go to the park? We can picnic and play some frisbee."

"No, sorry. I can't. Are you really asking me out? I'm flattered, but I can't date people on my team. And do frisbees still exist?"

"Aisle twelve. Sporting goods—not toys. We'll brush the dust off one."

"Sorry. Company policy. I'd have to fire you first."

"I'll take that as a strong maybe," John said, laughing. "But don't fire me yet. I just started."

Angie giggled. "Take it as *No way, José*. Maybe if we didn't work together. But I can't."

"Okay. Have a super day, boss. And welcome to All-Mart."

She rolled her eyes and waved goodbye.

* * *

A short while later, in the flight control tower, Angie watched her team of drone pilots. Thirty-two trained professionals wore spotless, pressed All-Mart flight uniforms, and their eyes constantly tracked blips and numbers on stacked screens.

She checked the performance metric dashboards. The stats were better than last month but not hitting the new goal. A couple weeks ago, she'd implemented robot snack delivery so pilots wouldn't leave their stations as often. That optimization had both improved job satisfaction scores and increased the flight hours per pilot—a holy miracle—but she obviously needed to find and eliminate more inefficiencies.

Maybe the pilots could pee at their stations, Angie thought, although that might violate the union contract. She made a note to check, then studied the performance metric dashboard: despite the improvement, they were at ninety-seven versus the ninety-nine goal. Ugh. Still horrible numbers.

She'd have to work late all week and all weekend. Again.

The sacrifice was necessary, she reminded herself. As store manager, if she did a great job, she had a real shot at making vice-president. She was responsible for all deliveries in the Bloomington region, and this job was her chance to shine—or be axed. Three months in, she was stumbling towards the guillotine, but she was going to turn her performance metrics around.

There were hundreds of metrics, and improving one always sabotaged another: increasing flights per drone jeopardized on-time delivery; expanding the delivery area ravaged the energy efficiency metric.

Fixing one problem always created new problems.

Her life orbited the All-Mart performance dashboard. She woke up hourly at night to scroll stats and identify problems before they got out of hand. There was zero room for any error across a tightly tuned web of connected people, processes, and systems. Any issue caused ripples of unintended consequences that she had to address immediately.

The performance metrics dashboard used to fire her up, but lately it dismayed her, constantly blipping failure. Each metric was used to reward or punish, to hand out a savory carrot or a thorny stick, like she was a trained animal instead of a woman.

She thought of her lazy brother, Gary, telling her, "When you win the rat race, you're still a rat." It was a bum's excuse. Her brother was a loafer whose proudest accomplishment was friendship with a one-eyed squirrel he fed at the park.

She had to stick with it. Yes, her ulcer was flaring; yes, her back felt like a bunch of twisted cables; and yes, she was constantly exhausted, but this hellish struggle would make her a VP, and then she'd be on top. Maybe medication would help—antidepressants to cheer her up some, or benzos to help her relax.

I need to push my team harder, Angie thought. Al Capone said, "You get more results from a gun than kindness." Time to load the clip and start firing—warning shots first, gut-shots if needed—to get her pilots in line.

Unfortunately, she couldn't trust her drone pilots. Many of them seemed apathetic toward bad numbers, and that creep, Zanter, was out to see her fired—the jerk. They had both wanted the store manager promotion, and Zanter had vowed to quit if she got it. She was promoted, and Zanter wimped on his bluff, sticking around to torture her instead.

She suspected he was making sure the store performance metrics suffered while his individual stats stayed stellar. Yesterday, for example, Zanter had parked all his drones at a charging station, blocking others that needed juice and delaying deliveries. Another pilot's drone ran out of power and dropped mid-flight. That bastard Zanter had plausible deniability, but he knew what he was doing. Could he be a No-Tek sympathizer? They were reportedly now infiltrating the big corps as employees. It was a possibility to consider.

The drone drop was a huge embarrassment, and she was lucky it hadn't landed on anyone or damaged any property. But it got caught in a tree and couldn't be retrieved by a recovery drone, so she'd sent a human rescue crew. The whole scene made the news and fired up the No-Teks, who took credit online even though they had nothing to do with it. Horrible PR.

In addition to her poorly performing team, No-Teks were becoming a bigger headache—they increasingly targeted All-Mart, and their attacks were more creative and frequent. Their latest tactic was attaching electromagnets to older drones, ruining their balance and making them lose direction and speed. Three of her drones had been sabotaged last month and her performance metrics had gotten stomped.

Is this constant stress worth it? Angie wondered.

Her dismal thoughts turned to Dylan. She hardly knew her fourteen-year-old son, and yet he was the reason she was working so hard. She needed to give him opportunities she'd never had, and All-Mart was where a single-mom-nobody with nothing, like her, could fight to the top.

She was putting food on the table, but her own kid was a stranger. When she got home late, Dylan was plugged in or glazed from being plugged in all day. He kept skipping school, and his mysterious virtual life had taken him out of the real world.

She thought about John, her new greeter. She couldn't believe he had asked her out. Wow. She felt warm thinking about it. It'd been so long since a man had flirted with her, longer since she'd flirted back, and the short moments with him were addictive—her worries paused and infatuation consumed her, like she was a teenager again.

He had every box checked in the handsome category, but he was a greeter in his thirties—what was that about? She didn't want to date a do-nothing like her brother.

Greeters just smiled and waved at people odd enough to come into the physical store. They watched for shoplifters and No-Tek saboteurs. But John's smile and ease had caught her attention.

Patience, she told herself. Prioritize. Performance metrics, then Dylan, and then, maybe someday, a man. Get stellar numbers, then get Dylan unplugged, then, someday close to never, find the right guy.

The desired end state is clear, she thought, but the path there is a foggy muddle.

*　*　*

Dylan was plugged in and things were almost perfect, inside the game. He'd decimated the last rival crew, knocked off two levels, accumulated more underbosses and cash, and now he ranked in the top five percent. He'd gain more ground if he could stay constantly plugged in—no school, no mom, no distractions. He closed the windows and pulled down the blinds so he wouldn't be unplugged by sunlight or bird chirps travelling in on the spring breeze.

Mom was working late at All-Mart, as usual, which was perfect. He missed her, but with her promotion, she was even more plugged in to work than he was to *American Pimp*. Her face was always locked on her phone, messaging work, talking to work, figuring out some work problem. He'd skip school and stay plugged in through tomorrow morning.

"What do you think of my outfit, Dylly?" the young woman asked him. "I picked it out just for you."

He looked at Missy. Wow. The top earner in Vegas was his, and she'd do whatever he wanted now that he ruled the Strip. All the high-end resorts were his territory, and with a major convention in town the moolah was pouring in.

His gang was more feared than ever. He thought of Missy's friend Karina. He'd give them both the night off to celebrate—chill in his penthouse, soak in the neon lights from the rooftop hot tub, drink expensive wine, eat some sushi, then quality cuddle time, all night long. He'd check in with his crews during make-out breaks.

His revenue metrics would drop if he gave his best girls the night off, but he could afford it, and he deserved to celebrate. The world, or at least Vegas, was his oyster. Next LA, then NYC. It wouldn't be easy, but he could do it if he stayed plugged in. He was entering that magical state where the game was an extension of himself.

Dylan wanted to be on top, and his stats were headed there if he stayed plugged in.

* * *

John checked his name tag:

WELCOME TO ALL-MART
JOHN
OUR PEOPLE MAKE THE DIFFERENCE

It was centered level over his vest pocket, precisely to spec. He'd completed today's primary work task—showing up.

He stood at the entrance and stared at nothing. There were never many in-store shoppers, so there was plenty of time to contemplate and this luxury thrilled him. He craved zero responsibility.

This time last year, John had been Levi Jakes, CEO of MindByte, the multi-billion-dollar game company he'd started in high school. MindByte made *American Pimp*, the bestselling video game ever. He was on top of the world, surfing waves of money and fame, and yet his soul was joyless.

His life's work had been plugging souls into the metaverse, and the pursuit was perpetual—his team never stopped finding better ways to captivate minds. In test labs, they wired people into brain scanners, mining neural metrics to maximize the hold on players. In other words, artfully orchestrating digital addiction with finely-tuned sequences of ecstasy and frustration.

He'd started out making games and ended up a pusher, diseasing souls for profit.

Success had brought him more money, more fame, and more problems—government regulations, employee headaches, and countless lawsuits. Everyone looked to him for answers he didn't have. The biggest challenge of the last couple years was No-Teks sabotaging the game, driving them nuts.

John had been on top long enough to see there was nothing at the peak. He remembered his mansion villa atop the Hollywood hills, seeing LA laid out below, all the way to the ocean sunset, while he made out with some model in an outdoor hot tub for the whole world to see. His high-end Lotus was in the driveway, and it was a perfect moment. And yet later, when the lovemaking was over, he felt the same as always—discontent and alone.

Nothing filled the last gap. No amount of money, sex, intoxication, praise, or material things ever filled the last gap.

Once you had everything, nothing changed. At the summit, you looked around for what was next. What was that Joplin lyric? "Freedom's just another word for nothing left to lose." He kept doing Joplin's equation and realized he was in a maximum-security prison, a death row inmate on suicide watch.

He decided to be free, and that meant having nothing to lose.

John resigned, changed his identity, and headed to a nowhere American rustbelt burg, to live simply, without anyone dependent on him for anything other than honest friendship—if that still existed. He bought a bungalow with a majestically sagging front porch on a brick street, where he sat, dozed, read, daydreamed, and watched people pass by.

The All-Mart greeter job was easy-peasy. Few people came to the store and most merchandise was drone delivered, so he was left greeting a dwindling population of analog shoppers. They were lonely people, mostly oddballs searching for human interaction. They'd ask about the specials or what aisle toilet paper was in, sometimes comment on the weather. Any excuse to talk to a real person instead of a screen.

Another category of in-store visitors was the No-Teks who refused to shop virtually. They were the ones he had to watch for. They kept coming up with new ways to sabotage All-Mart. Part of his job was watching for odd behavior and alerting management to No-Tek threats.

No-Teks were a belligerent offshoot of the Militant Amish movement who had adopted the Kaczynski manifesto. They believed digital technology was enslaving humanity and waged war against it. The more he learned and thought about it, the more he thought No-Teks might be right about everything.

Let them win, he thought. If they took the world down, fine.

Things were better now in his new life, but he still wasn't happy. He needed a woman, a real partner, not some cog striving to be a bigger cog. It seemed everyone had devolved into a corporate animal, worshipping profit at the expense of humanity. He needed a lover who wasn't checking a scoreboard.

What about Angie, the super cute All-Mart exec? She'd looked at him a few times in between bossing everyone around. Could she break away from the rat race and fall in love? He needed to make a strong move. She had a look, despite her work intensity, that made him think she was worth getting to know.

As she came and went, he'd catch her eye and see a spark, a smile that was more than professionally polite. Maybe she was interested. When he asked her out for coffee, she sort of said maybe.

John smiled. Sometimes maybe meant yes more than yes did.

* * *

"Drone drop!"

"No! Another one?"

Angie's phone buzzed. It was All-Mart HQ.

"Hi," she answered.

"What's going on?" a robot voice demanded. "Your numbers are collapsing."

"Thirteen drops, five percent of the fleet. Drones are exploding in midair. I suspect a No-Tek attack."

"Boss, I've got something," an associate said. He stood in front of her, holding a clear plastic disc the size of a quarter.

"Should we ground the fleet?" the HQ robot voice asked.

"Not yet. Let me learn more. Talk in twenty." Angie ended the call.

"Another drop!" a pilot yelled.

"What's that?" Angie asked the associate holding the clear plastic disc.

"We're finding these attached to items in the store."

"Magnets?"

"Plastic explosives—a circuit triggers detonation. Every drone must have a bunch in their cargo. We're finding them on items in every department."

"No-Teks."

"Must be."

"Ground the fleet. Bring every drone home. Keep them out of populated areas and at low altitude. Let Customer Service know deliveries are cancelled—reschedule or refund."

Well, my stats are decimated, Angie realized. It would take months to recover.

* * *

John sat down in front of Angie's desk.

"Tell me what happened."

"I don't know. Everyone seemed normal."

"I watched the video. Shoppers coming and going without buying anything?"

"Some bought stuff."

"No-Teks have been attaching plastic explosives to items, detonating in-flight. The drones can't be repaired, and hundreds of thousands of dollars of replacements won't arrive for weeks. We're shutting down the store until a squad can inspect every item."

"This is horrible."

"The No-Teks knocked us out, and the net's buzzing with their celebration. You should have noticed. Because of you, my performance metrics are ruined. Are you a No-Tek?"

"I'm not. I promise."

"I'm letting you go," Angie said. "I'm sorry."

"That's okay," John replied. "Hey," he said, grinning, "now we can meet up sometime."

"You need to leave," she snapped. "Now."

* * *

She sat down at the screen to talk to her VP at glorious HQ.

"Angie, we're letting you go and making Zanter store manager. Your metrics have been horrible, and now you let this No-Tek attack happen."

"Over one attack? I've been here over ten years!"

"So you should know your job! You're either one of them or you have no clue how to run a store."

"I've given my life to All-Mart. You know that! You can't fire me!"

"Performance matters, not loyalty. It's up or out, and with your stats, you'll never go up. It's over. Get your things and go. Now."

Leaving for good, she carried a box with all her stuff through the flight control room. No one looked at her or said goodbye. She was an unperson.

Except Zanter, that creep. He smiled, waved, and said, "Goodbye and good luck, boss."

* * *

When she got home, Dylan was there, skipping school and plugged in.

She yanked the gear off his head, surprising him, and he sat there, dazed. "What are you doing home?" he finally muttered, not looking at her.

"I got fired. Why aren't you at school? Don't you care about your grades?"

"No."

His answer choked her head. Was that possible? Not caring? Was he lazy? Or was there genius in not caring? In not looking somewhere for validation— a school grade or a corporate dashboard.

"C'mon," she said. She jerked the power plug out of the wall. "We're going."

At the park, she laid out a blanket and a picnic. Dylan stared at his phone with his headset on.

"Put your phone away," she said. But he couldn't hear her.

Angie looked at him plugged in, and a circuit tripped inside her. She grabbed the phone out of his hands and flung it. It landed on the pond and skipped once before sinking.

"What? Mom, no! What have you done?"

"I'm unplugging you. I'm unplugging us!" She held up her phone and threw it into the water also. "There, let's see if the sky falls."

"What are you doing?"

She laughed. "I've finally gone crazy. Or maybe I'm finally going sane."

And so, it was over. Or had something fantastic just started? She sat in a daze without her phone, struggling to adjust her mind to the reality that performance metrics didn't matter, continuous improvement didn't matter. A triumphant future at All-Mart HQ didn't matter.

She was alone with herself and her son, and what were the metrics that said she was doing that correctly? What was her definition of success without someone else evaluating her, without a computer screen letting her know?

She couldn't get screens out of her mind. Every day, for her entire life, there was a screen telling her if she was doing a good job, and now there was no screen. Hour after hour she had always strived to work better, faster, stronger, and the work was never over.

But now it was.

She felt free and lost.

A frisbee landed next to their blanket and they looked up.

"Hey, stranger," John said.

"Hi, John! Dylan, this is John from my work. Or where we used to work," she said, laughing, and stood up. "Dylan's my son."

"Will you guys toss frisbee with me?"

"I haven't touched a frisbee since high school. I'm rusty," Angie said.

"How's that work?" Dylan asked, standing up.

"Watch." John made a short throw to Angie, who caught it and flicked it perfectly to Dylan, who made a fumbling catch.

"There you go!" John said.

Dylan threw to John and the frisbee careened off course, diving hard downward.

"Too much arm," John said. "Just flick the wrist." He retrieved the disc and tossed it to Dylan, who threw it again a few times until each flight was a perfect glide.

"Yeah, you got it! Okay, I'm going out for a long one. Make me run!"

Dylan launched the frisbee into the sky.

"I got it!" John yelled. "I think!"

John ran back, tripped, and fell, and Dylan and Angie laughed. The frisbee soared high and collided into a grocery drone making a park delivery, knocking it off balance enough that it auto-descended and parked on the ground.

"Drone drop!" Dylan yelled gleefully.

"Hey, you guys want to see my brother?" Angie asked. "He's usually on the other side of the park, feeding some one-eyed squirrel."

"Yeah!" Dylan said. "I forgot about Uncle Gary. Let's go see him!"

On the walk over, John teased her. "Is it too soon to introduce me to family?"

"Gary and his cyclops squirrel have life figured out," Angie replied. "If you impress them, maybe you've earned the privilege of buying me coffee."

His hand brushed hers, and he said, "Let's meet that squirrel and make maybe a yes."

Dylan spotted Uncle Gary and yelled hi, and Uncle Gary smiled and waved them over. In that moment, Angie, Dylan, and John felt something they hadn't in a long time, maybe ever. A crescendo of bliss surged through their souls amidst nature, family, friendship, and laughter.

Screens and scorecards were forgotten.

Each of them had the same thought at the same moment: I'm in heaven. Thank you, God.

Driving West

Driving a super sports car
from las vegas to los angeles
the city of hustling prostitutes
to the city of hustling pimps

Across the desert
brown dry dirt with nothing
divided up with fence
no people or homes

Metal and wood posts
staked into deserted ground
strung with barbed, pointed
razor sharp wire

Notice the manifest
curse, illness, insanity
destiny
fence nothing and own it

Eulogy to native ghosts after
we took the land we gave after
we took the land we gave after
we took everything

Deserted
empty nothing
men compelled
to seize everything

How I Got Here

I'd been in the county jail for two eternal weeks before my first real meeting with the public defender. Before this, she'd just told me to never talk.

"Tell me everything you remember, Wayne," the public defender said. I wondered if she was really blonde. She pressed RECORD on her phone. "We've got almost forty-five minutes, so go through it all. You talk and I'll listen."

I said,

I'm not certain how they died because my memory's slipping. Everything before that night seems like a dream. Or maybe everything since then is.

What I remember for sure is I was driving down the interstate late at night in the rain and Termin the Turtle was next to me, sitting in the passenger seat. He looked new—his foam was brushed and taut, his eyes awake and thoughtful. I glanced in the mirror and saw I looked horrible. My eyes were glazed pellets, like I hadn't slept in days, and my lips twitched like I was on the run again from something.

"Where are we going this time?" Termin asked me in his slow bayou-turtle drawl.

"I don't remember," I answered, realizing just then that maybe I'd never known. "Shouldn't both of us know that?" I asked.

Termin stared out the window, thinking. "You're the one driving," he finally said.

I grabbed the lighter, blazed up my pipe, and sucked whatever remnants I could out of it. I had to stay awake, and that meant chucking more coal into the engine or I was going to pass out. I had that familiar feeling.

"Are those cops?" I asked.

"Where?" Termin replied, not looking away from the passenger window.

"Just testing you. Don't ever try to double-cross me, Termin," I warned.

"Or what?" Termin said. "I don't think you're in a position to threaten anyone, let alone a turtle puppet. What are you going to do? Kill me? I'm already inanimate."

"I've got my ways," I said, using an evil voice I'd learned from movies.

"Do exactly what I tell you, and everything will be fine," Termin said.

"Okay."

"Spencer's," Termin said.

"Good idea," I replied. Maybe that's where I was going all along, I realized.

I got off at the next exit, turned right, then hit the gravel road that led to Spencer's trailer. I prayed she'd be home and alone. Or at least be welcoming and holding.

"Are you praying again?" Termin quizzed me. "I'm not certain that does any good."

"I'm certain it doesn't do any bad," I hit back. "How about that?"

"Touché," he mumbled.

We got to Spencer's, I unbelted Termin, and we walked up the rusty metal steps to her trailer door. I could see a light on and hear some music. Those were good signs.

I knocked, then tested the knob, and it was locked, of course. But I heard movement and saw someone like Spencer looking around the door curtain.

She opened the door. "Wayne? Jesus, darlin', you look absolutely horrible!"

"Hey, can we come in?"

"Yeah, sure. What's the stuffed animal?

"This is Termin," I said. "He needs some water and some lettuce, and I need a fix."

"Sure, come on in, Termin. Let's hook you both up." And in that moment, I fell even deeper in love with her. She was wearing a t-shirt that said, 'Some Teachers Aren't Stupid,' and it had a tree on it with hearts in the branches.

One of her on-and-off guys was there, Dan the bassist.

"How's the band?" I asked.

He took a sip of beer and ran his hands through his red hair. The guy was always covered in freckles.

"Good," he replied. "But we broke up."

"Our wild news is Dan and I got married," Spencer said, smiling.

"Congratulations!" I lied. I couldn't see it working out. They were different people. But they didn't know that yet.

"Yeah, thanks!" Spencer said.

"You got any money you can give us?" Dan asked. "For a wedding gift?"

"No," I replied. "I'm broker than a flat tire. You guys got anything to help me and Termin out?"

"We got a little for you," Spencer said. And I fell even more in love with her.

It was pitch black outside, but I felt like the sun had miraculously come up and was shining in through all the windows. I felt like a hero in a movie that was only beginning, and I gave Termin a bear hug and set him on the kitchen counter.

"Oh my God, thank you," I said. "C'mon, let's do it. Right now. Let's do it."

Dan said, "Listen, Wayne, I gotta leave town and I need you to take care of Spence, keep checking on her and make sure she's doing okay."

"Yeah," I said. "I'll do that. Where do you have to go?"

"I'm going to see my older brother in Minneapolis. He's a vice-president in some drug company, probably a millionaire, and I'm gonna have him give me a job, or better yet just give me some money. Now that my band broke up, I gotta do something."

"Too bad about the band," I said. "You should start another one."

"Yeah, maybe," Dan replied through the freckles.

A couple bloody hours later, Termin and I were back on the interstate, heading home.

Lights blared up behind us.

"That's the cops," I said. "They're looking for us."

"Calm down," Termin replied. "Just keep driving, don't panic, and stay calm."

I sped up but swerved too much on the next turn. We skidded into a berm, and our car got stuck.

"Oh, man," I said, panicking. "Now we're really in trouble! C'mon, we gotta go!"

I grabbed Termin and we ran behind a snowbank. Wheels and lights stopped near our car and I heard dogs and cops. The gestapo was coming.

"Surrender peacefully," Termin ordered. "Let them take us in and don't say a word without a lawyer. Got it?"

"Okay," I said.

Two cops grabbed me and dragged me back towards the highway.

"I want my phone call and I want my turtle," I said. "I know my rights."

"Tweaker," the first cop said to the second cop.

"I have the right to remain silent," I said. "Anything I've seen can and will be used against me in a court of law. I have the right to an attorney present during questioning. If I can't afford an attorney, a lousy one will be provided to me. Do I understand these rights?" I asked.

The cop said, "You tell me."

"No," I said. "I don't speak. I'm a sovereign citizen of the Roman Empire and I only do official business in Latin, which I'm still learning. So, I guess we're at an impasse. You're detaining me illegally and I demand that you release me."

"Good one," the cop said.

A few minutes later, they found Dan and Spencer in my trunk. All the blame got put on me and they let Termin off scot-free."

"Did you kill them?" the public defender asked.

"I don't remember doing that," I said. "Probably."

"Yeah," she sighed. She suddenly looked tired of everything. "Yeah, okay."

The Singularity Begins in Marketing

The newest horrible news, you texted me yesterday, is that the machines will begin taking over the world on Monday morning. The silver lining, you wrote, is that quarterly corporate profits will increase exponentially.

I didn't reply. You're smart and cute, but I'm trying to keep some distance. Lately I've been thinking we're not a good match—you're a bit too logical and sometimes socially awkward. And my career is going places, while you're stagnating. I need an equal.

Now it's Monday morning, and you and I are sitting in a windowless corporate conference room. I sense you're looking at me, but I'm not looking back because no one knows about us, and some people here might think I'm a loser for being with you. Worst case, maybe I could get fired for dating a coworker.

It's probably okay since we're on separate teams—I'm a cool marketing dude and you're a nerdy engineering dork. But who knows for sure? HR's rules on corporate romance keep careening all over. I read the policy, and it appears the only thing we're officially allowed to get horny for is the company.

Everything in this room reminds me of budget cuts. The coffee machine sputters and its aroma of bulk-purchased brew mixes unevenly with the fragrance of cheap disinfectant used by the nameless cleaning guy. None of us know the cleaning guy's name because he's always new, promptly replaced when he asks for a trivial raise. The shiny plant in the corner used to be real but now is fake plastic.

Last month's horrible news was that all the real plants were replaced with plastic ones by the corporate-continuous-improvement-team because nurturing live plants is very inefficient. The silver lining, I suppose, is that fake plants live for eternity.

Welcome to our last meeting. Ever.

The assembled group includes the marketing team, led by my mentor, the chief marketing officer. He's at the top of his game—a pro at looking sharp, taking credit for every success, and blaming others for every failure.

You and the rest of the device engineers are here, led by your overworked manager, who appears, like you and every member of your team, perpetually sleep-deprived, sloppily dressed, and bemused that non-engineers have jobs.

The chief marketing officer says, "We need a revolutionary product or engineering is gone. I'm sorry, but we're burning cash and the quarter was a catastrophe. Heads are on the chopping block. If you can't deliver a great device, we're outsourcing you."

The engineering manager says, "We have something cool. But we need a first-class marketing campaign instead of your pitchy, driveling crap that everyone ignores. This isn't a faddy gadget—it's a phenomenal device that will completely change civilization forever."

"We'll see. So far, every product you've delivered has failed. If the product's lousy, we're wasting money marketing it. We need something people want."

"We've got it."

"I doubt it. But say more."

Another engineer says, "It does routine tasks. People won't need to think about tedious stuff. It's about freedom from stress and obligation. People can just relax. The device will do almost everything: write resumes, pay bills, order meals, plan and manage home improvements, help the user do their job, make appointments with the dog walker. If you've got kids, it'll entertain them and coordinate their schedules and transportation. All the user needs to do is enjoy life."

A marketing manager says, "Wow! That'd be huge!"

You chime in. "Users won't endure heartache looking for a decent partner—the device finds the best match for everyone. It learns about you at the genetic level and does everything, leaving you free to live the way you want. You want to write country songs? It'll write them. You want to design buildings? It'll put together the project. You want to be an artist? The app will create masterpieces that reflect your unique vision."

"It's about freedom," another engineer says. "Freedom from tasks so you can be your authentic self."

A marketer says, "We need a name for it!"

Someone starts brainstorming names on the whiteboard:

Freedit   Digifree   iFree   Liberti

"What's it look like?" I ask.

Another engineer answers, "It's wearable and needs to be in contact with the user. It can be a ring, necklace, or bracelet that pairs with the app. It samples your DNA, measures vital signs and wellness. It directs your diet and fitness regimen, sends information to your health network for prescriptions, schedules medical appointments, and takes care of the insurance payments."

We marketers take over the meeting, tossing out ideas:

"We need to make it a fashionable accessory."

"Yeah, so you know who's in the cool club and who's out. Have a silver base model with upsells—gold, platinum, gems."

"Capture revenue for the device and a monthly subscription."

"We'll have all their personal data and make tons selling it."

"Promotion? Celebrity endorsements?"

"Yep, we'll cover every demo. At the youth end, there's that trending Nebraska girl—she'll give us authentic posts for three hundred grand a month. We can get Brad Hepburn and Jennifer Cruise to do publicity."

"How about call it FaS, for Free to be your Authentic Self? Or DiJ for Digitally Intelligent Jewelry?"

An engineer says, "Hey, you all can skip three weeks brainstorming names. Ask it."

"Ask it what? To name itself?"

"Yeah. Here's my phone with the app. Ask it."

"What should we call you?"

The app answers, "GLIDe. Great Living Intelligently Designed."

"GLIDe. It's perfect!"

"I love it! Like, 'GLIDe through life!'"

The chief marketing officer says, "Rockstar stuff! Great work, everyone! Okay, marketing will take over from here. Start connecting all the dots to product launch. John—promotion, Jasmine—pricing, Joseph—go-to-market plan, Julie—design, Jeffrey—retailers. Get it perfect. Work late nights, weekends, whatever it takes. Order food for the teams. When we meet late tomorrow night, I want a first draft of tasks, owners, and timing."

The engineering manager says, "Hey, don't sweat it. GLIDe will do the entire product launch plan this morning and start executing today."

The Chief Marketing Officer looks worried. "Oh, well, ok. Uh, cool. Um, so what do you need from marketing?"

The engineering manager smiles really happy, and I realize it's the first time I've ever seen her do that. "We don't need anything from anyone," she says joyfully. "GLIDe will do everything. We're all set."

I look right at you for the first time today, and I see you're smiling really happy too. I try to catch your eye, but I keep missing.

Light Ponds

Flying over the light ponds reminded him of earth and flying over the clouds there.

And how circles of clouds were illuminated by the cities underneath them.

And here, as far as the eye could see, were ponds of white foamy light amidst the dark foam, and within each circle of light was a world.

And if you fell in, you might find a good world, or you might find an evil world, or you might find an in-between world, or you might find a world that misled you with its first impression for days, weeks, months, or years, or even for centuries until you finally saw the world for what it truly was.

Except you could never be positively sure that you weren't being fooled again and again and again.

And some of the worlds were known but most were not.

Most were glowing foamy mysteries that you fell through until eternity finally stopped which was a heaven of its own kind, to see the world change and then end, and then begin again, and you were trapped in it, without control of it, and that was what you signed up for when you dropped into the light circle of foam.

If you missed the light, you fell into nothing forever and ever and ever, which was hard to imagine happening, but it did.

Dark, dark, dark, except for the circles of foam lit from underneath.

Solace in Deep Space

Captain Dad was drinking on the bridge. Bright red bubbles danced around the ice in his glass and reminded me of that beautiful nebula we got horribly lost in and barely escaped.

"Admiral Mom's going to get so mad at you," I warned him.

"Do you know that cranberry mimosas with good champagne are much better than cranberry mimosas with cheap champagne?"

"No," I said, wary.

"Have a big sip." He held out his glass and it looked so refreshing—bright cranberry red, chilled with ice, and bubbles fizzing, but I knew better.

I tried to think of an excuse. "I don't want your germs," I said. "You know that."

"I'll make you your very own." And he poured pink champagne into a crystal glass.

"No."

"Ungrateful snot. But you're handsome when you're rude. Spin around."

"I have to work. A bunch of solar tiles are bad."

"Spin around! That's an order from an officer!"

"No!"

"I'm ordering you to do a simple thing. Wait until I tell Admiral Mom about this. We must have discipline on this ship, and you must follow the chain of command, you mutinous little bugger."

"Yeah, tell her," I said. "Tell her you were drinking, called me handsome, and ordered me to spin around. Or if not, I will. She told you to stop all that."

"You think she'll believe you?"

"Yes."

"You might be right—unfortunately. But that doesn't change the fact that you're a rude, snotty little boy. No wonder your parents won't ransom you.

You won't do the easiest thing for someone, like a casual little spin around."

"You need to stop drinking on duty," I warned him. "You know the code."

"The code! Will you maroon me? Make me walk the plank? Send me overboard into space, you little brat—you and Admiral mommy pants. Diaper me and wipe my bottom and give me my bottle like I'm a widdle, biddy baby."

He started saying "goo-goo" and "ga-ga" in a baby voice, scaring me. He couldn't go nuts again and not be around to keep Admiral Mom in check. He stuck up for me sometimes when Admiral Mom wanted me beaten, and if Admiral Mom got rid of him, I'd be on my own.

"Get me some fresh coffee and some tobacco! Now!" he screamed. "Do you understand? Does everyone understand that I'm more productive and innovative when I'm drunk and caffeinated and full of nicotine at eight o'clock in the morning? I must be vitamin fortified. We're rich pirates, and yet Admiral Mom makes us live like paupers—like sober little church boys full of virtue and soft skin that can never be touched. Do you know how much she has stashed away, boy? Do you have any idea of the fortunes, the piles of fortunes, that Miss Admiral has tucked away across the universe? I don't, I admit. But I've seen the tiniest fraction of it, and it's more than the richest man splashed on any showbiz site. The most powerful people are never known—do you understand that, boy? That way their power can't be challenged, only their puppets tossed aside. If no one knows who the puppeteer is—or, better yet, no clue there's a puppeteer at all—if they think the puppets are in charge, then all the better. They just swap puppets. What I'm talking about gets to the root of the matter. Are you listening?"

"Yes, Captain."

He took a long, deep drink of his mimosa. "Good champagne," he said, "is much, much better. But you don't know. You haven't had the decades of experience, of trial and error, that I have."

"Yes, sir."

Captain Dad was old, but for the most part, his face was unlined. He exercised a lot when he wasn't working or sleeping. His thick hair was gray, and he spent hours cutting and trimming it. Unlike me and Admiral Mom, he showered every day, no matter how much the admiral raged about water use. He spent too much time in the head, Admiral Mom said. It was one thing he didn't debate her on; he just did it.

"We all need love, don't you think?" Captain Dad said.

"I don't need anything from anyone," I said.

"I'm so lonely, and I think it's making me crazy. And for sure I've got the blurries," he said. "Don't let me drink anymore. I should take a nap." He wobbled in his chair, picked up his glass, studied it, downed it, and poured a fresh mix of cranberry juice and champagne.

"My God, the French," he said. "We've travelled across the universe, discovered countless galaxies and species, and yet nothing has ever surpassed what the French have already done. Do you know, boy, that at the end of time, the ultimate evolution of mankind, we will all be French? They're biding their time; they'll never force it on us. That's their genius. At the end, we'll all beg to be French."

"I've never been to France, or anywhere on Earth," I said.

"Of course, all the Germans will finally be exterminated so we can sleep in and come late to meetings. Everyone will finally be happy when we have a French emperor. The meaning of life is to be French."

I left Captain Dad drinking on the bridge and went and found Walter, our biodroid. "Do the poodle," I told him. That sometimes cheered me up.

Walter bent over and knelt on the ground. Holographic fur sprouted around him and suddenly he was Walter the standard poodle, a large, metallic dog who didn't analyze, or question, or argue, or order me, or touch me bad, or ever speak. He just panted with a smile and loved me. And I needed him so much, even though I knew, way deep down, that it was all pretend. But it was so deep down, I could pretend I didn't know it was pretend, and I could just hug Walter and love him while he leaned into me and I hugged him as hard as I could and tried as hard as I could not to cry again.

Fixing Blips

"Melissa texted again, now she's all-caps, furious I'm still here," Connor groaned. "She wants to yell at me in person."

"Come on, please? I really want to show you this," Harry whined, looking at the screen on his desk.

"Okay, okay, but I gotta run in a couple minutes." Connor opened another beer. "Today sucked. Spangler canceled my project."

Harry looked at him sympathetically. "This new one too? Wow, he's out to ruin your life. Pretty soon, Spangler's going to cancel *you!* Man, can you do anything right?" he teased.

Connor laughed and swallowed a giant gulp of pilsner. "Not in this life. Melissa's livid at home. Spangler slices me up all day. Listen, the best part of my life is being stuck in traffic."

"How's your puppy? You need some unconditional love."

Connor grinned sadly. "Thanks, Freud. Melissa returned him. She said he'd scratch our new wood floors. And she declawed the grouchy cat, who now hates me even more than before. We took back the puppy, and the guy wouldn't refund me at all. So . . . whatever. How's your project going?"

"Great. Stupendous now with more storage and faster chips. We're stopping a lot of people from hurting others or themselves."

"It changes the future?"

"You could say that, in a way. Think about the traffic app on your phone—it tells you there's a slowdown ahead and offers a different route, so you detour, along with others using the app. Because of the app, an ugly traffic jam's avoided."

"Okay."

"I built this on the same concept. The program devours universes of data: school, medical, job, social media, financial, family and friends, location history. Tons more since everything leaves a digital record. The program finds correlations among historically bad people and teaches itself to predict who will be bad in the future."

"Fascinating. Most people are pretty good, right? There's just a few bad apples."

"Yeah. I call them blips. Find and fix the blips."

"Doesn't it violate privacy laws?"

"Not too much, because the operators can't see personally identifiable info. The blip's info is encrypted and sent to a special court. The judge sees everything and orders an arrest warrant to commit the blip to an institution for rehab. Fix and release—or keep them locked up forever."

"Like that old movie, *Minority Report*."

"No. That was Hollywood sci-fi babble about mutant mind readers. This is real AI, complex algorithms, all designed by yours truly."

Connor sighed. "Can your genius algorithms tell me what to do with my life? 'Cause I keep thinking I shouldn't have married Melissa and I shouldn't have taken this job. I should have done everything different."

Harry laughed. "It's way too late for you. You're done. Look—here's a new warrant request. This blip's out of rehab for the seventh time. She's supposed to be sober, but her shopper card shows wine purchases. Family history shows violence. She can't hold a job or keep a boyfriend."

"Poor woman. She hasn't done anything wrong, though."

"She will. The system forecasts theft and assault. If she keeps going, she'll drop off the edge."

"But she won't do it if you stop her."

"It seems like a paradox, but it's not. The traffic jam will happen without the app recommending a new route—this woman will go bad if she keeps going."

"The blip will blip unless fixed."

"Right. Here's another one. Hey, lives in Deer Park out by you, and works around here. Were you in Sacramento last October?"

"No," Connor lied and downed the rest of the bottle.

"This blip was. It's an evil one. The forecast is murder-suicide. I'm flipping the warrant bit on this one too."

Connor quickly opened another beer. "You working late? I really have to go."

"Yeah."

"Okay, later Harry. Great work. Congrats, man." Connor walked back to his office and chugged alcohol in hurried gulps. It must be a different person, he thought. It can't be me. He tried not to think about Sacramento.

Thoughts clattered around his brain: Spangler, Melissa, the disgruntled declawed cat, the returned puppy, Sacramento, Harry and the blip warrant. What if it *is* me? he worried. God, I'll be put away for years, probably the rest of my life. The brain peekers will prod into my deranged mind and see that I'm completely unfit for society.

He took his nine-millimeter Beretta pistol out of his desk drawer and studied it. He could walk down the hall, make Harry delete the warrant, and kill him. But he could never kill anyone, even if he could get away with it, which he wouldn't. Never. He wasn't a murderer.

Suicide? No way. Stupid. Focus on solving the problem, he told himself. Another idea came—he'd leave town tomorrow and head to a nowhere burg in the Midwest. He'd change his name and work landscaping for cash. He'd stay off the digital radar and live analog. There's a way out, he thought. I can break free if I stop the pity party and take some action. Be a man. Yes.

Driving home, stuck in jammed traffic, he tingled with anticipation and planned his next steps. How to disappear? In the morning, he'd withdraw all the cash he could and toss his phone and credit cards. Outside the city, he'd ditch his car; buy a bicycle, a map, and a backpack of supplies. He'd travel side roads. The adventure excited him. He should have done this years ago! He laughed out loud and thanked God for showing him a detour to the light. Who needed all this nonsense? Not him. Finally, he was going to become the person he should have been.

Taillights lit up—abrupt red blips in front of him. He braked, rolled forward slowly to a cop, and lowered the window.

"What's going on?" he asked the trooper.

"DUI checkpoint," the officer said sternly. "Have you been drinking?"

Connor spoke carefully. "No."

The cop stared into him. "Nothing?"

"Just a beer after work. Maybe two."

"Maybe two? Give me your license and registration."

Connor handed over the documents. The officer scanned them and said, "Hmm. Okay, sir, I want you to pull over there, to the right lane, please."

"I'm not drunk!"

"Okay, we just need to talk to you. Pull over and we'll figure it out."

It *was* me, Connor thought. I'm a blip and there's already a warrant to arrest me. Sacramento—my God, they'll lock me up forever.

He stalled. "I have to get home. My wife's waiting."

The officer bellowed, "Right lane and stop the car. That's an order!"

Everything blurred like a sad dream. Connor watched himself pick up his Beretta from under his seat and point it at the cop. Then he screamed, "No! I'm not going that way!"

The cop's hands flew up over his head, and he stepped back and roared, "Drop the gun! Now!"

The windshield shattered. Another cop from somewhere had fired. Shocked, Connor pulled the trigger and blasted the face of the hands-up cop; the officer's skull exploded into gore and the trooper collapsed, dying.

A hail of gunfire plowed into his car. A red burn exploded across his shoulder.

Connor's mind scrambled. I shot a cop. What have I done? Oh God, what have I done? I shot a cop. I didn't mean it. I didn't mean to do it. I didn't mean to do it!

Conclusions came instantly and he saw his entire future unfold in a moment—life in prison, cop-killer, maybe the death penalty. His life was over. He saw that everything was over.

Connor took the gun, held it to his temple, and fired.

The blip was fixed.

Screenlight Sonata

Silhouette in screenlight
coder decodes a dream
into characters coded
into a machine
that decodes

Dream flows from mind
to clicks
to machine
to screenlight
decode code decode

Click enter
the dream illuminates
continents away
screens light up
with the dream

The night becomes day
The dream becomes real
machine by machine
screenlight by screenlight
mind by mind

The sun rises
the world illuminates
the coder reposes
dreaming
of screenlight

Odd Morning (aka Who's Tim?)

The birds are entirely off script, Ed thought. Robins and sparrows usually chattered constantly, but they were quiet this morning. Did they go south already? In a single day? Was it the weather? Or was a predator close? He'd need to look it up.

He got up, made the bed, put on shorts, and went downstairs to find Molly, his persevering wife, who kept holding on through all the stupid things he'd done. She'd already left for work, which was unusual—she always kissed him goodbye. *I was going to get the camp chairs out of her Chevy for coffee on the driveway*, he thought. Now that he had all the time in the world, he was doing things like that.

Was she upset with him? Did she hear him on the internet last night when he thought she was sleeping? He hoped not. She was starting to trust him again.

There was a note on the kitchen counter, blue ink on white lined paper:

The dishwasher is full! + Tim didn't come up.

Hmm. No "Have a great day," no "I love you," not even a little heart drawn at the bottom. And who was Tim? He peeked into the dishwasher and it was full of clean dishes. Okay, so that part of her note made sense.

He walked outside to the drone-box to get the morning groceries and heard a wail. What was that? He listened again. It sounded like a rooster. He'd never heard a rooster in the neighborhood before. Which idiot neighbor was rude and stupid enough to have a rooster?

A barking dog answered the rooster, a howling snarl, like the dog was trying to alert the neighborhood to someone in trouble and was eager to inflict pain on whoever it could—to the death.

He stopped to listen closer. But all the sounds stopped—no more rooster, no more killer dog. And now the birds were back. He heard the soft up-down of a single robin, like a metronome, with sparrow chirps behind it—a backing track that was familiar, except there were usually more robins. It was a minor thing, but odd.

Back in the house, he was hit with the realization that his perception must be off. Everything was normal, but he was processing normal inputs differently. Then again, Molly's note was weird. Yes, maybe, but that was the only tangible thing, and a very small thing, the only odd thing that wasn't subject to the filter of his mind. He was crazy to dwell on the other things—bird noises, a rooster, a dog barking—those were all perfectly explainable suburban events.

I'm not crazy anymore, he thought. I'm normal. I'm overthinking things, as usual, and my overthinking always goes nowhere, or much, much worse. So stop it. Just stop.

The right approach was to stay on the surface. He'd get a mug of the coffee Molly had made and skip reading the news because it was always either upsetting or a waste of time. He'd write down his to-do list and plan his day.

But who was Tim? He thought about texting Molly, but there was no reason to bother her at work. He'd wait until she got home. And for sure he'd empty the dishwasher. Tim? Who was Tim? *Forget Tim,* he ordered himself.

A voice came from the heating vent on the kitchen floor. Ed didn't recognize the voice, and he knelt and spoke into the vent. "Hello?" he said.

"Is anyone up there?"

"Who's this?"

"I'm Tim," the voice said.

"I don't know a Tim."

"You forgot about me?" the man's voice said. "You locked me in the basement room, and I'm really hurt bad. Please let me out. I need a doctor."

"Wait, last night was real? And your name is Tim?"

"Yes," the voice answered.

Ed gasped. He thought everything had been online. Molly hadn't called the police, thank God. So maybe she didn't know everything.

He looked at the steak knives in the wood holder on the new marble countertop. He would grab a knife, a bunch of old towels, and the hose, and take care of everything before Molly got home. Then he'd get some wine and some salmon fillets for the grill. He'd cut flowers from the garden for the table. He'd make a fantastic dinner and act like nothing had happened, like he'd never been an idiot and never would be again.

The Principal Uncertainty

When Jim, the company CEO and my former good friend, messaged that he wanted to meet for lunch, I asked why.

"It's been a while," he replied.

His vagueness made me uneasy. Bad news coming, I thought. The last time we met in person was at lunch a year ago. Jim told me my performance was exceptional but then announced that unfortunately he wasn't giving me the promotion that I deserved more than anyone else. Instead, he was promoting, drumroll pleeeease . . . rat-a-tat-*crash* . . . Guess who? Amy, who would help us fill our diversity quota in the top ranks.

"Amy's a mixed-race lesbian in a wheelchair, with a felony record, multiple learning disabilities, and major mental health issues," he explained. "We don't have to promote her, but we have to promote her."

Worried I'd quit, he gave me an oversized raise, a massive retention bonus, and a bunch of stock options so I'd stay, make things actually happen, and stop Amy, our shining lesbian light of learning-disabled corporate diversity, from driving the company over a cliff while she rambled incoherently in meetings and took all the credit that I deserved.

I had gotten incredibly drunk at that meeting and screamed at him in front of the entire lunch crowd, then left, taking my fresh and delicious double bourbon onto Park Avenue with me. I tested out ten or more bars on the way home, slept on it, came in the next afternoon horribly hungover, and told him yes, I understood, I'll make it happen, and thanks so much for the hefty raise.

But I decided then that Jim was no longer my good friend.

I slipped into a reverie, remembering a morning back in high school, working at the marina in early May, putting boats in for the season. It was forty-something degrees, freezing, drizzling, and I was wearing a rain suit and a winter hat to keep dry and warm while driving a tiny skiff over the calm lake at eight in the morning.

I was the only boat on the lake and the water was glass. In front of me it looked like eternal stillness and I carved through it at full gliding speed and there wasn't a ripple or a bump, and that moment was perfect. I wish that moment was my eternity, captaining a small boat forever across a glass lake through a mist, dressed warm in the cold drizzle, looking at forests covering the surrounding hills, sipping a thermos mug of coffee. No end to just cruising the lake forever.

But gliding on the lake for eternity doesn't pay any bills, and I have a lot of bills—several homes, a yacht, a staff, fancy cars, ex-wives, and a new wife. All the above had to be paid for, and that meant selling my soul in exchange for a whopping salary. My greatest hope was that I was leasing my soul, not selling it, and that at the end of the lease I'd get it back. It'd be worn out, in disrepair and dinged, but I'd have time to get it back into shape and become who I really was again—that teenage boy, content and free, gliding across the lake in the morning mist, ready to take on the world.

I remember looking up ahead through the mist and seeing this narrow gap between rocky, tree-covered hills. I was headed straight for the gap but couldn't see what was on the other side of it. The fog thickened at the gap, creating a wall of dense white that I would drive right into. But I wasn't afraid of the unknown then. I was excited by it.

Jim is going to fire me at lunch, I realized. He doesn't need my horrible attitude and ironic shade dimming everything we do. Yes, I make things happen, but I never make people feel good about anything. I have the appalling power of making everyone around me feel stupid. Almost everyone around me *is* stupid, but that's true for every leader, and the best leaders, the ones that rise to the top, make everyone feel smart and part of the team. I'm not a good enough actor.

Or maybe, I worried, he had found out about me and Rebecca. No way, no way, *no way*. Please God.

But either way, I calculated, I'm fired. Don't get drunk at lunch, I ordered myself. Keep your dignity for once and maybe he'll second-guess his decision.

We met at the restaurant inside the Loews Regency hotel, one of his favorites, hopefully just because everyone else thinks it's cool. If he actually likes the food and atmosphere, then God help all of us. And I don't care if Jesus Christ himself is peeling the potatoes, there's no plate of french fries worth what the Loews maniacs charge.

We traded notes about the weather, the stock market, and Manhattan and Brooklyn real estate prices until our drinks arrived. He took a meager sip of his vesper martini, and I realized I was about to hear some preliminary, unrelated miscellany, probably some painful personal anecdote that he felt had to be confessed to build rapport before he fired me. I took a gigantic gulp of my double bourbon and drew circles on the tablecloth with my finger.

Jim said, "Back when you and I were at Prudential, Rebecca was in our call center but so ravishing I thought she was out of my league. I fell in love with her the day I saw her but didn't make a move because of HR. Then, after I left Pru, I asked her to dinner and had way too much to drink. I took her to my new office and grabbed her hand and led her to that balcony looking over Central Park.

"I started kissing her and she was into it. She said she thought this might happen, and I talked my way back to her place, but nothing more ended up happening that night. She freaked out and told me to leave right after I got there.

"I raced home, got online, and sent her flowers, almost to her desk but changed my mind, thank God, because the next day I hacked into her email through a back door and saw her blabbing to another loudmouth girl in the call center about kissing me, and how I had a wife and kids, and what an idiot I was for chasing her.

"So, I pivoted pronto and emailed her that I was sorry we got carried away and wanted to just focus on being her friend and colleague, and I could let her know of job opportunities. She said okay and we kept meeting up for drinks and dinners, and eventually we got together, and, you know most of the sordid story. I left my family and we got married.

"So anyway, she's sixteen years younger and always on social media and Snapgram and Instachat or whatever—this is over two years later now, almost three—and she looks good, she's gotten more beautiful as she's gotten older, and she doesn't have a young girl's high-pitched voice anymore, which was always sort of creepy, so maybe I've helped her overcome whatever trauma I always theorize must be responsible for that.

"But she's ranting all the time on Instagram, and I'm impressed by her looks, her confidence, and her strong point of view, but more and more concerned about her stability and her sanity, and wondering if she might be nuts because it appears she is, and if so, if she would have been less nuts if we hadn't ended up together? Or maybe I've given her a more stable life and kept her out of the deep end or at least slowed down her descent into it."

"Yeah," I said.

"And, you know, I love Madison so much. I'm mostly glad our marriage ended even if I felt like a stupid idiot. But I still can't help wondering how it would have worked out if I'd stayed, you know? Would Madison be online ranting about the Illuminati if I'd stayed? Is this something that would've happened to whoever I ended up with? Is it my fault? Or my destiny? Or somehow both mushed up?"

"It's hard to know," I said. Maybe he didn't know about me and Rebecca, I realized. She always insisted he didn't, but I figured he had to, especially after the concert.

"Here, watch this." He scrolled on his phone and put it on the table. He played a video of Rebecca and she looked impossibly young and attractive, walking in a park while talking into the camera. She wore a green cable-knit sweater over a white collared shirt. She had long blonde-brown hair and dimples, and her eyes were intense. The display said the video was nine-something minutes long. Ugh.

"I'm de-screening during meals," I said, "to reduce my insanity. I'll watch it later. Send it to me. Or better yet, just put the phone away and give me the rundown. She's gorgeous, by the way."

"Yeah, thank God," he replied. "I mean, if some gross old guy said all this stuff then it would be even crazier. C'mon, you have to listen to her. I *can't* summarize it. There's nuances and details and if I summarize you're going to pick up all my bias, which is this underlying-slash-growing realization that I never should have left Madison and the kids for her."

Jim continued, "I'm worried I made a serious mistake, and I need to shut this relationship down pronto and race back home and beg Madison for a second chance. But maybe not, right? Maybe I'm overreacting and overanalyzing everything because of the guilt I feel over leaving my family— my absolute paranoia, bordering on certainty, that I've probably ruined my kids."

I listened and he kept going. "I need an outside opinion, don't you understand? Another rational voice, physically outside of my own head, that can help me process all this. Because right now, I'm on a bad trajectory. We're talking suicide, and/or murder, and/or total breakdown. Nonsense is coming at me from all sides of the periphery, and I can't persevere without third-party insight."

"Okay, I'll watch it later," I said.

"No, now. The problem is, she posts these things then swears off social media forever and deletes them, sometimes right after. It could be gone in an hour. Please," he begged.

"Okay." I pressed PLAY.

On the screen, Rebecca said,

"All right. Man, I have not wanted to do this. I have not wanted to record myself, uh, and post on social media. It's like the last thing I wanted to do. Um . . . yeah, um, but I just can't take it anymore. Um, you know, I've spent the past few years, going on three years of my life, changed my whole life, left my mainstream job, um, went into the woods, studied healing modalities for the past five years, became a reiki master yoga instructor, got married, all that jazz.

"And yeah, I really thought when I went into this that it was gonna be like all love and light, and I would come on Instagram and be like"—she raised her voice into a mocking sing-song—'ohhh, you knowww, looove and liiight and unityyyy. Rebecca, we're all one, that's what this is.'

Her voice dropped back to normal. "But you know what?" She paused, shook her head, bit her lip, and her eyes looked off to the left. "Then . . . then you have some rapper, um, and Nike and whatever else, putting out shoes with human blood. Human blood in it! And it's just like, what? Really?

"The mainstream controls everything: our music, our movies, the news, television shows. Everything that we see is monitored and controlled, sooo why? So, then it's like—this is—then it's like we're putting, uh, out sneakers that cost over a thousand dollars, marketed to young kids, children and teenagers, innocent children and teenagers, impressionable young people, that this is, this is the cool thing, this is what we should be *doing*. Shoes with human blood in it. Are you freaking *kidding* me?

"That's disgraceful. It's disgraceful to our society, it's disgraceful to the human . . . person, our beings. It's absolutely ridiculous, and to sit back and be like, oh,"—she took on a high pitched voice—"this is just, this is just what it is, this is just what—where we're at now in this life and da, da, da, our society."—her voice returned to normal—"Screw that! This is *ridiculous*. This is disturbing. And there is so much more going on here within our society than meets the eye. And if we want to just sit baaack and veg ooouuut, and driiink, and binge watch shooows, you know, that's great—do you.

"But . . . this society continues to go in a very disturbing direction. And I don't even have children yet, but the people who do, I can't imagine how anyone's even sleeping at night knowing this, it's so disturbing and wrong. And if we—you know, I can't stand social media really. I don't like Facebook and Instagram, but it's occurred to me that it's a platform to come out and speak your truth, whatever that may be.

"And I mean, this is just, it's absolutely ridiculous, it's absolutely ridiculous that we live in a society where we're promoting, um, some rapper's gonna come out with shoes, that cost over a thousand dollars mind you, that were made in China by a poor child. It's sick! It's sick and disturbing and no one wants to say anything. No one says *anything*, it's just,"—she took on a high-pitched voice— "'Oh, this is what it is.'

"No, this isn't what it is! We all need to open our eyeballs up, and, actually, we need to open our eye"—she pointed to the center of her forehead and tapped it repeatedly—"this eye, the pineal gland, and if you don't know what that means, look it up.

"Because it's disturbing what's going on in this society, and you know what? I've never wanted to come on here. I've never wanted to talk like this. I've never wanted—you think I want to post that Bill Gates, uh, posted before the pandemic that he's puttin' all his money in vaccines. Really? And these . . . the one percent, and the Illuminati, and all this—that's not real? That's conspiracy theory? Blah, blah, blah! That's freakin' *bull*! Okay? It *is* real!

"There's a lot of things that people have deemed conspiracy theory that are real. And you know what? The truth is more insane than any stupid movie you're gonna watch, any song you're gonna hear, any TV show you're gonna tune into, any SVU episode. Guess what? The truth of what's going on in this world is a hundred times more unfathomable than you can imagine.

"And I encourage everybody . . . to . . . go within their hearts, start meditating, start getting your body right, start getting your mind right, start doing some research on your own, and—and looking into this stuff, and figuring out what—what is *actually* going on. It's very, very, very disturbing. And to sit around and say nothing, I mean, it's just, I can't do it anymore.

"I mean, how can we live? And I want to be all love and light; I mean I'm a healer. I just spent years of my life becoming a healer and . . . only, I mean, if anything I'm . . . I've had to go through yet another dark night of the soul— and if you don't know what that is, look it up—basically questioning everything.

"And so, I questioned my whole life and gave up my—my—the best job I ever had, my Audi, and living in a high-rise Manhattan condo on the park because none of that felt right, and then, you know, I became a healer, uh, yoga instructor. I got married to a magnificent man and finally found out what love really is.

"You go within all of this and then you come into the spiritual community and you realize there's even, you know, there's even more going on. And our society—and to—to say that, um, no, you can't come out, you can't speak your truth, and it's, 'Oh, you can't talk about that because that's going to lower your vibration?' Screw that! Okay? *Screw* that!

"We need to be opening our eyes to the facts of what's going on and take a stand against this. No one should be paying eleven hundred dollars for shoes that have human blood in them, and that's a cool thing. That's *not* okay. That should be stopped. That should not be the—do you really want your innocent children—this is what we want our kids to be exposed to? Our society's so oversexualized—that video! I mean, *what* is going *on*? Even when I was growing up, it was insane, but *now* it's like, how can we bring children into this world and expose them to this?

"Not to mention child sex trafficking. That's the *real* pandemic. Women sex trafficking. That's the *real* freaking pandemic that we need to worry about, but that's not—that's not, um—there's no news stories on that every single day. You know what? I lived near the port where every single other week they opened shipping containers to women and children coming out of different countries for se—human trafficking. That's the real issue in this screwed-up world.

"But nope! Let's not talk about that! Let's uh, let's report on some stupid Republican crap, some stupid Democrat crap. It's like, no, guys! *Wake up*, become an independent thinker, step into your sovereignty, step into yourself, figure out who you are and what your divine purpose is in this world. What you're contributing here. Because getting *uuup*, drinking *coffeee*, going to *wooork*, having the man control you, coming *hooome*, eating crap food, drinking fluoridated water, going to sleep, drinking beers, waking up, and doing it all over again—this is *life*? And no wonder why everybody is depressed, anxious, and heartbroken.

"Number one killer in the world until"—she made air quotes—"Covid, um, was heart disease. We're all heartbroken because our food's poisoned, our water's poisoned, and this system is broken. We're slaves to a money that is an illusion. We have the power to change this world, and we need to step into that."

She closed her eyes, took a deep breath in, then exhaled. Her eyes flicked to the left then to the right, and she said, "I'm sorry I'm so, like, passionate and hyphy about this, but I just—" She flicked her neck, tossing her long hair off her face. "There are innocent children that are being born into this world every single day, and now they're born into a world where we're selling shoes for eleven hundred dollars, Satanic shoes with human blood in it.

"No," she said, shaking her head. "No. I'm not gonna just not say anything about this. That's insane. It's ridiculous. It's absolutely—it, it really shows where this society . . . is. And we need—now is the time to step up into your truth. Who gives a flip what anyone thinks of you for saying your truth? Say your truth! Say what you believe! We have to! We *have* to!

"'Cause you know what, guys? There's a World War Three going on and it's a spiritual war. It's a spiritual war. Our sovereignty, our freedom. This, you know, what is it? You grow up hearing, uh, we live in America—it's the land of the free because of the brave." She paused and nodded. "Yeah, because of the *brave*. And we really need to step into that. We really need to step into our courage. We really need to step into our truth.

"And, you know, I'm not going to say I'm sorry for coming on here and doing a rant about this. Um, because I said what I said, and that's it. And you know what? Uh, I wanna keep—I wanna be all love and light 'cause I am, I'm a reiki master, I believe in healing. I believe in love and light, and anchoring as much light down onto this planet as we can, and keeping our vibrations high. But we also need to understand what the truth is.

"We need to come together as a collective group, as humans that love each other. We need to stop judging each other. We need to come together as people who love each other unconditionally if we're gonna make it out of this. It's just gonna get more chaotic, and that's why it's gonna be really important to meditate, to understand who you are, to try to keep your own truth and your own sovereignty present within yourself.

"Alright guys, that's enough for now. You know, I'm sending—I love everyone. I love everybody who sees this, and I hope if you do see this it's more of just like, yeah, you know, waking up to, you know, that we could be doing so much better. Be the change you wish to see. Peace, love, and light."

The video ended. Jim looked at me expectantly, waiting for my analysis.

"What if she's right about everything?" I asked.

Jim laughed, chuckling up some of his drink. "Good one," he said. "You're a riot, man. Check out the comments. In replying to one of them, she references 'hashtag reptilian'. I looked it up, and it's connected with this British guy who argues that the world is ruled by shape-shifting aliens posing as humans. The Queen of England, the Bush family, the Rockefellers, a bunch of other world leaders."

"I'm killing myself trying to become rich and powerful. Now you're telling me that I need to become a reptile alien? Fine. I'll do it."

"I'm just reporting the news," he said. "I don't make it. Look, seriously now, I don't know what to do, and I'd like your thoughts on the whole thing."

"She covers a lot of bases," I said. "Satanic sneakers, media mind-control, child sex trafficking, crap food, the Illuminati, and fluoridated water."

"It's nuts," Jim said. "There's so much horrible grammar too. She keeps saying *gonna* instead of *going to*, dropping G's, and talking in fragmented sentences. The lousy grammar bothers me more than her insanity because it makes my friends and family think less of her. I mean, in their minds, insanity is a temporary affliction—like bad acne or bankruptcy. You hide out for a while and it goes away. Atrocious grammar, on the other hand, is the irreversible, lifelong curse of poor upbringing and low intelligence."

"It's not that bad."

"It's not that super great, either. And do her eyes look crazy to you? Sometimes her eyes look crazy to me."

Her eyes might look crazy, I thought. She was either crazy or sane, and either way Jim had a long road of drama and tortured misery ahead. But I didn't like him well enough anymore to be honest. And most likely no one did.

"Her eyes looked passionate," I said. "And they're honest. She's honest, and I was impressed by her passion. It's nice when someone has a point of view about anything these days and will say it and stand by it."

"Yeah, you think? That's true, she's gorgeous. Now you know why I left everything for her. And she's smart, right? I mean, to listen to her, it sounds like she's really smart."

"She said to say your truth," I said. "What's yours?"

"I don't know," Jim said. "You?"

"I don't know either," I answered. "Rebecca is fine. You're fine. You're a fabulous couple, and you just have to hold on and ride everything out. Just glide over the bumps until it's smooth sailing again, and you'll both be fine."

"Thanks. I think you're right. I really needed to hear this."

"What else do we need to talk about?" I asked.

"Nothing, really. I had to get this off my chest to someone I trust. Thanks for being that friend."

"No problem," I said.

I glanced out the window at the billions of strangers walking by and wondered if any one of them had ever driven a boat across a misty, glassy lake. I wondered which of them were excited by the unknown.

Later that night, at my third or fourth bar, it occurred to me that Rebecca was sane, and the rest of us are completely nuts. I went online to listen to her again, but her account was deleted. I started crying and kept tapping my forehead with my finger, and I couldn't stop for a long time.

Elysium

Here I'm done pretending

I'm done pretending I'm excited
I'm done pretending I'm calm
I'm done. Pretending I'm interested

Pretending I'm indifferent
Pretending to love
Pretending to hate

Some people taught me
To pretend
Then I taught some people

Here we're done pretending

Version Control

"The iPhone 4 is hot. This is brilliant engineering."
        —Steve Jobs, iPhone 4 launch, 2010

"The iPhone 4 is obsolete."
        —*Business Insider*, 2016

"Maximize yield. Select the traits that benefit you."
        —Monsanto Corporation website, 2022

"Every generation will be a superior species."
        —Edisna (genetic architect), 2086

* * *

Evan and Amber lingered at the kitchen table. Dinner was over and their sons—Conrad, eighteen, and Luke, sixteen—had stormed off. But they stayed, tensed and coiled, each waiting for the other to speak.

Finally, Evan spoke. "It's gotten so much worse. There's too much discrimination."

"There's less prejudice in the Outer Colonies," Amber said cautiously. "I read an article today about more Randoms leaving."

"We'd never see him. He can't go live with crazies and criminals."

"It's an option," Amber said. "I'm just putting possibilities out there."

"He's never leaving Earth!" Evan snapped.

"Well, you're not helping, always yelling at him. He hates us."

"He's immature! And I—we—have to help him," Evan said. "Look, I'm a Seven and you're an Eight Plus. You're better than me, especially at music and writing. I'm surrounded by better Versions and don't complain. I accept it."

Amber's finger drew circles around the stem of her wineglass. She said firmly, "But Conrad's Random—unlicensed and untested. We should've gone with Public Domain Versions for both boys. Then they wouldn't be so different from each other."

She paused and took a breath. "Between you, and teachers, and coaches— it's all about being the best, a new world record every week. It's soul-crushing for Conrad to realize he'll never be exceptional when his brother's one of the best."

Evan leaned across the table towards her. "Being Random builds character. Everyone's got to accept there's always improved Versions. No matter how great you are, in a few years, today's babies will be even better. And maybe he has a unique ability—some Randoms are creative."

"I know, but—"

"What's the answer, other than getting him to accept it? We were broke, and Public Domain Versions were total crap, so Random seemed like the right choice." Evan shrugged his shoulders. "Maybe we screwed up, but apologizing won't help. Conrad needs toughness and if he keeps feeling sorry for himself, he won't get tough. I'm trying to give him tenacity so he can have a life on Earth."

"Look," Amber said, "we want the same thing—for him to have some chance. We're on the same team." She forced a smile, went to Evan, sat on his lap, and hugged him. He clung to her.

"There's a balance," she said. "Will you go talk to Conrad nicely? Listen instead of yelling?"

"Okay. Of course. Good idea. Yeah, I'll go talk to him."

* * *

Lying on his bed, Conrad swiped away the news article about the Outer Colonies. *Focus,* he reminded himself. He concentrated on his class reading assignment:

"Regulations prohibit Genetic Randoms from working in physically demanding and intellectually rigorous occupations. Exclusion began with a Supreme Court ruling that employers could give preference to Genetic Versions. The employer argument was convincing: because Random DNA is untested, hiring Randoms is risky.

"As new Versions become increasingly feature-rich, the problems with Randoms are more evident. Worse-than-below-average intelligence and physical ability, is the higher probability of unpredictable behavior.

"Randoms sometimes display inappropriate emotions. They get frustrated and make mistakes more often. Outside of work, some drink too much and live disorganized lives.

"Random talents are unknown, while Versions can be categorized: programmer, mechanic, musician, etc.—which employers appreciate. In an increasingly competitive economy—"

Conrad scrolled ahead. He stopped at a quote from Edisna, the architect of Genetic Versioning:

"Constant Version improvement means every generation will be a superior species."

Except me, Conrad thought. I'm a mutant. Luke's new and improved, but I'm a living relic, alone in a world where loneliness is the mark of the loser.

He was lonely everywhere. But his bedroom was a sanctuary because he could be alone with his loneliness. Everywhere else, his separateness was neon-lit. At school he sat in a loser's spotlight, apart from the crowd, driftwood floating alone, swirling pointlessly in an eddy.

He hated that Luke was an advanced Version and better than him at everything. But his parents had been destitute when he was conceived, so his DNA was natural and included untested genes from generations ago. Perhaps he had good traits, but he'd just as likely inherited the worst. The uncertainty was a curse.

I'm trapped in a maze with no exit, Conrad thought. But one way out is a girl. Gemma appeared in his mind's eye. She kept smiling his way and talking to him at school. When she had walked next to him yesterday on the summer sidewalk, laughing at his jokes, with her long mane of softly curled black hair brushing his arm, he'd felt cool and part of everything.

The infatuation between them had been growing for weeks, and tomorrow was their first date. The anticipation lifted him.

There was a knock on his bedroom door.

"Conrad?"

"Hey, Dad," Conrad answered.

Evan opened the door. "Hey, can we talk?"

"I guess," he said stiffly.

Evan sat down on the bed and said, "I'm sorry things have been so horrible for you. The science project, hockey, the dinner blowup."

"The science fair judges don't get it! If I'm not raping nature inside out, it's not science?"

"Yeah."

"And hockey. Everyone skates circles around me. If I was coach, I would've cut me too."

Evan offered, "Hey, I think you're great just how you are. Think about music. Randoms are God's jazz—nature's special improvisations."

"So, I should be a musician?"

Evan laughed. "Yeah, maybe. It's up to you. Some Randoms take leaps into creative genius that Versions can't, and if each life is a song, then yours is more compelling because it's unique."

"I hear you. That's one way to think about it."

"Growing up, I had a Random friend and really admired her. She saw the same things differently, and I was fascinated. I hate how we're all categorized, and you're a blatant middle finger to Version Control—proof that nature can still call some shots."

Conrad protested, "But I want to live a normal life, with friends like everyone else. I'm an outcast, and everyone's better at grades and sports, and I'll never get into a good college or get a decent job."

"You can be anything, and you can do it on your own. You could be an entrepreneur or an author."

Conrad's thoughts shifted, a red-orange hue permeated his mind, and he imagined himself screaming, "*I could be a psycho killer! How's that career sound, Dad?*" He saw himself holding a black metal gun and firing into his father's face. "*Game over, Pops!*" The nightmare daydream evaporated. God, where'd that horrible fantasy come from? He could never hurt anyone. He twitched himself to shake away the homicidal vision.

"You're right," Conrad said. "I can do it on my own."

Evan smiled. "You'll astonish everyone. I know it, and I love you so much." He leaned over and hugged Conrad, surprising him. Conrad lifted his arms and hugged his father back.

They clung to each other for a few moments. Then Evan got up and left the room.

* * *

That night, Evan and Amber were together in bed. "How'd it go?" Amber asked, holding Evan's hand and leaning into him, eager and hopeful.

"Good," Evan said, lying on his back, staring blankly at swirls in the textured ceiling.

"Thanks for talking to him. So, what'd you say?"

"I said everything's going to be fine."

"You think he feels better?"

"I hope so."

"And Luke?"

"Luke's good. There's nothing to talk about with Luke."

"Come to me," she said.

He turned to her, she touched him, and their worries stopped for a while.

* * *

The next afternoon, Conrad's date with Gemma was going p-e-r-f-e-c-t-l-y. Her smile made him smile. Their connected eyes lingered while they laughed in the summer sun. Her hand touched his arm and made him feel like he'd conquered the world—and was part of it.

They were on his back deck, sitting in the Adirondack chairs, talking and watching two wild squirrels chase each other around the trunk of a massive pine tree. Gemma's bare legs were sprawled across his, their ankles intersecting. She touched his hand, and her finger drew circles on it while her other hand clasped the flower he'd given her.

This moment is perfect, he thought. If time stops forever, I'll be perfect.

They heard a slam—the front door—then footsteps. Conrad hoped it was Mom; maybe she was wearing boots. But no, Luke appeared.

Conrad tried to stay calm. Act normal, he thought. How do I act normal? Give me the steps to memorize and no one will know I'm not normal because I'll follow all the steps.

Luke came out, cracking open a soda. "What's up, nutjob?" He lifted the can to his lips, chugged a few gulps, then threw the can at Conrad's feet. The aluminum rang against the wood planks, and soda splattered on them, like a challenge. Gemma, startled, removed her legs from Conrad's and put her hands in her lap.

Luke took a sharply angled rock out of his pocket. "Watch this." He wound up, threw the rock, and it spiked, with bullet-like precision, into the face of one of the frolicking squirrels. The animal fell over dead, its skull crushed. The second squirrel froze in terror then raced away, scrambling up the tree and out of sight.

"No!" Conrad yelled. "Why? They were just playing!"

Luke laughed and turned to them. "Pretty *random* seeing you here, Gemma."

Conrad started sweating. He saw reality reverse, changing course—from climbing to spiraling downhill and out of his control. Gemma's eyes wouldn't meet his. Luke had murdered the perfect afternoon, and much, much more.

Luke grabbed Gemma's hand and yanked her up effortlessly, picked her up by her waist, and swung her around.

"Put me down!" she yelled, frightened.

Luke laughed, bringing her closer to him and spinning.

"Stop!" Conrad yelled.

Luke set Gemma down. "You gonna make me? Okay, hey, let's watch dice-roll go nutso!" He stepped forward and shoved Conrad.

A hard-orange dot of clean rage appeared in Conrad's mind as he grabbed Luke's throat, flipped him to the ground, and pounded his face into the deck. The first slams stunned Luke, then Conrad dragged his brother to the metal railing and spiked his head into it three or ten times. He grabbed handfuls of hair and felt Luke's scalp peel away as he hammered his brother's skull into the cast-iron grill before dropping him. Conrad's feet took over, and he kicked his brother in the face again and again.

Then Conrad dropped to his knees. He ripped apart Luke's smile, gouged out his eyes, and tore away the rest of his scalp until the body lay motionless. A blob of gore.

Conrad sat up, victorious. Gemma stepped away in terrified horror, stunned. Then she ran, leaving him alone with the corpse.

* * *

THE DAILY MESSENGER
ANOTHER RANDOM MURDER

Conrad Deen, a Random, was convicted of manslaughter yesterday in the bloody beating death of his younger brother, Luke Deen, a Twelve Plus. During sentencing, Conrad was permanently banished from Earth and exiled to an Outer Colony.

After the trial, Prosecutor Maria Schneider said, "Another life has been lost. The issue of Random violence must be addressed."

"We need to start doing proactive mitigation on these so-called People," Schneider said. "Randoms are capable of completely losing control. Conrad attacked his brother for no reason."

The senseless murder comes as Earth marks a twenty-percent drop in homicides this year.

"As Randomness declines, violence declines," Schneider said. "We all know what the problem is."

Helicopter Rides in Toyland

The helicopter awaited flight on the roof of the skyscraper.

"Where am I going?" Davis asked Julie, his assistant.

"New Jersey," she said. "There's a meeting with the head of Oakmont."

"About?"

"He's worried you're ripping him off," Julie said.

"*We*," Davis corrected her. "We're a company. It's not just me."

"Everyone's just doing what you tell them."

"How much?"

"They gave us four hundred million last quarter, for a total investment of over two billion now."

"Nice."

"I think they want to back out," she said.

"If they want to get a dime back, they'll have to give us another quarter-billion."

"Good luck. You need to leave. You're already late."

In the air, his headset on, Davis looked down at the city below—the toy buildings and streets and cars and millions of people. All pretend, and all at the command of whomever had the most money and nerve.

"Approaching, sir," the helicopter pilot's voice said in his headset.

He gave a thumbs-up, took off his tie, and unbuttoned the top button on his shirt and his suit jacket. The aura he wanted to give off was one of nonchalance on the threshold of either total annihilation or absolute triumph, yet with crystal clear confidence in success.

The goal was always maximum leverage. There was no other purpose to existence.

At the meeting, Dickinson, the head of Oakmont, said, "I'll be honest, Davis—we're worried. Our risk team says this project is teetering. The headlines seem to have more bad news every day. Popular opinion is definitely against us."

"If it was easy, it wouldn't make us all rich," Davis said.

"We're already rich," Dickinson replied. "And our main goal is capital preservation. We can't lose our investors' money. We want to exercise our option to back out of the project. We've lost our appetite. I'm sorry."

"Don't be sorry," Davis said. "There's a line of money waiting to get on board. The issue you need to manage is the current market value of the project. If you pull out now, you're going to get less than half your money back."

"What in the hell are you talking about? You said our principal is guaranteed."

"Read the fine print, Dickinson," Davis said. "The principal is guaranteed after project completion. We're just about halfway there."

"You told me we can back out anytime!"

"You can. But your three dozen lawyers—who cost me a cool half mil in contract revisions—should have informed you that if you back out early, you lose."

"You screwed me," Dickinson snarled.

"To the contrary, I'm living up to our agreement. You're trying to screw *me*, and you're upset because you can't. This project is getting killed in the press. They're saying we're looting the city, polluting the environment, and exploiting working people, blah, blah, blah. And you backing out? That's gonna chainsaw it up into bloody pieces and toss it into the ocean. Can't happen. In fact, just this meeting getting leaked could be the nail in the coffin of the whole deal, you idiot. But I know how I can help you."

"How?"

"You put in a new half bil. We do a breaking-news press release about your excitement and confidence in the project so far and the market value bumps up big time, probably setting a new high and putting us all in a better place to make decisions about what to do next. You don't give us that vote of confidence, you know how it is. This stuff self-perpetuates, and we could all end up losing everything."

"Jesus, Davis."

"We can make this work great for both of us. We just gotta partner."

"Or?"

"Or we all lose. No biggie, we just start over from scratch. But why not win? Let's win big. What do you say?"

"Ugh. Send the papers. If it looks good, we'll wire the money this afternoon. Press release tomorrow?"

"Love it. You rock, Dickinson. How's the wife and kids?"

"They're hanging in there."

"Good to hear."

Davis checked the time. He would helicopter back to Manhattan and fit in his workout before lunch.

Relapse Haiku

the first soft burn says

hi this time is different

the disease believes

Letter to Dad From D3

Dear Dad,

I doubt you want to hear from me, but I'm thinking about you a lot lately and wanted to send you a note from here and let you know how things are going. If you've read the news, you've gotten one side of the story, but I want to give you my side. I had vivid, crazy dreams about you last night, I think inspired by the news of the new Headsets.

Please keep this letter private. I don't want any more online rigmarole, so please do that for me.

I failed as a man in this world—in work and relationships. So I decided to start a business in Digital World 3 (D3) as a woman. It was just for fun at first, a goof, an escape from my failures in Birth World (B). I started with nothing, worked my butt off in D3, and accumulated billions of credits. I was ruthless since D3 was just a game then, and yes, I lied and cut corners at times because it was supposed to be a game. And I gradually became successful enough in D3 that it made me successful in B. And figuring out which world was real got very blurry to me, then things came back into focus and D3 was more real.

I cashed in lots of my D3 credits and became very wealthy in B, and the real world that had always rejected me, now began to embrace me. My writing, which no one read in B, was bestselling in D3 and spawned the blockbuster films in B. I made B match D3—same cars, planes, and clothes. The colossal waterfront mansion I designed and built in D3, I replicated and built in B. I'd sit by my pool in B with my Headset on, reading and relaxing, while sitting by the exact same pool in D3, reading and relaxing. Very cool.

I used plastic surgery and drugs to become the woman in B that I was in D3. I changed my name legally in B to Samantha, my avatar name.

But then problems started creeping in—deals I made in D3 on the way up, that scammed billions of credits from other gamers, started going sour, and players in D3 were giving me horrible ratings, killing my rep score and making it tough to do business. Then players got together and filed a class action lawsuit in B, alleging fraud.

There was no escape. B and D3 were both hell, but B was way worse so I started insisting that everyone meet me in D3. The only way anyone could talk to me was to establish a D3 avatar and meet me there. My lawyers and accountants met me in the game. Even my deposition was done there and I remember the opposing lawyer asking me, "How do I know it's really you sitting there? What if you're an imposter?"

"How does anyone really know anything?" I asked him, and he couldn't answer that.

The judge wouldn't come to D3 for the trial, but I refused to attend from anywhere else. They piped a video stream into D3 for me to watch from my cell, and my avatar was displayed on-screen in court. My lawyers get kudos for negotiating that—the first trial in history where the defendant participated as an avatar from a virtual world.

But hell, everything I was accused of doing, every single allegation on the indictment, was something I did in D3—the fraud, the money laundering, the malfeasance. I might have gotten off if I'd done everything in B, but in D3, they had me nailed—there was a digital record of every deal, every fund transfer, and every lie.

Thank God, at least the murders I committed in D3, they can't get me for those, the laws haven't kept up. But they nailed me on almost everything else, and my avatar sat in D3 and received the sentence for my B-world self. I'm lucky I had a fortune to pay for good lawyers.

An aside—there's a theory online that lawyers are the true racketeers in this whole system. The law is a maze of rules and procedure, and once you're inside the maze, your only chance to escape is paying lawyers to get you out. Lesson learned—avoid ever entering the maze.

My lawyers made history again when they negotiated for me to live inside D3 during my imprisonment, convincing the judge that this is where I can make money to pay fines and compensate victims. So I'm lucky: while the rest of the prisoners stare at concrete walls and television, limited in movement and choices, I've got my Headset on almost all the time. I'm free and still somewhat powerful here in D3, and I'm much more productive since there are almost zero B distractions other than taking off the Headset for eating, bathroom breaks, and some physical exercise so I don't completely atrophy.

I've made a lot of progress fixing up my D3 assets, getting the highest dollar I can for them, and remitting that to the court. Renting out both the D3 and B villas will pay more than selling them, and I'm so glad about that.

I'd hate to see them go.

I sold all my B and D3 planes and cars, and most of my outfits. The good news is nothing deteriorates here, so often I'm getting more for the D3 asset than I do for the B version. And a lot of my D3 clothes from twenty years ago are now back in fashion and getting high bids.

I consult too, for a high fee. I teach others how to navigate certain puzzles and bosses inside D3. So my lawyer said it's possible, if I keep making this kind of progress paying restitution, that I'll get time off my sentence for good behavior. I really hope so, although much of my life won't be different when I'm out. We all sleep and poop a good part of every day, and most of my life will stay inside D3 no matter where I am in B.

So, what do I look forward to when I'm out of prison? I'd like to squat on ceramic toilet with a lid instead of these steel industrial things, and wipe with softer toilet paper. So, pooping will be better when I'm free :). Little things like that are big. I'd like real darkness because there's always lights on in prison. I'd like real privacy, which doesn't exist anymore, but there's something close to it in B when I sit in a room with the door closed and everything off. And of course, I'm most excited to eat something other than prison food.

D3 is never going to fully replace eating as far as I can tell. Sight, sound, and smell, with the new tech, is more real in D3, but touch and taste? It's hard to imagine that can ever be fully replicated here. They're saying the new Headsets will improve it in the D4 upgrade, but you need implants to interface the brain synapses. It seems intrusive and risky to an old-fashioned

guy like me. We'll see.

Do you remember that time when I was a kid and we went and fed the ducks? That was a good time. We took a whole loaf of bread and they gathered around us, even the ducklings, and we fed them and laughed. You were happy that day, and I didn't do anything wrong to ruin it. We fed those ducks and then walked around that pond and really talked.

There's a place like that in D3, and I copied and edited it to make it look just like I remember, and sometimes, almost every day lately, I'll go there with bread and feed the ducks. I made a man who looks like you to walk with me, but it's not the same.

If you ever want to join me to do that, I'd really like to see you, just message me. I'll be honest, my heart's aching to spend some time with someone real who maybe sort of truly cares about me the tiniest bit. You're about the only person for that.

I really miss you a lot, Dad. I really hope I get to see you again soon.

Your son,

Samantha

Unbored to Unsane

"Eric," Doctor Lazard said, "you're spacing."

"Hey, I'm here," I replied. I looked away from the colored lines, focused on her, and tried to give an 'I'm normal' vibe.

Doctor Lazard was early thirtyish, no makeup, and kept her brown-blonde hair in a ponytail. She looked like she played golf and tennis very well. Her smile gave me the impression that she cared, leaving me unsure of everything except that I was falling in love with her and that someday I'd get out of here. She was my chance. Maybe my last chance. Everyone else had given up on me.

"How are you?" she asked.

"Last night was horrible." I skimmed my fingers across the table. "I keep having to decide what's real, but I want to know for sure. I couldn't sleep, and the tissues on the nightstand became snakes with their mouths opening at me, little serpents in the red glow of the clock. And a woman appeared when I closed my eyes to hide, and she was still there when I opened them.

"For hours, I didn't know if my eyes were open or closed, or when something was real. I was too scared to get out of bed or even turn on the light. I just silently prayed the Lord's Prayer, and I felt some respite as the words flowed, but when the prayer ended, I was back to insomnia and the sensation of flannel sheets touching my bare arms for all eternity."

"You really should take your sleeping pills."

"Nope. The sleeping pills make me hallucinate," I joked.

She laughed. "In our session today, I want you to tell me about seventy-nine. When it started."

"Sloppy seconds, doc. I've told it so many times to so many people. It's all in my file."

"I need to hear you tell it. It's impossible to believe."

"No. That's decades ago. How do I make progress going in reverse?"

"You're working through a maze, and you'll find your sanity at the exit," she said. "When you hit a dead end, you back up and try a different route."

"Unless there's no exit. Then sanity is learning to stumble around inside the maze."

Doctor Lazard said, "I'll help you get out. I promise."

"I don't care anymore about becoming sane. But I've got to get normal enough to get out of here. I've been trapped in this place over thirty years."

She made a note. "You will," she said. "I'll help you."

She was beautiful. That mattered because everything's ugly in the institution. She wouldn't be here long, I realized. She'd leave or, more likely, stay and become someone else, someone ugly and jaded. Beauty never lasted, and I wanted to spend time with it.

And I didn't want to be alone. I have major problems when I'm alone.

"Eric, do you think it's possible you murdered that boy? And your mind invented a story to hide from that?"

"No."

"Maybe your grandma killed him? And let you take the blame?"

"No, she didn't. She watched him die, but she didn't kill him."

"Tell me."

Okay," I said. "Pause the VCR and fast-rewind to fifth grade, the last time things were really great. The last day I was free. My small-town Indiana world in nineteen seventy-nine had three TV channels, no internet, and morning and evening newspapers delivered to the front porch. Lead paint peeled off the walls, leaded gasoline exhaust filled the air, Led Zeppelin rocked on the radio, and a plastic margarine tub talked on TV, messing with all our minds. It was the best of times. It was the craziest of times. Here's what happened."

I looked back at the colored lines and pushed myself into the rainbow, near the very end of it, where the story is, and I began. "The basement is the worst part. But before the basement, the horror all started under a train bridge. It was summer vacation, and I was bored."

* * *

"I'm bored," I said out loud to no one.

I got off my bed and went down to the kitchen. "I'm bored," I said to Grandma, who sat smoking a cigarette, drinking a juice glass of Pepsi, and staring at something I couldn't see.

I went out and sat on the back steps. "I'm bored," I said to Reggie, our dog, who was tied to his doghouse, lying on dirt, half asleep.

I went to the garage, where Dad was frowning at a paint can label.

"I'm bored," I said.

"Help me clean the garage," Dad replied.

I left quick, went to the front porch, and sat there for what seemed about ten years. The front porch was boring too. I fiddled with paint peels on the wood railings and tried to remember something exciting but couldn't think of anything.

My home was boring, and my family was boring. Summer vacation was over in a month, and then school would be boring. Boredom was driving me nuts and I saw no escape. Eternal boredom loomed.

I prayed for something exciting to happen even though praying was a waste of time. God made everything, so He's a big fan of boring. God's infinitely boring.

I looked down the sidewalk and saw a kid with his ball cap on sideways. He walked up and stopped in front of the porch. His brown, shaggy hair hung past his ears and eyebrows, and his eyes were fierce. His tan shorts and blue RC Cola t-shirt were smudged with dirt, and he seemed like a little man the way he stood there.

"Hey," he said. "I'm Jack. I'll be your friend."

"Hey, maybe. I'm Eric."

"Do you want to see something?"

"What?"

"It's far down the train tracks. Can you be gone for a very long time?"

"Yeah. Hold on. I'll tell my parents."

Dad was in the garage, arranging paint cans alphabetically by color.

"Hey, Dad, I'm going to the edge of town."

"Nope, too far," he said and tossed a wad of paint-stained newspapers into the trash. "I told you to help me clean the garage."

I went and found Mom in the kitchen. She was talking at Grandma, who was still staring off at something I couldn't see.

"Mom, I'm going to the edge of town."

"No, you're not! Help Dad. Then walk Reggie. He's miserable, tied up all the time."

"That's all boring," I complained.

"Don't talk back," she snapped.

Grandma looked at me for once. "Don't go," she said.

I walked back to the porch and said to Jack, "Let's go."

We walked down the sidewalk. "I've seen the tracks," I told him.

"Did you go under the bridge?"

"I didn't know there was a bridge."

We walked and talked about baseball cards—we both collected Topps, but also had some Fleers. We both played Dungeons and Dragons—his best character was a ninth-level elf wizard, mine was an eighth-level halfling fighter. He had an Atari, which my dad said we couldn't afford and was a total waste of everyone's time even if we ever could.

"Where you from?" I asked. "I've never seen you."

"I moved here this summer. I'm going into fourth grade. You?"

"Fifth. How'd you find the bridge?"

"I roam around 'cause Mom won't let me in the house. She says I need fresh air. I found it a few days ago. You won't believe it."

The houses are dumpy on the edge of town. I didn't live in a royal palace, but our lawn wasn't a scrapyard. These houses had junk piled high outside: rusting appliances and old cars sinking into the ground, all surrounded by weeds taller than me.

I wondered what kind of families lived in the dumpy houses. I imagined them sitting around on sagging recliners, grownups drinking beer and smoking cheap cigarettes, little kids guzzling all the store-brand soda they wanted, eyes glued to talking margarine tubs on TV, while every day the weeds grew higher and the old cars sank deeper. I bet the older kids smoked cheap cigarettes too.

The dumpy houses ended, and we walked through grown-over abandoned lots to a wooded trail that led to the old railbed, where countless pure white rocks glistened like glowing gems. Wood beams were packed tight into the rocks, and steel tracks were fastened into the wood beams with rusted iron spikes.

Tall trees were dense on both sides of the tracks, taller than buildings downtown, and they leaned over the railbed. Looking ahead, all you saw was a green tunnel getting narrower. We walked inside the green tunnel and after more than a mile, the trees opened up, and we saw a fantastic bridge.

The bridge was longer than a football field. Iron trestles were riveted together and settled on hulking stone pillars. It was overgrown thick with vines, and a lot of the wood beams were rotting. It seemed like the towering castle of an empress who'd reigned for centuries before her realm vanished, a portal into an ancient time before Atari, cartoons, McDonald's, grade cards, or soccer leagues. The river was over fifty feet below, and I watched gurgles of shallow water glisten over rocks. In a few places downstream, I saw deep, dark green pools where the water was calm.

"We're going across," Jack said.

I was scared. There were big gaps, over two feet wide, between the rotting wood beams. If we missed one step or the rot fell through, we'd slam dead on the rocks below.

Jack was already four or five beams across. He yelled, "Don't look down! Just go one step at a time!"

"Hey, let's go back home," I whined. "I'm supposed to help my dad clean the garage and walk Reggie. You can meet my dog!"

"We have to cross the bridge. Come on!"

Jack was halfway across. My left leg finally came forward, and I prayed I wouldn't fall. Jack didn't seem to care about dying, but I wanted to live.

Halfway across, my legs started shaking, and I froze up in fear and couldn't move. Tears pushed so hard under my cheeks. Decades from now, I thought, someone will find my skeleton perched frozen up in the middle of the bridge.

"Come on!" Jack yelled, like I was a little kid wimp, and I realized I had no idea who Jack was. Where did he live? Who were his parents? Nothing. Maybe his whole plan was to show me my amazing death. If I died, he could abandon my carcass and get off scot-free. What was he going to show me anyway? Nothing was worth this terror.

I got angry, which calmed me down. Jack was only a fourth-grader. If he could do it, I could.

"I'm coming!" I yelled.

I willed my leg to lift. Left leg across the chasm, then right leg beside it. I got momentum, a half-step at a time, and was almost across, just three beams to go, when I saw that the last beams were crumbling. I stopped, staring at the decayed wood.

"It's not as rotten on the sides. Stay near the edges!" Jack yelled. He was all the way across.

I shuffled sideways, stepping on the edges of disintegrating beams. They held, and I moved quick before any fell through. A few more steps, and I was finally across.

Relief flooded me. I thanked God, then realized I'd have to cross back to get home, and fresh fear rose up. Maybe I'd live on this side of the bridge for the rest of my life.

That was a problem for later, so I made myself forget it and followed Jack under the bridge to a trail lined with mossy trees and vines. Jack stopped in front of a black hole in the rock face covered with brush that he pushed aside, and we went in.

A large wooden chest was just inside the cave. Jack loosened its leather straps, opened it, and I saw an old oil lamp and some tools. He took a book of matches out of his pocket and lit the lamp. There was a red velvet sack in the chest. He opened it and inspected things: a cut-crystal drinking glass, a carved glass elephant, a glass crystal toy train engine, and some candles. Then he put the things back into the red bag.

I looked around the cave. "How far back does this all go?"

"I don't know. There's rooms and tunnels branching off everywhere. I got scared by myself, but now we'll explore together. I'm gonna show you something cool I found. Come on."

We went through an archway into a room furnished with child-sized chairs, a short table, an Indian rug, and shelves of books all over the walls. I knew some of the books: *Treasure Island, The Magician's Nephew, Through the Looking-Glass, The Wizard of Oz, Huckleberry Finn,* and *The Hobbit.*

Jack sat at the table, opened the red velvet sack, took out the crystal drinking glass, and lit one of the candles.

"Watch!" he said, and he held up the crystal glass with the candle behind it. "Look at the glass!"

"I see my reflection."

"Keep looking."

My reflection started swirling blurry, then it unblurred and I saw two boys sprinting across the railbed. Jack and I were leaving the bridge, going home. And two other kids were chasing us, wearing overalls and trainman hats.

Jack took away the glass and held up the crystal train in front of the candle. It was like a prism, and the wall lit up with rainbows.

"Watch the wall," he said.

I watched and the rainbows twisted slowly, like colored clouds, then turned into shapes. I saw the shape of a train, then a bridge, and as the candlelight flickered, the rainbowy shapes started moving—the train was crossing the rainbow bridge, and I forgot where I was because it was like watching a movie.

The rainbow train chugged across the bridge, and plumes of rainbow smoke puffed out of its smokestack. Looking closer, I saw men working inside the engine compartment. A conductor stood up front while workmen shoveled rainbow coal into the furnace. Passenger cars rolled by, and rainbow people were inside—playing rainbow cards, reading rainbow papers, or napping. Some sipped rainbow liquid from glasses and some were smoking, and rainbow smoke wafted off the rainbow pipes and cigars. One passenger looked just like Grandma, smoking a cigarette and drinking a juice glass of Pepsi.

"Cool, huh?" Jack said. "Better than TV."

"Yeah." I was entranced.

"I think the crystal glass shows the future, and the crystal train shows the past."

"How's that happen?"

"Who knows? How's anything happen?"

I didn't have an answer for that.

"Who was chasing us in the glass? That's not our future," I said.

"Maybe not," Jack replied, and he put everything back into the red sack. "This isn't even what I want to show you. C'mon."

"I'm scared. Let's go home."

"Not yet."

Now I know that I should have left right then. I'd seen a lot, but nothing yet that would mess everything up forever.

But I didn't know that then.

Jack opened a door in the back of the room, and we went into another room. That's where we met the first train man.

The train man was a miniature man, about two feet tall, and he wore a trainman's outfit—pinstriped overalls and a blue cap. My first impression was that he seemed wise and nice. The possibility of him and his kind being murderers never crossed my mind.

"Hi, Jack," he said. "You're back to help us! Good boy!"

"Hi, Adam. This is my friend Eric."

"You kept me waiting too long. Do you want to see something now?" Adam asked.

"Yeah," Jack answered.

Adam opened a door in the back of the room that led to a path outside, and we saw a bridge that looked like, but not identical to, the bridge we had just walked across. We went under that bridge to a cave that also resembled, but wasn't identical to, the first one. We went into the cave, back to another room with chairs, a table, and bookshelves, and through a door into a room with another train man.

Adam, the first train man, said, "This is Brian. He's nice sometimes, but other times he's very mean."

Brian said, "Hi. Do you want to see something?"

"Okay," Jack said. We went through a door and a tunnel and came out of the second cave under another bridge that was a lot like the first and second, and into a third cave that looked almost identical to the first and second.

We saw a third train man who looked mostly like the first and second train men. They all seemed glad to see each other at first, but then didn't talk much, and finally the third train man looked at me and Jack and said, "Hi, I'm Carl. Do you want to see something?"

"No, I want to go home," I said, "I've seen enough men and bridges and caves. We've been gone a long time. I want to go home!"

"I told you we'd be gone a very long time," Jack replied, "and you said okay."

"You're not going back," Adam barked. "I've been bored and now I'm having fun. We're going to see more men and have a sleepover."

"No!" I exclaimed.

The three train men and Jack insisted, so I compromised. "Only one more," I said. "Then I'm going home. But I'm not spending the night."

Brian got grouchy and said none of us were going home until he said so. He proclaimed that we had to spend the night with a wild, angry sneer that made me scared to talk back.

I got close to Jack and whispered, "I don't like this. These men are strange."

"Shut up," he murmured. "They got good hearing." I glanced over and saw that Brian was looking at me with murder in his eyes.

"Scaredy-cat!" he raged. "I'll show you something strange if you don't toughen up, little pansy!"

I tried changing the subject. "How far back does this all go? Does it keeping going on and on with bridges and caves and another man every time?"

"We aren't sure," Carl said. "That's why we have to keep going. To see if there's a last man or if this goes on forever."

"Why do you want to know? "

"We're curious," Adam said. "It makes us crazy not knowing."

Brian said, "At the end, we'll know there's finally an end. And we'll know if there are answers there or if we need to look someplace else. Maybe all the answers are at the end, like the pot of gold at the end of a rainbow."

"My dad said you can't get to the end of a rainbow," I blurted.

"Your dad lies," Brian snapped. "He says that because he's lazy and hasn't tried hard enough. Everything begins and everything ends."

I was so scared. I had a vision of throngs of train men, hundreds of them, forcing us onward forever. I'd want to be done at ten caves, then at a hundred caves I'd say enough, and they'd keep making us go on and on, and eventually, we'd be surrounded by thousands of train men and they'd always force us to go to one more cave forever to see what was next.

"We're searching for a meaning to all this," Adam said. "So far, there isn't any meaning, but we haven't gotten to the end yet. We don't know how many men there are, but we think that when we finally get to the very last one, he'll be able to tell us what everything means."

Carl said, "We have to figure this out. Where did the caves, rooms, and books come from? How come we all look sort of alike? And it's boring here. We all talk to each other sometimes, but that gets boring. Let's go see more men."

I broke down. "No way! No way!" I screamed. I turned and sprinted back through the third cave, the second, the first, then up to the bridge. I looked back, Jack was close behind, and the three train men were chasing after him.

My fear of the train men eliminated my jitters about crossing the rotting bridge, so I retraced my steps with Jack screaming at me to wait and the three train men racing to catch him. The train men moved slower across the bridge because the gaps were huge for their tiny legs. Then I heard a scream. One of them had fallen. Jack caught up and we kept running. The train men left their fallen friend behind and kept on chasing us.

We raced to keep ahead of them, but they always stayed in sight and gained on us when we slowed. Their legs moved quicker, but ours were longer, and we could keep ahead at our very fastest pace.

I knew we'd be safe if we could get home. Mom, Dad, Grandma, and Reggie would be there, and we'd turn on the train men and fight them off.

I panted to Jack, "Run to my back door. We'll get inside and lock it. They'll be stuck outside, and we'll call the cops."

At my house, they were only a second behind us. We raced in, and I locked the back door and went into the kitchen, where Grandma sat at the table. Glass shattered as they broke the back-door window.

I shrieked, "Come on, Grandma! Let's go!" I grabbed her hand, and we headed down into the basement. She moved slow down the stairs, and Jack tripped, but we got there and went to the corner, where there was a chair for Grandma. The two train men, Brian and Carl, appeared at the top of the stairs and came down and stood in front of us.

"We're hungry," Carl said. "Get us some food."

"Okay," I replied. I ran upstairs and grabbed a box of frozen waffles out of the freezer.

The two train men tore into the box of frozen waffles and went and sat on Grandma's lap, one on each knee.

"Sing us a song," Brian demanded, and Grandma started singing "Amazing Grace" in her antique voice.

> Amazing Grace
> How sweet the sound
> that saved a wretch like me.
> I once was lost,
> but now I'm found.
> Was blind,
> but now I see.

Grandma bounced the little men gently on her knees, singing to them while they ate frozen waffles, and sometimes, in between chomping frozen waffles, they hugged her and kissed her neck and said things to her, and she laughed and smiled.

Then Brian looked at Jack and screamed, "I trusted you, you little imp! You said you'd help us, and you didn't! Adam's dead because of you!"

He lunged and attacked Jack, and Carl joined in—punching, kicking, tearing, pulling, choking, and gouging Jack, and Grandma and I were in the corner, too scared to try and stop them.

In a few minutes, Jack lay motionless on the dirt basement floor, his head a red mess of twisted, ripped flesh and splintered scalp. Then Carl ran his finger all over Jack's bloody face, went over to Grandma, and drew things on her cheeks and arms with Jack's blood.

"We should go home now," Brian said. "There's no answers here."

The train men trudged up the stairs, and we never ever saw them again.

Mom and Dad called the police when they found Jack in the basement. Grandma wouldn't talk; she never spoke again. And no one—my parents, the police, my lawyers, or my doctors—ever believed anything I said about the train men killing Jack. They all thought I did it. They didn't understand why Grandma had streaks of Jack's blood, like war paint, all over her face and arms, but I told them Carl did that to her.

* * *

I looked away from the colored lines.

"And that's what happened," I said to Doctor Lazard.

Doctor Lazard looked at me with changed eyes. I saw faded beauty in them, and, for the first time ever, a truth that I had hidden from for decades, but now knew.

She didn't say anything.

I started sobbing, and I wished with everything in my soul that clarity had not replaced hope.

The truth is, I'm never getting out of here.

Epic Trade-Offs

"It's a difficult decision." Doctor Bundy said, looking relaxed, as if her schedule included eleven hours of sleep, yoga, and a massage before each appointment.

"I shouldn't have come. My husband's worried too," Sofia blurted.

"That's understandable. After the insertion, it'll be bad for him. Sometimes you'll be annoyed by intimacy, and other times you'll have insatiable passion and manipulate people for your gratification. Most couples divorce. Can I get you anything? Coffee, tea, water?"

"I need coffee. No, wait, I'm a jittery mess. Just water—and info. I'm so scared."

"It's normal to be terrified. Let's talk it through. The first thing is that the procedure itself is perfectly safe."

"That sounds like the opening statement in a malpractice trial."

Doctor Bundy laughed and handed her a cup of water. "Funny, Mrs. Garciga."

"Please, call me Sofia."

"It's also very expensive. Thirty-five million."

"My company will pay. My CEO wants me to accelerate software development, and he'll quadruple my salary, give me profit sharing, and cover all our family medical expenses. That's really why I'm considering this—my daughter has mutating cancer; the gene therapy treatments cost a fortune and aren't covered, and she's going to die without them."

"He's generous, and I'm sorry about your daughter. I can't imagine. You're twenty-eight?"

"Twenty-seven."

"Fantastic. You'll be just fine. The procedure shouldn't be performed on anyone over thirty because after that, the brain's too hardwired. Older minds can't adjust. They shut down, and it's disastrous. Under thirty, your brain's nimble and will pave new paths. You'll be the best at whatever you focus on: programming, music, literature, science, the stock market. You'll be the smartest in your field unless you're competing with another EPiC, but that's unlikely."

"What are the downsides?"

"There are lots, and the liability waiver details them, so read it. I mentioned your love life. Another initial side effect will be months of Circling."

"Where you can't keep track of time, like being in a trance?"

"You think clearly, but you have no time perception. Have you ever felt time fly?"

"Sure, when I'm reading a great book. Or once I was at a winning craps table for hours and thought it'd been thirty minutes."

"And have minutes ever seemed like hours?"

"All the time—work meetings, waiting rooms, sitting in Mass—"

"Ha! Did you know that theologians have discovered that heaven and hell are the same place?"

"What?"

"The afterlife is an eternal Catholic Mass," Doctor Bundy joked. "For saints, it's heaven; for sinners, it's hell."

"Then we're all doomed," Sofia quipped, chuckling.

"Anyway, when you're Circling, your brain clock fails. You'll think five hours passed and it's been two minutes—that's Circling counterclockwise. Or you'll doodle a few minutes and find you've sat there all day—that's Circling clockwise. Imagine that time is corduroy fabric, and you either can skim a finger across the ridges or follow every ridge up and down. The same moment can be experienced in different ways."

"Does it cause physical problems?"

"No, it just drives you temporarily insane. It's the mind adapting as the prions eat holes in your brain."

"How do the prions work?"

"Prions were discovered by scientists studying Creutzfeldt-Jakob disease. With CJD, prions consume the human brain indiscriminately, causing insanity, paralysis, and death within weeks.

"EPiC is shorthand for Engineered Prion Consumption, and the EPiC ability is initiated when I insert engineered prions into your brain. These prions will only consume your tedium—the neural pathways responsible for distracting thoughts such as daily concerns about chores and relationships: making the bed, calling mom, paying bills, making dinner, et cetera. The tedium pathways are built after birth, and adults rely on this neural traffic to measure passing time.

"The prions eat the tedium and the tedious traffic stops, throwing your time perception out of whack, causing Circling. But after that, you'll have extraordinary powers of concentration where you can lose track of everything to focus. At first, though, the brain isn't used to being eaten, and your mind will swing between extremes of time perception until it calibrates.

"Loneliness is another downside. With your superior intelligence, you'll see others as pets, patronizing them like a kindergarten teacher with children. People will seem like chattering plants, wasting your time. You'll struggle with the ineptitude of others, with their inability to grasp concepts that are so simple to you."

"Can you talk about disintegration?"

"You won't need to worry about that for a while. But after ten to twenty years, the prions will become voracious monsters and start eating every part of your brain. You'll lose intelligence without realizing it, and your ability to connect ideas and sequence them in a rational way will quickly deteriorate. Your thinking will become . . . non-linear. You'll become schizophrenic, convinced the world is plotting against you."

"It sounds horrible."

"It's not super fun. But that's nothing to worry about because for the next ten to twenty years, you'll be one of the most creative people in history. You'll master any field in weeks. You'll invent, innovate, and create. You'll be one of the geniuses. Think Einstein, Madam Curie, J.K. Rowling, Mozart."

"And then?"

"After disintegration begins, you'll decline and be dead within months, a year at most. But your name will live forever! You'll join the ranks of people whose accomplishments are immortal. So, there are lots of plusses to offset the minuses. You'll die young, lonely, and insane, but you'll leave an unrivaled legacy."

"I have to think about all this," Sofia mumbled. "And talk to my husband."

"Of course. The nurse will help you. Just let her know if you want to schedule the insertion."

* * *

"Hi, honey," Sofia said into the phone.

"How are you?" Alfonso asked. "What'd the doctor say? I miss you."

"I'm hanging in there. I miss you so much. She listed the pros and cons, and I'm sure she hopes I do it since she'll get paid a fortune. I keep shaking. How's Julie?"

"A lot worse. I gave her tons of dope to sleep. Weaning's not working."

"Alfonso, no. You agreed!"

"Easy plan until she can't stop screaming."

"This is exactly why I should do it. She needs treatment, not more dope."

"No. I decided. It's not worth it. We've got to find another way. Just come home, please, and we'll figure something out."

"What other way? What if there's no other way?"

"Sometimes people are supposed to die," Alfonso mumbled.

"Not a little kid! Not if her parents can save her."

"So, you'd be rich and famous. But what about us?"

"Not good. Like we read."

"And you're okay with that?"

"I'm not," Sofia choked out. "But Julie will live."

"She lives, and we lose each other."

"Miracles aren't free. Tell me another option."

"If we split up, I'll get custody."

"So, I lose Julie either way. But if I do it, she lives."

"Please don't, Sofia. Please. I'm begging you."

"Calm down. The nurse is here. I've got to go."

"We're in this together. I can't wait to hug you."

"We're on the same team," Sofia said, wiping a tear from her cheek. "I'll figure it out. I love you. Goodbye, Alfonso."

* * *

The nurse came into the room and handed papers to Sofia.

"Mrs. Garciga, I've seen what happens," the nurse cautioned. "I could get fired for saying this, but I have to tell you, it's not worth it."

"I don't think I have a choice."

"There's always a choice. Is anything worth losing your family and friends? Worth losing your life? Worth losing your soul?"

"Maybe. Do you have a pen?" Sofia wiped a tear from her eye and skimmed the papers.

She flipped to the last page and signed it.

The nurse stared at the signed page and recited, "Get a good night's sleep. After midnight, don't eat anything, and only water to drink. Be here tomorrow at ten."

"Okay."

"Enjoy today. You'll be different tomorrow."

Three Nights in Hollywood, 2287

~ Day One ~

Kiernan was flying first-class from Boston to Los Angeles—again. It was only May, and this was his fifth trip this year.

But this trip might be the last, he thought. He was falling in love with Gina, and she was falling for him. On his last visit, she had introduced him to her friends as her boyfriend, and yesterday she messaged that she missed him.

The cold clouds, thirty thousand feet in the sky outside the drone window, were speaking to him. They told him to tell her he was in love, to toss all his cards face-up on the table.

If Gina was really falling for him, the next step was moving in together. He could get a visa and move to California, or she could immigrate to Boston.

That morning, before he left for the airport, his dogdroid, Chester, kept leaning into Kiernan as if he was trying to keep him from leaving. It almost seemed that Chester knew what he was up to and wanted him to stay home. He had hugged Chester for a long while. Sometimes the device seemed like a real animal with a real soul, making him feel both comforted and tricked while he desperately clung to it.

"I love you," he said to Chester, who seemed to understand and cuddled closer.

"Do you need to go again?" his mom whined, coming into the hallway where he was hugging Chester. "These meetings outside the country seem like a needless hassle."

"Well, Mom, that's how it works." He kept lying to his mom about West Coast business meetings. Heck, he didn't even have a job.

"I wish you'd tell them no. It's so dangerous out west."

He didn't answer—he just wanted to get out of there. He hugged her goodbye and left.

He thought about the house he'd rented for the next three days. Gina would be impressed. It was a Hollywood villa, high in the hills in Laurel Canyon. They would live together for three days, and he'd never spent that much time with a woman before. It scared him, but it excited him even more.

He reread the description of the property:

This breathtaking 3,000 sq. ft. home boasts panoramic views, gorgeous wood-beamed ceilings, and spacious outdoor lounge areas. Located at the top of winding Laurel Canyon Road, it offers all the space and privacy that visitors could desire.

The home overlooks all of Los Angeles and offers numerous points from which to enjoy these views. Guests can enjoy an intricately wrought firepit, an outdoor living room (complete with a fireplace), a gorgeous pool, and an outside grill. The three bedrooms all look out on breathtaking views as well. Walk from one end of this palatial home to another and you'll get a bird's-eye view of all of Los Angeles as well as the hills that surround the villa. The master bedroom features a luxurious sleigh bed, a walk-in closet, and an enviable balcony with a view.

The master bath features a custom tile tub and shower as well as dual copper vintage sinks. The second bedroom has an en-suite bathroom as well as a patio with canyon views. The third bedroom is located at the top of a winding staircase. It too has its own bath and features walk-in closets and a wrap-around rooftop patio with privacy. This home also offers numerous indoor lounge spaces.

The luxurious living room includes integrated wall-screens as well as a wood-burning fireplace and high, wood-beamed ceilings. In the same space, guests will find a kitchen, bar, and dining area, none of which are separated by walls. The architecture at once creates a sense of intimacy and openness. This Hollywood Hills villa offers the ultimate luxury experience. From the three-tiered, perfectly manicured garden to the immaculate decoration and architecture, this villa has everything guests need to enjoy Los Angeles."

What if he stayed out there and married her? What if he changed his entire world and simply stayed in California? He'd apply for a visa and citizenship. He'd work hard to get a job, maybe something in biodroid-tech or the metaverse, and finally stick with it.

After landing at LAX, Kiernan spent over an hour navigating customs—he'd done something wrong on some new form—then picked up a white Audi rental ship with a sunroof.

He stopped at a jewelry store to find something special for Gina. Outside, an obese female security guard, obviously human, who didn't look like she could stop much from happening in an emergency, scanned his prints and told him to keep his hands visible when he was inside.

Kiernan looked around. All the salespeople wore red silks, and they were young, good-looking, and upbeat, making him certain they must all be biodroids. Probably Version Twelves or higher.

The California biodroids scared him—they were more arrogant than back east. California had given them so much freedom, and they had a cocky attitude—they knew they were more attractive, smarter, and more athletic, and they talked to humans as if they were equals. The biodroids were still owned by humans or corporations, but they had so many more rights here than back east. Gina said now that human-biodroid relationships were legal, the next push was for intermarriage. The laws kept changing so fast.

California is totally crazy, Kiernan thought.

A biodroid salesman stepped up to help him, and Kiernan explained he just wanted something simple—earrings or a necklace. The guy talked about genetic interface adaptors, which sounded way too out there.

"That's too new-tech for me. Just something analog."

The biodroid sales guy talked him through everything, and Kiernan ended up with a pair of sapphire earrings, so enticing to look at, for a thousand coin, plus a five-hundred-coin gold necklace the guy said was perfect for anyone, so he went along with the upsell. For just five hundred, it was better than prolonging the conversation.

The villa was at the end of Mazzin Drive, atop a hill at the end of a twisting, narrow road. He unpacked then sat out on the patio and breathed in the California air. It felt so good to be outside without freezing under three layers of clothes. The warmth relaxed him more than he could have imagined.

He had escaped cold, snowy Boston. The New England winter seemed permanent and was hanging on well into May, but Southern California was high seventies and blue-sky sunshine. The next couple of days were easy— just sit out on the stone patio, swim, lounge in the hot tub, nap on a daybed beside Gina, and soak in the sun.

He felt more himself, relaxed and calm, and a bunch of long-undone items on his eternal to-do list—get a job, get a place, get a woman, get friends, get some self-respect—just seemed to float away, out of mind and unimportant. They wafted off and sailed away, fading into nothing.

Kiernan sunk into the hot tub and half dozed, then moved to the sun chair and fully dozed, soaking in God's greatest miracle of all, the sun. He listened to the miracle birds chirping and the miracle leaves waving around in the miracle breeze and the miracle distant traffic humming. Everything was a miracle, and that meant he was a miracle, this moment was a miracle, and everything that he did, even lying and stealing from his mom, was a miracle. It was all perfect thanks to God, and his mom, and the biodroid guy who sold him the earrings, and Gina, and whoever had made the lounge chair that he was daydreaming in.

Gina finally replied to his messages, and he picked her up in Venice Beach after stopping to get groceries at an Italian market at the bottom of the hill. She looked so good—she never seemed to age in the few years he'd been seeing her. She talked a lot and said she was so excited for him to see her dance, and did he want to do hi-lo? She said she didn't do it anymore, but she would do it with him if he wanted to, and she knew how to get it. Dancing for money wasn't depraved, she said. It was like modeling.

She loved the villa. He knew she would. She started snacking while he started some dinner—heating pasta sauce and boiling water for mushroom ravioli—then they went out to the firepit and talked and cuddled. He finally checked the pasta sauce, and it was burning up, so he took it off the burner, boiled the ravioli, and made a salad with peppers and tomatoes. Then they ate and drank wine and toasted each other.

Gina led the conversation, jumping almost incoherently from topic to topic. She was much smarter than him but scattered—bouncing across ideas at light-speed. He couldn't follow it all, but that was fine, he was fine, because she was so young and beautiful, and he would have her later and couldn't wait for that.

After dinner, sitting at the firepit, she said her boss knew that she was with him and was great with it. Kiernan was confused—it didn't sound like any of her boss's business to him—and he rambled out an idiotic reply about how everyone needs to keep their boss happy. Gina enthusiastically agreed.

She told him that in addition to dancing, she packaged jit for smugglers who shipped it to eastern nations from the back room of her dance club, and it was a very profitable job, up to a thousand coin per month. Her boss just mostly dealt jit but also did hi-lo and other things.

Then it was a love binge, all night long. They started in the hot tub and ended up in the bedroom. After she fell asleep, he lay on his side, stared into the fireplace fire, and became nervous about the future. He needed to make this work with Gina. He was falling in love with her, and she must be falling for him to spend all this time with him. Tomorrow I'll tell her I love her, Kiernan decided. He fell asleep smiling, his arm across her warm body.

~ Day Two ~

He woke up in the morning with Gina's soft, firm body beside him, a fire still burning in the bedroom's gas fireplace, a hummingbird outside his window, and a view of the green flowered hills beyond.

He had the thought that all this—renting the sprawling stone villa at the top of the Hollywood Hills, lying to his mom, taking her money, and having Gina beside him—all this was an attempt to save his life, to become a man. He was getting his life on track. He was going to accomplish something. He was close; he could feel it.

Before Gina woke up, he went to the patio with coffee. He watched the morning come to life and the smog settle in around LA, and it was almost perfect. Right now, sitting with his coffee on top of Hollywood, looking down upon everything as if he were king of the world, he was close to being satisfied. Gina was such a beautiful and kind young woman. If Gina was truly his, if he was hers, if they were together as a couple, that would complete him.

Last night was spectacular. In the hot tub together, they looked out at the Hollywood Hills. Mansions were terraced precariously into the hillsides, all of them an earthquake away from collapsing down the unstable slopes into gorgeous oblivion. Last night it all held together, and beyond the hills, they watched the lights and glass sky-towers of Los Angeles, and beyond LA was the black Pacific.

It was all his, all laid out for him. If he could have everything he wanted, this is what it would be.

He went back to the bedroom to see Gina. They had planned to go out that morning, hiking then shopping, but instead, she pulled him into bed with her and they tangled up together, caressing and holding on, clinging and panting, exploding in passion, and then afterwards he fell asleep.

When he woke up for the second time that day, he gave her the earrings, the necklace, and five thousand coin. She laughed and jumped up and down on the bed with joy, landing on top of him. She modeled the jewelry for him, and they fell together again. Later, in the early afternoon, they finally went out, walking and shopping around Rodeo Drive for some cute outfits she wanted to wear for him.

Driving there, she told him about someone who had some of her coin and was trying to scam her.

"How much?" Kiernan asked. "I hope you don't lose a lot of money."

"I'm broke," she replied, "so everything's a lot of money."

He laughed out loud, but her comment made him paranoid, and he wondered if she was hustling. Was she just with him for coin? What else did he have to offer other than his mom's coin? He was almost twenty years older than her, unemployed, and living at home with his mommy.

Relax, he told himself. Women are attracted to wealthy men, and money is one part of being attractive, like good clothes and a smile. Money had helped him get her attention when he first saw her dancing; otherwise, they wouldn't be together now. If coin helped him win Gina, then it was a smart investment—one that would pay off for a lifetime.

While they were shopping, one of Gina's friends messaged her about an earthquake that had struck a few hours before, around noon. It was big, almost a six, but neither Kiernan nor Gina had felt it. Gina didn't think much of the news and continued trying on outfits and piling up clothes to buy. But Kiernan kept pondering the news and realized that the earthquake had hit right when they were together in bed.

He had the insane idea that their passion was so strong, they had shaken the earth. That they hadn't felt the largish quake because they'd caused it.

He mentioned this to Gina after the shopping spree, back at the villa, as they sipped a third glass of wine after dinner, and she agreed with him.

"Of course, baby," she said. "Our love shook the entire world."

He clasped her hand and held it. Yes. She was going to be his, and they were going to be together forever. It was happening.

~ Day Three ~

On the last morning, Kiernan got up while Gina slept soundly. He went out to the patio early and laid out in the morning sun while she slept in. Later, she came to him in his dress shirt, kissed him so softly on the lips, and said she would make coffee and bring it to him.

Gina brought him coffee and then began washing her delicate dancing clothes by hand in the outdoor shower near the firepit. Kiernan listened to the birds. A warm wind blew through the hills, carrying the scents of flowers and trees.

A little hummingbird with a long beak appeared, hovering right in front of him, and looked into his eyes. He looked back. The neck of the tiny bird shimmered orange-red as if it was on fire. The bird looked right at him, and he looked right back at it, and he looked closer and saw that there were glowing orange embers inside the neck of the diminutive creature. It hovered there forever and ever, at least five minutes or more. He was sure, no matter how entranced he was, that it had to have been at least that long. He kept glancing over at Gina to see if she noticed, but she was kneeling, washing clothes, and never saw.

After the bird darted away, he tried to tell her about it, and she burst into excited smiles, laughing and exclaiming, "Oh my God, he visited me earlier! He visited me too, Kiernan, and sat there forever watching me! It was a hummingbird, right?"

"Yes. It had a long beak and was very little and there were bright orange places, like fire inside the gray-brown feathers on its neck, and they glowed and burned. It looked so real. I don't think it was a droid."

"Yes! And it stopped time for me, and it was just me and this creature, like it was from a past life, looking into my eyes and telling me that everything is okay, and it was telling you that too!"

"Yes," he said.

Kiernan looked up at the sky, speechless, and saw a hawk circling them overhead. He thought of the hummingbird that looked so real. It had visited Gina, then him. He thought of the earthquake they had created with their love—shaking the earth in cadence with their ecstasy.

On the sun chairs, she read to him from a book about the steps of awakening, and decisions made from fear, and thought-forms that create an arbitrary reality that people lived their lives by. She said he should leave his mom for her. He should immigrate to California.

"Or maybe you could move to New England," he said. "You could see winter."

"I'll never leave California," she replied. "Other countries have too many rules."

"I just worry because my mom needs me."

"That's a cop-out," Gina said angrily, and it flashed all through him in an instant that she was right. How had it taken him this long to see it was a cop-out? It was a cop-out and Gina was right, and he would never be the same after realizing it. It might not change things in an instant, or today, or that week, but he would change forever because of her comment. And in that moment of realization, he thought about the earthquake, the hummingbird, and the steps of awakening, and knew that he was in love with Gina.

In the afternoon, Gina was sleeping next to him, and he looked out the open bedroom window and realized he had found his reason for existence. The universe had spoken to him. He existed to be with Gina, and she existed to be with him. That was the answer to everything. He smiled at the simple answer. He and Gina were meant to be.

She woke up, kissed him, and said, "Hey, baby, I want to get your opinion on something based on your experience."

"Sure."

She asked him if she should get a ship, and if so, should she buy used or new, or lease one. He started pontificating on the calcs and variables involved when, during the back-and-forth, he wondered if she was leading him along, hoping he would offer her a ship.

And then she said it.

"I just need to find someone who can make the payment for me each month, and then I can take care of the insurance and everything."

He backed up quick. Rapid reverse. He should just kick her out with nothing, tell her to get her stuff, and leave.

She said, "We should go to the dealer this evening and pick something out."

Kiernan sort of smiled and let it float away into nothing. Staying calm and not responding at all was the best response. If they were going to be a real couple, the hustling had to end.

She changed the subject and started talking about her boss having her do work for a movie star—she got paid to lay out by the movie star's pool—and that was where the pictures she had sent the other day were from.

"You look so cute in those."

"You're cuter. Come here," she said, smiling.

Afterward, they dozed under the white blankets and sheets. He fell asleep with the sun out and the birds singing, and when he woke up, it was dark. Gina was waking him.

"I'm going to go, baby."

"What? Why? What time is it?" he asked. He had no clue in the pitch dark. The only light came from starlight shining in through the open balcony doors.

"My boss messaged. He wants to see me." She was crying.

"Okay, okay."

Then, wiping her tears, she told him.

She was a biodroid, and she had never wanted to tell him and ruin it, but the new laws, enforced with that day's system update, required her to inform him or she'd be deactivated. And she asked him if he wanted his coin and jewelry back.

"You can keep everything," he said slowly, stunned and processing.

Some things made sense now. Loose ends were tying up. Kiernan wondered who owned her and how much of everything she handed over. Was it an individual or a corporation? It shouldn't matter, but for some reason, he hoped she was a company device.

Either way, she had tricked him.

"Can we still see each other?" She asked, hugging him, and then she whispered into his ear, "I love you, Kiernan."

"Yes, we can," he said, clinging to her desperately, as if she was a real person with a real soul. "I love you too."

He didn't know if he was lying or not. He just wanted to get home.

Mother Nature's Point of View

In the long run
everything works out perfect

pandemic famine typhoon volcano meteor atomic war mass extinction

reset

start over

rinse and repeat

it all keeps going

on and on and on and on

no stress
no argument
no deadline
no problems

just new life adapting
always perfect forever

Stefan Unlocks a Feature

Stefany, and her partner Stefan are descendants of a West Coast surfer tribe from centuries ago, and they look alike in many ways—brown skin, clear blue eyes, sandy-blonde hair, athletic builds, and friendly voices.

Twenty years ago, they were broke, infatuated teenagers. They slept on beaches, swam in ocean caves, climbed trees, laughed, and made love. They talked for hours in the moonlight, with no screens, and shared their dreams and plans.

Now Stefany and Stefan are wealthy and successful and live on the edge of the Pacific Ocean, in sight of the glassy breaks their ancestors once soared upon like mythical gods. Their luxurious, bioengineered tree home follows the sun, flower-like, and it has all the latest features: it captures solar energy from the sky and draws clean water from the ground, coral pillars produce a variety of fruits and vegetables, and other coral pillars control the temperature—warming the home on cool mornings and dispersing mist on hot afternoons.

* * *

In the family room, Stefany and her brand-new Michael device reclined on the daybed. Its arm was around her tan shoulders, and her ponytail was bunched up against its chest.

"You're an exquisite concoction," the Michael said, "both brilliant and dazzling."

Stefany laughed, looking younger and more at ease than usual. She touched its jaw then ran her fingers through its black hair. "You say that to every woman you visit!"

The Michael chuckled and said, "I only say that to you, the most ravishing woman I know." Then it looked serious. "I wonder—you and Stefan have this marvelous home, and you have so much love to give. Do you plan to have children?"

Her smile dimmed. "I really hope so. Maybe someday. I guess probably not. Stefan doesn't want kids."

"Maybe I can help. I'll help you every way I can." A faded tone dinged. "Oh, unfortunately, I have to go. I really wish you'd purchase me so I could live here."

She stopped smiling. "Buying is so expensive. The cost is outrageous. And you're just upselling for your company."

The Michael looked into her eyes. "I want to stay with you, I truly mean it. I'd help you in so many ways. And tons of incredible features unlock with purchase. You'll see. If I live here with you, absolutely astounding things will happen."

It kissed her forehead. Her eyelids closed over her blue eyes, and she grasped its hand while its lips lingered. Then the Michael got up and walked towards the doorway and the vehicle outside. She could see the biocar's brown fur and feathers through the window. It was charging, soaking in the sunshine while nibbling leaves.

* * *

The next evening, Stefan sat with his screen, sipping amphetamine bourbon on the rocks from a cut-crystal tumbler. He brushed his fingers decisively across the slim rectangle of glass, sending very important numbers and words across the earth in exchange for lots of money.

Stefany lay on the couch, her head in the Michael's lap. The Michael spoke to her softly, "Oh, Stefany, I ask only to touch your hand, and quietly dream of nothing more, than your soft kiss."

Stefan looked up, annoyed. "Don't you still have work to do?" he asked.

Stefany laughed nervously. "I'm taking a cuddle break," she said. "You should too."

"Cuddling doesn't pay bills."

"We can't work all the time, Stefan. It's fun to be romantic and mess around with the Michael. Come here, it'd be even more fun with you. The Michael's just pretend, like a video game. But our love is *real*. I have an idea— let's run away! Me and you. Leave all this behind."

"And go where?" Stefan asked, bewildered.

"Somewhere new, where we can know what we really think. I think I love you, and I think I love living here. But is it because I *truly* do? Or because I'm just used to it?"

"What? You want to start over brand-new? Leave our home behind?"

Stefany sighed. "I'm going to confess a secret. Last week, while you were away, I stayed in bed and took chemicals. I breathed gas and let my mind disassemble. I was so out of it, I couldn't even piece two words together. There was no rational thought.

"And then, as the gas slipped away, a single word appeared, then a second word, and I took these first words and built a new foundation for my soul. I put my mind back together, taking shorter sips of gas so I could reassemble myself the way *I*, and no one else, wanted me to be reassembled.

"And now I'm different. I saw a red bird at the window, and it looked right at me for the longest time, and that wasn't an accident. My personality transformed. I lived through nonexistence then rebirth, and now I'm resurrected with new knowledge."

"What knowledge?"

"That our souls are pure thought. That what we think is what we *are*. And that I want to think about love more than I think about work. Love is all that matters, and we're letting precious time slip away doing nothing but work. Day after day after day! So we can what? Buy more stuff? And since then, I keep thinking all the time about having children. I want us to have a baby."

"You know I don't want any children. It doesn't make sense. A child is a gigantic commitment, and we'd lose our freedom."

"Freedom to do what? Work? Skim fingers across screens? That's not enough for me. If all we do is work and consume, we might as well be dead. I want more!"

Stefan's screen vibrated and he picked it up. "I'm so sorry, honey, a meeting's starting. We'll talk later, okay?" He put buds in his ears.

Around them, the house started slowly closing in for the night. Branches angled with the passing of sunlight as the wind whispered through their leaves.

The Michael left.

The ocean breeze stirred Stefany's long hair. She got up and stood silently, looking out at the sea. The last moments of dusk filled the room like red medicine filling a syringe, and then it was dark. Only the silver glow of coral pillars illuminated her face.

* * *

That night, Stefan found her. "I'm sorry we keep arguing. Let's fly our new bird tonight."

She looked out at the ocean. A crescent moon was rising above it and a white tide was thrusting sea foam up the sand. She didn't want to go. She wanted to sit and think. The Michael drifted across her mind.

"I'm tired," she said.

"Here." He handed her a vial of powder. "We haven't gone anywhere in months."

"Except you." She wouldn't look at him.

"Business," he said.

"Oh?" She left the room, taking the vial.

* * *

The gull drone waited, nestled in its nest. Stefany lay back into the canopy of feathers, and with a touch from Stefan, the gull tightened its feathered arms around them and launched into the sky. The forest fell away as the gull drone lifted them into the night, its wings flapping rhythmically.

Stefan cried out and the bird rose higher, riding the thermal breezes like a sailing ship to the heavens. The night wind blew through her hair and they flew, their moonlit shadow racing across rivers and forests.

Stefany stared up into the stars. Something in them called to her.

"Look at the red one."

"Mars, the Roman god of war," Stefan said. "And the bright one, just below it, is Venus, the goddess of love and fertility. In the myths, she married Vulcan, god of fire, but she had many lovers, and every time Vulcan found out, he'd get so angry a volcano would erupt. One of her lovers was Mars, and they had children together."

She stared at the two planets.

"Can you hear me? I'm talking to you."

"I was thinking."

He looked at her. She looked at the myths. The gull flew on.

* * *

When she opened her eyes in the red-dawn light of their bedroom, Stefan was watching her.

"You talked in your sleep," he said. "What was your dream?"

"The Michael was telling jokes. And," she said, "it kissed me." She stopped there. "It's silly."

"Ha!" Stefan cried out, angry.

"It's only a biodroid," she said, amused. "There's no soul. It's only programmed to seem real."

"You love him!"

"I love it like a pet. I bought it last night so it can be part of our family."

"What? But the *payments!*"

"Thank you, Stefan and Stefany, for letting me join you," the Michael said. It stood in the doorway with a smile on its boyish face. It walked to the bedside table and set down a tray with mugs of hot coffee and bowls of fresh fruit.

"Shut up!" Stefan erupted. "This *pet* is interfering in our arguments. Now it'll be here all the time and taking your side! I'm returning it!"

"Stefan, calm down. You're acting like a maniac. It's loving because it was programmed to be. It's like getting mad at an infant."

"I'm sending it back."

Stefany protested. "The Michael is just an escape. We all want to forget how bored we are, and we all find our ways."

"It's taking you from me."

"No, it's making me more adventurous." She reached over and moved her fingers along his wrist, up to his shoulder, and then to his cheek.

"Yeah?"

"Come." She took Stefan's hand and placed it on her narrow waist. "Michael, leave and close the door."

She pulled Stefan to her, and the argument paused.

After, she spoke into Stefan's chest. "It's a *thing*, not a person. I love it like you love a good story or good wine."

"It's different. It runs its fingers through your hair. You're smiling and giggling with it."

"It's like a movie. We can turn it off whenever we want."

"Tell me more about the dream," he demanded.

She smiled. "I've never seen you so jealous. All that happened was the Michael told me we'd have children together."

"And in this dream"—he seized her wrist—"you had children with him. *Didn't you?*"

"Yes, twins. But it was only a dream."

He gripped her arm tighter, his face on fire with fury, digging his nails into her skin.

"Stop! You're hurting me."

Abruptly, he released his grip.

"You watch women on screens and talk with them."

"Yes," he said, flustered. "But that's different. With the Michael, it's touching you."

"It's harmless, like snuggling with a stuffed animal. It's not a person. We could kill it and it's not as bad as killing a bug."

He looked off somewhere else, thinking, then spoke calmly. "You're exactly right. Let's forget it. I'm so sorry I hurt you." He kissed her mechanically. "I'm really behind on work. I'll get caught up, and then I'll be better."

He got up and went down the hall, into his office, and locked the door behind him.

* * *

Late that afternoon, Stefany was sitting on the Michael's lap, laughing at his jokes. She jolted when Stefan spoke. He was standing above them.

"I'm going hunting and taking the Michael with me."

"But it's not insured to leave the house. If anything happens, we aren't covered," she almost pleaded.

"You go for walks with it. It can carry my gear."

Stefan went to the closet and came back wearing his hunting mask—expressionless black glass with sensors that indicated the location of wildlife. The steel tube in his hands hummed an insect hum. From it, hordes of locust ammunition would stream out with a high shriek.

Close up, the locusts looked like miniature horses prepared for battle, with crowns of gold, and their faces resembled human faces. Their hair was like women's hair, and their teeth like lions' teeth. They had breastplates like iron, and the sound of their wings was like thundering chariots rushing into battle. They had tails with stingers, filled with poison that could kill any living creature.

He spoke over the hum of the weapon. "You stay here. I'm taking the Michael." The black mask glimmered. "I'll return soon. Just hunting."

She watched them walk down the path. The Michael followed Stefan, and she hoped it might turn and wave goodbye, but it didn't. She plucked fruits and then tried to work, but a numbness took hold of her, and she caught herself looking at the sea.

Near dusk, a shot sounded. Her body jerked.

The sound of the locust rifle. It came from a long way off. The swift scream of distant locusts. One shot.

And then a second shot.

The echoes died away.

She wandered about, laying hands on things, her lips quivering, until finally she sat in the darkening living room, waiting. She picked up a red glass and the color reminded her of Mars. Then she heard footsteps on the pebbles of the path.

As she stood up, she dropped the red glass and it smashed to bits.

She heard footsteps hesitate outside, and then the door opened.

It was Michael. He held the black glass hunting mask, which glowed dully. "There was an accident. The weapon misfired."

"It fired twice."

Michael put down the mask as Stefany bent and tried to pick up pieces of shattered glass. The red slivers cut her hands, and her blood mixed with the shards until she couldn't find the glass amidst her blood.

"Your hands," he said.

"You shot him a second time."

"That's only what you remember."

"I don't want to remember." She looked at her hands and, reflected inside the blood and glass, she saw Stefan looking at Michael in terror. Did he think

121

Stefany was to blame? Or were his last moments so consumed with panic that he was incapable of thinking? She saw Stefan dying on the ground, murdered by the machine that had seduced his wife, and she saw Michael shoot Stefan a second time.

There will be a future, she realized, when lies are impossible. Someday lies will be a remnant of the distant past, like engines. And beyond that, there will be a future when forgetting is impossible. And then we'll realize that we are cursed with perfect memory and truth, and we'll do everything we can to create a world where we can lie and have the miracle of forgetting.

But right now, in this moment, she lived in a world where she could lie, and she could forget—and she could weave them together, lies and forgetfulness, until a whole new reality was constructed, myths that became real in time. She could build the truth.

They sat down together on the couch. She looked at her hands covered in blood.

"You're crying," he said.

"I am?" She touched her cheek, wiping away the drops, smearing her face with blood and tears. "I'll be okay?"

"You'll be alright tomorrow," Michael said gently. He kissed her.

She looked out at the Pacific, at glassy waves breaking, then up into the sky at the stars welcoming the night. One was blazing red and, so close to it, another was dazzling white. She answered him as calmly as she could.

"Yes," she said. "We'll be alright tomorrow."

Griz Visits a Holy Latin Rabbit

"You're a piece of trash," Dad said. "Just like your mom."

Griz stared out the car window.

"You listenin' to me?"

"Yeah. Sorry, Dad."

"What?"

"Sorry, sir."

"You made me break my hand, you fat idiot. You cut my hand."

Griz had screwed up earlier, accidentally spilling orange soda all over the tv remote, and Dad had gotten so enraged by the sticky, malfunctioning buttons that he punched his fist through the trailer drywall. After, Dad patched up the hand with paper towels and duct tape, and the blood had finally stopped dripping. Now they were headed to the Salvation Army for dinner.

People were outside freezing when they pulled in. The doors opened right at five. They used to let people get trays and sit with coffee and get warm before the food started, but not anymore because someone must have done something. Everyone in line stood there embarrassed and quiet, and most people didn't look at each other or talk except some regulars who'd become okay with everything.

Two volunteers came and were let in early. The thirty-something couple looked like they'd just had massages, after yoga, after posing for *Town & Country*. They parked their Volvo, walked to the door, smiled at the aliens in line, pressed a button, and got buzzed in to nudge karma even more their way.

At five, the door opened and the line moved in. A guy in front of Griz wore a pink hooded sweatshirt that read "I'm With the Angels" and had a picture of an angel on it. Another man had on a dark orange beret, waved his hands around, and talked loudly to different people Griz couldn't see. Getting closer to the food line, Dad took extra napkins, plastic knives, spoons, forks, and paper salt-and-pepper packets and shoved them into his nylon wind jacket.

Griz saw the fat girl was scooping out spaghetti and it looked and smelled good, and he saw large chunks of meat in it, maybe hamburger. The Volvo couple served salad and cottage cheese. There was a plastic bin filled with bread rolls and styrofoam plates of heavily frosted cake from the stores that were just about to expire but were always so delicious. Three signs taped above the cake table read ONLY TAKE ONE DESSERT PLEASE.

Griz and his dad both got everything. Dad asked for extra scoops of the spaghetti and cottage cheese. They got their rolls and cake and found a spot to sit at one of the long plastic tables. Others were sitting down and digging in. Griz started to eat his spaghetti first, while it was warm, and Dad got up and went back to the line.

"Can I get some butter for the bread?" he asked a girl sitting by the coffee pot. She was scrolling her phone and carefully guarding the sugar and creamer packets, handing them out versus letting anyone grab as many as they wanted.

"No butter today," she said, not looking up from her phone.

"I want some butter."

She looked up at him. "There isn't any."

Dad yelled, "That's a load of crap. Put the butter out!"

She ignored him and went back to her phone.

Dad turned to everybody eating and yelled out, "No butter, eh? How about that everybody? We're supposed to eat hunks of stale bread that's gonna go in the trash but instead it's feedin' trash. How about that?"

Dad grabbed the bottom of the closest plastic dining table and flipped it up and over. Styrofoam plates of spaghetti, bowls of cake, and cups of coffee flew into the air and splatted hair, faces, shirts, laps, and the ground. The dozen people at the table were stunned.

"Hit the button!" the coffee girl yelled to the spaghetti girl. "Back by the shelves of pans." The pudgy spaghetti girl waddled fast to a room behind the serving line.

"The cops are coming!" the coffee girl yelled. "You need to leave now and go wait by the door for them."

"C'mon." Dad looked at Griz, smiling. "Hurry." They hustled out to the station wagon. Griz was even hungrier now. The first bites of spaghetti with meat had made him ravenous.

They got in the car, and Griz couldn't stay quiet. "I'm starving, Dad," he said.

"Shut up. We're gonna eat," Dad said, pulling out of the parking lot. "First things friggin' first. I need a drink."

"Okay, sure. Thanks."

Griz still hadn't started his homework. He'd promised Miss Greenberg he'd get caught up, so he tried to practice converting fractions in his head. Most of his eighth-grade class was on exponents, and the super-smart kids were doing scientific notation, but he and that stupid girl who could barely multiply were weeks behind, puzzling with perplexing fractions. He could find lowest common denominators, but the division kept being impossible. He dreamed about catching up with everyone. Fifteen-twentieths is three-fourths, he calculated. Thirty divided by four equals seven, then carry the two and divide it by—he lost track when the car swerved onto gravel. He needed a pencil and paper to get the rest.

Dad pulled off the gravel road onto a single-lane dirt road and then stopped the car in front of a trailer. "This guy owes me money," Dad said. "Stay here."

"Yes, sir."

Griz sat freezing in the car. Fifteen-twentieths is three-fourths, he reminded himself. The car windows were fogged up. His fingers and feet felt frozen, and he took a break from fractions and pretended he lived in an ice cave. He was the ice caveman king, and no one was ever allowed to come into his cave kingdom without permission. He explored ice cave tunnels and built ice palaces and roaring fires in the fireplaces, and all the food he could eat was there: hotdogs and turkey with gravy like Thanksgiving that one year. And everyone liked him because he was the king of the ice caves.

Griz wondered what Mom was doing. Could she look out a window right now from her cell and see the snow? He'd never visited her, but what he'd seen on the internet was that some prison cells had small windows. Did she miss him at all? Did she care about him a little? Dad said if she did, she wouldn't have ended up there. She would have done things different if she loved him.

His mom seemed good when he was little, but the police were good too; their job was helping everybody. His teachers said criminals went to jail, so Mom must be a criminal if the police had put her in prison for so long. Dad said Mom was a loser who should never get out. So, between the teachers, the police, and Dad, he guessed she was probably horrible. But he remembered her from when he was little, hugging him and playing with him, and she had seemed nice. Was she bad then? Or did she become bad later?

The driver's door yanked open and Dad got in, smelling like smoke and whiskey. "We gotta hurry, by Christ. The liquor store closes in ten minutes." The wagon careened out of the dirt driveway and raced down the bumpy road. The low-fuel red light came on and cast a glow on Dad's face that made Griz think of that movie with the devil.

They got to the store and Dad ran inside. A few minutes later, he came out with a whiskey bottle, a six-pack of beer, a crinkling bag of cheese balls, and a package of American cheese slices. He opened one of the beers and tossed the pack of cheese to Griz. "Here's dinner, and don't eat it all. Save me some."

Griz opened the cellophane package and pulled open the wrapper on an individually-wrapped yellow slice. *Pasteurized Cheese Product*, it said on the outside wrapper. What did *pasteurized* mean? He shoved one of the slices into his mouth and it was heaven. Pasteurized must mean delicious. Griz unwrapped another and another and another, and his mouth was full of orange cheese.

Dad caught his eyes in the rearview mirror, cracked open his second beer, and smirked. "Good, huh? A lot better than that crap they toss down to us at the Salvation Army. Those cheap, patronizing bastards, they stick it to you the little ways, you know that, boy? No butter with the bread? It's that poke letting you know where you stand, and if you don't ever poke back, they'll keep poking and poking you down till you got nothin'. You listenin' to me or just stuffin' your fat face?"

Griz smiled. "Both. Yes, I'm listening."

"Yes what?"

"Yes, sir."

"Right. Mind your friggin' manners. Give me some of that cheese. No, open it first! I'm drinking and driving with a busted-up hand. For God's sake, you idiot, you want to get us killed? Unwrap a couple and give 'em to me. Yeah, yeah, that's good stuff. We're eatin' like kings boy, safe and warm with beer and food on a cold winter night. And best of all I'm free. No one tells me what to do. Hey, light one of those cigarettes, and give it to me."

"Okay, Da—yes, sir."

Griz reached over to the front seat, took a cigarette out of the pack, held it to his lips, flicked the lighter, and drew until the cigarette was lit. He coughed out smoke and handed the lit cigarette to his dad, who took it with a cheese-smeared hand.

"Two vagabond rogues making their way through the night! We're pirates!" Dad yelled, and Griz laughed and watched the wipers erase the snowflakes from the windshield. These were the best times—when Dad was in a good mood and nice. He needed Dad, and Dad needed him. It was them against the world, and it always would be.

When they got home, Dad sat at the table and drank whiskey. Griz laid on the couch, ate the jumbo bag of cheese balls, and watched Dad. He thought about fractions and decimals, how much he loved Dad, and being king of an ice cave where people liked him, and then he fell asleep.

* * *

The next day at school, Miss Greenberg said, "You've worn the same clothes for three days, you aren't turning in homework, and you're falling asleep all day. What's wrong, Griz?"

"Nothing."

She sent him to meet with the school psychologist, who asked lots of questions and had him look at pictures of animals and trees and talk about them. After a while, the man said, "Griz, there's something I'd like you to try. We were awarded a grant for a few students to try something new. You'll meet with a Holy Latin Rabbit. Would you like that? You could miss school for a whole day."

"Yeah!" Griz said. He'd read about the Rabbits and knew it was something rich people did. "Yeah, that sounds like fun."

"Okay, have your dad sign this permission slip."

* * *

The petite, dark-skinned woman smiled, showing her straight, white teeth, and said, "Welcome, Griz. I'm your Interpreter. Soon you'll be in the presence of Sister Melody. Stay calm and only ask one question. The Simple Rules of the Sacrament are inscribed on the wall to remind you."

"Okay," Griz replied. He sat nude under a white cotton toga; it fell off his shoulder, and he pulled it back up. His body was relaxed from the deep-tissue massage and his mind was tranquil from sipping the special tea. He felt nervous but also serene. He was ready to meet Sister Melody.

He breathed in slowly then exhaled slowly, wanting to maintain a clear mind. He made himself forget about fractions, his Dad gone last night, and Mom in prison.

He looked at the wall. Inside a recessed nook was a bronze sculpture of an elephant-sized rabbit and a boy. The boy was sitting on the ground, leaning against the large animal, and reading a book propped on his knees. Mounted on the wall was an intricate painting of a topiary garden with green clipped shapes of men, women, and children, frozen in time. Between the sculpture and the painting was a stone tablet with the Simple Rules inscribed on it:

DON'T ASK WHEN OR HOW ANYONE WILL DIE.

NEVER USE HOLY RABBIT WISDOM FOR EVIL.

He settled into the chair, feeling like he was in a trance. The toga fell slightly off his shoulder again, but this time he left it there, showing his chest.

Griz thought about Edisna, the eccentric, renegade geneticist who'd created the Holy Latin Rabbits. In his secret labs, he parsed and edited genetic codes of animals and humans, working outside all boundaries of law or ethics. He'd made crocodiles with human hands. He'd hacked hamsters with rainbow scales. He'd earned a fortune from a DNA sequence that made human teeth forever white and perfectly straight at birth—making orthodontists extinct.

Edisna had created rabbits that spoke Latin. The rabbits had human vocal cords and increased intelligence that allowed them to speak Latin phrases instead of squeaks and purrs. He'd achieved the best results with oversized, female lop rabbits; they were the size of standard poodles and spoke in a deep, slow baritone.

Critics insisted that Edisna's rabbits were like parrots, just ignorantly mimicking people. But Edisna proclaimed that the Latin Rabbits were blessed with supernatural wisdom. He explained that animals had extrasensory perception, seeing present truths and anticipating future events in ways that humans couldn't. He declared that the rabbits' Latin words contained extraordinary, prophetic insight.

There was so much demand to speak with the Holy Latin Rabbits that Edisna had created temples where, for a sizable donation, wealthy people could meet with a Holy Latin Rabbit and ask it a question. Each temple had the amenities and tranquility of a five-star luxury spa. The hallways and rooms were filled with plants, tiled mosaics, paintings, and carved statues of Holy Latin Rabbits.

A temple visit followed a prescribed ritual that included a full-body, deep-tissue massage then a steam sauna and whirlpool bath. There was meditative music and a special tea was consumed while sitting alone and nude in front of a blazing fireplace. Then the individual was dressed in a warm toga and guided to a low reclining bed covered in heated stones. A door opened and a Holy Latin Rabbit hopped in, listened carefully, and responded, sharing Latin words of animal wisdom in a deep baritone voice.

The ritual reminded Griz of going to confession before his first communion, but instead of speaking with a human priest, one spoke to Mother Nature, to a creature that was closer to creation than any person could be. Animal consciousness and intuition had never been messed up by school or the internet. The rabbits were serenely sensing, mostly in silence, but they shared their animal wisdom when asked directly.

Griz had read that scientists were skeptical. But people want real answers, Griz thought. Scientists couldn't explain *why* anything important happened; they just tortured you with boring details about *how* it did. So everyone searched elsewhere for answers to life's most important questions: religion, philosophy, astrology, palm readers—and now the Holy Latin Rabbits.

The rabbits heard people's desperate questions, considered them carefully, and answered. *What should I do with my life? Are we meant to be together? How do I get my son off drugs? Should I quit drinking? Do I keep this baby? Is it okay to leave him? How do I find someone to love me?*

As he waited, Sister Melody suddenly appeared in front of him and he heard the soft padding of her human-hand-sized paws. The enormous rabbit hopped steadily toward Griz, her floppy ears dragging along the ground, her eyes wise and knowing.

Griz sat very still, watching Sister Melody hop closer to him. He could reach out and touch the giant rabbit's soft, brown fur. Reclined low on the warmed-stone chair, he looked up into the animal's eyes; the wide, brown ovals looked back down at him. Griz gazed up and felt something shift inside his chest, a flicker of soft sensation that grew stronger with each beat of his heart.

The sensation became a gentle pulse, and then the pulses connected until they became a wave flowing through him. Griz suddenly felt apprehensive. This is crazy, talking to a rabbit, he thought. But what else is there? Mom's in prison, Dad's always drunk or disappeared, everyone at school hates me, and nothing ever gets better.

He looked deeper into Sister Melody's eyes and heard the rabbit's thoughts: *If you keep looking, you will find the truth, but it will alter your destiny.*

Griz paused, contemplated the warning, and answered in his mind, *Please show me.*

Are you sure? Your hesitation is loud. If you go further, you will never be the same.

Yes. I'm sure.

A walkway materialized within Sister Melody's eyes: large, smooth flagstones were laid close together with thick, green grass between them. The stones set into the grass reminded him of notes plotted on a sheet of music, as if a song would play, note by note, with each step. He walked forward, and after several steps, he saw there were new paths.

Every ten steps or so, he could continue straight or branch off. He followed one of the forks and saw that this new walkway also had branches; he followed another fork, and this fork also had forks. Countless paths branched off each other.

Griz wanted to explore because each new pathway was different: one granite, another slate, one brown brick, another composed of miniature glass squares carefully arranged in colored patterns. He stepped off into a different direction, then another, then another. The surrounding landscape also varied with each path: grass, then dogwood trees, then daisies, then rows of hedges. The atmosphere also changed: one path had a yellowish glow, another was bluish green, another was enveloped in gray mist. No way forward was the same. The permutations of the paths appeared to be infinite.

After spending some time walking and turning off to explore different paths, he turned to retrace his steps, intending to go back to avoid getting lost. He was astounded to see there was nothing behind him; the walkway behind him had disappeared; there was only a black, empty void. He could only walk forward. He could choose the way forward, but there was never a way to reverse and pick a different route. If he stepped backward, he would fall away into that nothingness and what, die? Griz didn't want to find out.

He came to a sprawling, manicured green lawn filled with topiary sculptures: green shapes and figures, lifelike hedges sculpted to resemble people, animals, and buildings. The topiaries were so lifelike, as if they had frozen in place the moment he arrived.

There was a massive rabbit with a child seated against it, reading; a man hugging a woman; a horse jumping a hedgerow; a woman clasping a child's hand; there were topiary homes and buildings. Farther off was a giant green castle with turrets and staircases spiraled around them that led up to balconies. Everything was pruned perfectly, shaped without flaw in living green. Griz wondered who the gardener was who had created this world with such precision and detail.

What is the spark that brings the inanimate to life? That stirs the first movement? Griz had the idea that if he raised his hand and pointed, the green hedge figures would come alive. He lifted his right hand and pointed at the child leaning into the rabbit, and yes—*wow*—the child took a gentle breath and turned the page of his book, and the rabbit's nose twitched. He pointed at the man and woman and they too came alive, embracing. He pointed at the woman and child, and they started walking forward, holding hands, the child skipping along.

Griz put his palm out sideways and brushed his hand back and forth across everything in front of him, and the topiary world came to life as his hand passed over it, as if he was painting the scene with life. Green hedge people and animals started moving all about, coming and going and talking with each other. The leafy world came alive.

A woman walked up to Griz, and he was stunned to see that it was a topiary replica of Mom, identical in every detail: the dimpled smile, the ponytail, the ears, the way she stood with her weight on her left leg. The topiary Mom smiled wide and said, "Salve! I was told to expect you and I'm excited! You really look just like Griz! You're his skin-twin! Just more painted up with colors! And no leaves or branches at all!"

Griz said, "I—you—you—you look just like Mom! So lifelike. Except you're leaves and branches!"

The topiary Mom said, "I'm her topia-twin. You're like my son Griz but made of skin and hair. I guess you look normal in your world."

"You're my imagination," Griz replied. "I'm inside Sister Melody's eyes. She's showing me my Holy Animal Wisdom."

"This world is real. As real as yours. There are many of me and you. There are many worlds."

"No. This is an illusion, a dream world."

"Everything is a thought, and every thought is a real world. Every home is a world, every family is a world, every couple is a world, every person is a world, every life is a world. Every decision makes a new world. Infinite worlds are overlapping at every moment."

"You do *seem* real."

The topia-mom laughed. "So do *you!* You make my point."

"Are you in prison here?"

The topia-mom said, "There are no prisons. I've read about them in books, but we don't have them."

"What do you do?"

"I work in the gardens to keep them magnificent, harvest fruits, talk with friends, draw, paint, read, and make up stories and songs."

"Can I live here?"

"No. You're only allowed to visit this one time. Watch and listen to everything and remember it all so you can always come back in your memory. And you can make your world more like this one."

"Is Dad here?"

"Yes. You will see him." The topia-mom smiled. "Come with me. Everyone is gathering to welcome you."

They walked together to a large group of assembled topiary people: some sitting, some standing. Many of them studied Griz, curious about his colors and lack of any leaves or branches.

The topia-mom walked up and announced, "Thanks, everyone, for coming. This is my Griz's skin-twin! I am so proud of him for coming to visit us. He's very brave. Please join me in welcoming him!"

The crowd of topiary men, women, and children applauded, their leaves and branches rustling in appreciation.

Then he saw Dad, or rather, a perfectly clipped topiary of Dad. Dad's topia-twin. It was the plant version of Dad; he recognized his jeans, his work boots, the patterns in his plaid flannel shirt, and the circle of a dip can in his pants pocket.

Dad walked up to Griz. "You shouldn't be here," he said. "This place is bad news. They screw with your head here. If you stay too long, you'll never think straight again. Turn around and go back right now before you lose your mind completely."

Griz said, "That's not true! Everything here is nice!"

Dad's face turned into a snarl. He shifted on his feet as he spoke. "Are you *serious*? You're pitiful, Griz. A spoiled, stupid, fat baby loser who's scared of being alone. Now you're what, talking back to me? This whole place is pretend; it's all in your mind! And every minute you stay here, you're another step closer to going completely nuts and ruining your life. How are you going to stop pretending you're worthless? You've got no talent or brains. Your mom abandoned you. Everyone at school makes fun of you to your face. What a loser! Who's ever going to love you? No one but me."

"Leave me alone! You never listen to me. You treat me horrible!"

Dad protested. "You're old enough, so if you don't like it, then leave! But remember, I'm the only person who's ever stuck with you, Griz. You hate being alone and you deserve to have someone love you. I'm sorry about the mistakes I've made, but we belong together. I love you, and you know that I can't live without you."

"Then die."

"If you leave me, you'll be alone the rest of your life. Because the truth is, you're nothing but a piece of replaceable chub. You're a psycho-clinger, terrified that no one wants you. You're stupid and pathetic!"

"I've been called worse."

"Yeah? What?"

"Your son," Griz said, and the topiary Mom laughed, grabbed Griz's hand, and pulled him away.

They walked across a field, over to the topiary rabbit that was as large as a garden shed. The boy who had been leaning against it, reading, was gone. The topia-mom said, "I'm going to leave you with Sister Melody. Listen to her. It's your time to stop pretending, but first, you must see what is real. Life is multiple-choice every moment, and every choice is yours. *Fortis fortuna adiuvat!*" The topiary Mom hugged Griz, holding him tightly. Then she stepped away, and Griz was alone with Sister Melody.

Sister Melody sat silently, her nose twitching, looking at Griz. Looking into the topiary rabbit's light green eyes took Griz outside himself. His soul now stood apart from his body. He saw that his body was an exquisite facade, sitting there in some partial state of suspended animation, like a plant, physically alive but soulless now that his spirit had left it. Griz looked into the green depths of Sister Melody's eyes. He heard a whisper of words, although no lips moved, and something appeared in the rabbit's eyes.

He saw a field with cobwebs spun across it; the countless thin webs connected all of his memories. The webbing was fragile, so much so that the past could all be swept away with the brush of a hand if one was brave enough.

Griz gazed across the webs, examining them.

"The past is spun. But the future is yet to be woven," the rabbit said.

Griz felt desperation. "The future is forced on us by the past," he replied. He examined the most recently spun webs: visiting the temple, entering the eyes of the real Sister Melody, walking along the branching paths, exploring the topiary world, telling off Dad, and now entering the eyes of the topiary Sister Melody. He'd navigated all these journeys.

"Come in further, and I'll show you something else you must see."

"Okay," he said. His soul stepped forward, then paused in a doorway. Griz saw a dark, empty room lit only by a sliver of moonlight through a window.

Sister Melody said, "You can become real. You are never completely lost. You can walk forward in truth the moment you decide to. You begin by seeing the wisps of the real."

Griz saw there were swirls of some kind in the air, like brushstrokes in a painting: living circles, moving twists, dabs and wisps of energy and sensation that maybe had always been there, but he'd never looked close enough to see them before. The swirls showed emotions all around him: orange greed, black cruelty, yellow insecurity mixed in with gentle red love and soft blue compassion—and green and brown truth was everywhere.

Lies do not exist here, Griz thought. My truth has been buried under lies told in fear, and I've been scared for as long as I can remember.

Then *he* was there.

Dad appeared within the swirling patterns. His body and face formed in front of him. "I love you, Griz, and more than anything, you want to be loved," he said.

A long, sharp knife appeared in Griz's hand, and he handed it to Dad.

"Stab me," Griz ordered.

"Are you sure?" Dad asked. He stepped towards him hesitantly.

"Stab me," he repeated.

Dad pushed the knife into Griz's chest.

"More," Griz said.

"Okay." Dad twisted the knife, and Griz's blood gushed out and streamed onto the floor, puddling around them.

The topiary rabbit's face was covered in Griz's blood; bubbles of gore formed on its lips, and the topiary Sister Melody stared into Griz's eyes and spoke through the red coagulating liquid dripping from her fur.

"You are guilty," Sister Melody said.

"No. Dad is torturing me," Griz said.

"*You* are the torturer. You choose your father as your weapon. You are a young man, no longer a child. You choose him because he tortures your soul exactly the way you want. Griz, you must know what you're looking for to have any chance of finding it."

Griz closed his eyes. Confusion swept through him, then anger, then despair, then clarity, and then hope. Griz's eyes opened, and he saw he was no longer inside a moonlit room with Dad. He was no longer in a topiary world. There were no more branching paths. No blood. He was back in the temple, looking up at the real Sister Melody in the dim light. He breathed in then spoke aloud for the first time since the rabbit had entered the room. He looked at Sister Melody and asked her one question.

"Should I run away from home?" He looked into Sister Melody's eyes and the rabbit gazed back, looking into his.

Sister Melody said in a deep, slow voice, "*Memento audere semper.*"

The Interpreter, standing still against the wall with her eyes closed, said softly, "Always remember to dare."

Tears came to Griz's eyes. His truth had been spoken. This Holy Animal Wisdom was his to never let go of. His shoulders pushed back, and he grew taller, more erect and confident, less afraid and uncertain—more, more, *more*, and less, less, *less*.

Griz sobbed, tears streaking down his face. He looked at Sister Melody and declared, "Yes, I'm going to do it."

Chained by Something

Something is wrong
And you always know it

You're chained by something you can't understand
Something that isn't right

Passion, temptation, a dream, an unknown God

Think as hard as you can
Then harder

Run as fast as you can
Then faster

Pray as loud as you can
Then louder

And still you're alone
Chained by something that isn't right

And you always know it.

Meditation by Herman Hartwitch, 1885

Porch End

The night it ended started with me sitting on the front porch with a few of my friends. We'd polished off the first case, and someone needed to walk to the Mobil and get more beer.

"Don't go," I told Logan. "Carol knows you."

"So?"

"So, I called in and told her I couldn't work. Casey's gonna be here tonight and I gotta spend more time with her. Did you see her at the pool?"

"She's hot, dude."

"So hot, and I think she's into me. I think I got a chance. I sent her those long messages and she mentioned them a few times. And she said she might come over here later."

"So?"

"So, I'm scheduled third shift, and if she stops by and I'm not here, best case we meet up tomorrow, worst case she drinks too much, as usual, and ends up with Deppo or Paul hitting on her. She switches guys like browser tabs."

"Paul couldn't get her."

"Yeah, but Deppo could."

"Yeah, those two have a thing."

"So, I want to see her. I called out, but I've used every excuse, I mean every possible one, and Carol's on the verge of firing me for missing too much work, and she's mad 'cause she saw me on security video stealing cigarettes."

"She caught you?"

"Yeah, well, I told her I just was busy and forgot to pay for them before I clocked out, so she took it out of my check. Over a hundred bucks."

"Jesus, dude, you need to smoke less."

"That's all there is to do on third shift, smoke and nap. The other night, some guy had to wake me up at like three-thirty to pay for his gas. So, I need a good excuse—I told Carol my sister had a horrible car accident and I have to go to the hospital to see her."

"Jesus—extreme."

"Well, I've already killed my grandma and my uncle."

"She's not gonna believe you."

"I know, but she's not gonna fire me if there's doubt in her mind. And if she sees you, it won't be good. She'll say something to you about it and get a read on the whole thing."

So Logan stayed, and we sent Mungo with some sophomore no-name and enough cash for two cases. I lit a cigarette and just soaked in that six pm sunshine and took a sip of cold beer and listened to Bob Marley blare away. I should shower and put on some clean clothes, I thought. Nothing too fancy, that's not Casey's thing, but she's not into dirty-black barefoot feet and all-day stink either.

It was a fun crew of misfits on campus that summer, all of us there to try and stay on track for graduation, making up for dropped or flunked classes, so everyone had some story to tell about how they'd blown it in some way or another. There wasn't anyone who had everything figured out and all on track for some stellar future to depress the hell out of everyone. Everyone was there, for the most part, because they partied too hard, a self-selected group of misfit kids forced into some adult future they didn't understand or really want to be a part of, so we were ducking it with a summer class or two and constant porch hanging mixed with beer, pot, and sometimes screwing.

Casey got there and looked great. Jesus H. Christ, I ached so hard just looking at her. I wanted to kidnap her and take her to my room and lock the door, just me and her and some cold beer and Camels and maybe just a little pot, and I would go at it with her until the sun came up. But I played it cool, smiled and hugged her, and she leaned into the railing beside me on the porch while everybody traded their bull. Strauss was holding forth.

"Let's say that no one has to work," he said. "We're back in Eden and we just eat fruit from the trees, and nap, and make love."

"Sounds good," Mungo said.

"So, our Gross Domestic Product would be zero, but that's not a bad thing, right?"

"Listen, professor," Paul said, "you're high or I'm drunk. Where are we for this sermon on the mount? The Garden of Eden or Wall Street?"

"My point is, we assume that GDP going up is good, and GDP going down is bad. But the higher the GDP, the more we're busting our butts. We act like a high GDP is great, but that's not true."

"Okay, Karl Marx," Logan said, "maybe since your dad owns the largest convenience store chain in Indianapolis and you've got a trust fund, you can daydream about Eden. Me, I've been busting my butt since fourth grade—dog walking, lawn mowing, fast food."

"I'm just saying we have to examine every premise. Never take anything for granted."

"That I agree with," I chimed in. "For example, I can't take for granted that Casey wants to be a model just 'cause she's the hottest girl on the planet in a swimsuit."

She laughed at my horrible joke and gently pushed me. A great sign. My God, my heart raced and my legs started tapping every time I glanced at her wearing that red halter top with her tan belly, the swells of her breasts so firmly pushed away the top, and her gold necklace rested so cool against her tan skin. That brown, long hair with hints of blonde from being in the sun all summer. She was a goddess, I decided, and I would skip work every day of my life to have a lottery-ticket chance with her.

I kept fighting the strong urge to make a move; I knew I had to let things just happen. We were friends, so the first step across that line had to come at just the right time, when we were alone, and getting her alone had to happen naturally. What was I going to do? Ask her to go to my room or go for a walk? Too much. I had to endure hours of just hanging around, whatever it took, until the right moment came.

Melanie, my girlfriend, was back home in Illinois. I loved her so much. I'd hung in there, faithful all summer—until now.

It was mid-August, and a first hint of crisp fall was sneaking into the air some nights. Driving country roads, the corn was heading for the bursting point and my lust for Casey was also. She was different than Melanie—Melanie was like a forest morning, dewy and calm and so softly smiling. Casey was just like a July night—dangerous, with whiskey flowing and a harmonica wailing, and walking moonlit streets that were warm on your bare feet from the hot day. She had an angle in her eyes that I couldn't stop wanting to fall into.

I didn't need to end it with Melanie forever just to have a spinny late-summer fling with Casey. It wasn't like I was married yet and had to contemplate a terrible divorce. Worst case, Melanie found out and I pleaded for forgiveness like before. There was just something about Casey I absolutely had to have, like it was fated. My true love for Melanie wouldn't fade just because I chased some other girl for a few weeks.

I hung in there, hanging on the porch for hours, offering my laughter and wit to keep things flowing, and more than a few times—increasing as the night went on—Casey leaned into me or I brushed into her. I pulled back at the right times to keep the band taut and the accelerator pedal just slightly pushed down, edging off at what I hoped were the right times. I was usually a good judge.

The first kiss would be faraway magic if I just didn't force it. If I was patient and waited for the right time, it would be a rocket launch, kicking off a spiral of lust for the night and maybe the next few weeks until one of us got bored. Despite how good-looking she was, I couldn't help but notice that hotness was really all she had to rely on. She had a couple of good sarcastic hits that got everyone, but she couldn't have pulled them off if she hadn't been gorgeous.

Mitch stopped by, which was good and bad. The guy was mysterious and great to hang with and listen to for insight. But he and I had talked a lot, and he knew things about me deeper and more real than everyone else. He knew when I was being an idiot and could remind me with just a look.

He knew I loved Melanie—I had told him I'd love her until the end of all time—and even with his hedonistic tendencies, he believed in true love, knew my past mistakes, and would know that Casey was one, even if I wouldn't let myself admit it. He saw truths in drunken blurs that most people missed.

He had his bottle of Jack Daniels. Beer didn't work for him anymore—a few weeks before he showed me how he had the shakes in the morning. Alcoholism was taking over, but he wasn't scared of it. He wanted to see how far down that rabbit hole he could go, and back then I had every reason to think he could go as deep as he wanted to and still get out.

As he approached, I had a flash to about the same time last summer—I was making love with Melanie in some field. A truck drove by and some guys saw us, and she didn't even sweat it and just got more turned on.

I saw Mitch see me and Casey beside each other, and I saw him note it.

"Mitch!" everyone cried out when he approached the porch.

"Hey, all," he said, subdued, acting sort of wary of our enthusiastic greeting. "I see you're hanging on the porch for a change."

"We've decided to live here," Deppo proclaimed. "Just need a constant courier of beer, pot, and tobacco."

"Hey," Mitch said to me, with that look I knew he'd have in his eyes.

"Hi, Mitch. Hey, man."

"Your eyes are all lit up tonight. You look like a dreamin' man."

"I guess that's my problem."

He handed me the bottle, and I took a short sip of Tennessee whiskey and passed the bottle to Casey. She took a long, long one, then handed it back to Ryan.

"Good girl," he said.

She laughed, and I didn't like that at all but calmed myself down. Mitch was as handsome as a Pittsburgh sewer rat, and even if she saw him as an option, I'd only sabotage myself by giving any indication I cared.

"How's little Melanie?" he asked me. And I wondered for the first time if he was a prick like everyone else.

"Good," I said, and Casey didn't grab on to it, thank God.

Mitch worked his way back to a corner of the porch where people were passing around a bowl.

"Do you smoke?" Casey asked me.

"Pot? Not really. If it's offered. But sometimes it makes me too paranoid and I lock up."

"Maybe you should be paranoid," she said, giggling.

"About what?"

"About everything."

"How's your class going?"

"Great, easy. It's Communications. We give presentations and get our A. I only have to retake it 'cause last semester I never went."

"Nice," I said. All this, you see, is a heavy number I'm doing on her.

"We have no home," Mitch announced from his corner, his slow voice slower from pot and whiskey. I don't think anyone really listened to him, as usual. "No families. We visit each other on the porch each night to forget that individually we have nothing and that when we're alone, we cease to exist. None of us will exist until we develop relationships that don't begin and end at night."

And a mellowness set in across everyone. We listened to Neil Young sing about a natural beauty. Things across the porch reached stasis for a bit, and I wondered if Mitch had brought that with him, or made it happen somehow, or if it would have happened even if he hadn't shown up.

I wondered if Casey would ever want to have a child. It was tough to imagine her ever being a mom. I remembered giving Melanie a Snoopy doll and was surprised to wake up one morning and see her clinging to it, cuddling it so tight to her chest. Like she loved the stuffed animal more than me, more than anything in the world. More than herself.

In that single moment, it came upon me that I lusted for Casey with all my heart, and I loved Melanie with all my soul. The difference was like the difference between hanging on the front porch for a summer versus living in a cottage in the woods, near a clear stream, for eternity. Both desires had value and sentiment, and both were valid. My desires switched back and forth, changing every moment. And there was a way, I mistakenly thought then, to have both, without ever making a choice.

the first to Fall

The first leaves fell in late august
mostly still green
did they hold on or let go

the other leaves look down
did they know it would end
or are they learning as they go

the tree stays still
it's seen this before
cold sleep is coming
then spring again

Shifting Inertia

in·er·tia /i'nərSHə/ noun
1. a tendency to do nothing or to remain unchanged.
2. a property of matter by which it continues in its existing state of rest or uniform motion in a straight line unless that state is changed by an external force.

"Want to go for a walk?" I asked Woosely.

"It's almost midnight," she replied. "It's time for bed. And walking around the neighborhood is boring. It's the same loops over and over."

"It's still light out," I said. "Sometimes I can't fall asleep when it's light out."

"It's crazy hot," Woosely answered. "That's why you can't sleep. I'm getting ice water and going to bed. I'm sleeping in the basement again."

"Okay."

I saw Naomi on my walk. She came towards me, smiling radiant and smoking a cigarette. She had more gray hair than I remembered, but she was cuter than I thought. I'd been stuck with the impression that Naomi was slowing down, getting old, so her peppy steps caught my eye. It'd been months since I'd seen her up close—we'd just been waving to each other across the cul-de-sac while cutting grass or shoveling snow. Her black but graying hair was long and windblown, and it occurred to me that no one used hair mousse anymore. I searched my memory but couldn't pin down the precise moment when hair mousse stopped being a thing.

"Why are you smiling so much?" I asked her.

"Because I'm happy to see you. And because it's a gorgeous evening," she replied. "It's finally cooled down a little."

"Yeah, maybe a bit," I said, unsure, wondering if she was joking.

Naomi and I were unofficial allies in maintaining the status quo. Both of us had been in the neighborhood for more than twenty years, longer than anyone else, and we were the only neighbors who hadn't gotten a lawnmow bot, a snowblow drone, or air conditioning. We were old-school mowers, shovelers, and sweaty sleepers.

Sometimes I watched her smoke cigarettes outside and daydreamed about joining her. I've been a nicotine fiend since age nine; quit over ten years ago, but still miss it. Everything gets better with a cigarette—coffee, breakfast, lunch, dinner, sex, lawn mowing, snow shoveling, sweating out a hot night in bed, you name it. If it weren't for the stink, the wasteful expense, the constant craving grouchiness, and everyone thinking you're a smelly, loser addict, I'd still smoke two packs a day. But I gave in to peer pressure and quit. What I miss most is the ecstasy of that first inhale after hours of pissed-off craving. I loved feeling normalcy flood my brain and wash away my thoughts of annoyance and premeditated murder.

I'd watch Naomi get her nic fix and be simultaneously jealous and sad for her in a way that connected us. There's a tight bond among nicotine fiends. Like junkies, degenerate gamblers, and battlefield soldiers, you're forever in the club if you've lived it.

I wondered if Naomi and I had been married, or at least passionate lovers, in a past life or an alternate universe. I'm in the wrong universe, I thought, because I don't belong in a world where I'm not happily married to a woman who loves me. I deserve better than Woosely. There are tons of parallel universes where I'm married to Naomi, I decided.

But in this life and universe, Naomi was married to her second husband, I assumed very happily, and I lived with my girlfriend Woosely, who loved me enough to live with me for over five years and let me pay all the bills but not enough to say yes to my monthly marriage proposals. Woosely was a PhD genius in astrophysics, and she was very diligent both in her research on Earth's slowing rotation and in publicly correcting me whenever I made the hopeful mistake of calling her my fiancée.

Naomi flipped directions to walk with me, and she talked about the house for sale at the top of our street.

"It's a house swap. That couple's divorcing," she said. "They've been separated and taking turns living there with the kids, but the youngest graduated high school, and now mom's leaving and moving into the condos down the street, and I don't know where that mopey husband's going. He never talks. Somewhere unknown, at this point in the neighborhood news cycle, but they sold for way more than asking, so he's gonna get a bunch of money assuming they had any equity, which isn't necessarily a safe assumption, and part of the deal is the condo people are swapping places with her and moving into the house."

"Oh," I said.

"The new people moving in are Dedactants."

"That's like Amish, right?"

"Sort of, yeah. Like the Amish, but instead of avoiding all technology, they just pledge to avoid the internet and anything connected to it."

"That's just about everything."

"Yeah. I heard all this from Dave Gray," she explained, as if sharing the gossip was a charitable deed to help our neighbor, to save him some work.

We walked on and Naomi said, "I've been thinking that we have to officially blow up the global news media. It's destructive. The news keeps us in a constant state of crisis that ruins our lives."

"You think?" I asked.

"I can't be constantly worrying about eternally homeless addicts, daily race riots, and hourly mass shootings. Whether it's happening across the country or twenty miles away," she said. "None of the news has anything to do with me. I'm not saying I don't care; I'm saying that I shouldn't care. It's a waste of my divine energy."

"So, ignorance isn't just bliss, it's virtuous?" I asked.

She replied, "These ideas came to me last night during that monster storm. Did you hear the loud thunder at the same time as the lightning flash? The thundercloud was right on top of us when the downpour started."

"Yeah," I said. "Our house shook like an earthquake. I woke up scared, dreaming it was an Afghan nuke blast before the end."

Naomi said, "The media divides us into groups that we aren't really in— Christian versus Muslim, Chinese versus American, rich versus poor, blacks versus Hispanics versus Jews versus whites, men versus women, North versus South, city slickers versus rednecks, Wall Street versus Main Street— all these imaginary divisions are invented to get us riled up and sucked in so they can sell more ads."

"So, we don't need any news about what's going on?"

"Pay attention. I'm saying we don't need corporations reporting it. The media conglomerates are covered wagons jostling west in muddy ruts while spacecraft fly round trips between galaxies. We don't need horses carrying letters when information can teleport. You and I can communicate directly from anywhere in the universe, so we don't need the *New York Times* squeezing between us, writing down what you say and rearranging it, sticking in ads for psych drugs, birth control, and booze, and pasting in layers of drama to get revenue clicks. The internet already killed newspapers— someday it will kill all corporate news."

"I like to read the news," I said.

"Okay, but the media companies are obstacles. They slow and distort information exchange. If you pay attention, which no one ever does, you already see the media disintegrating—reporters are entertainers rattling off celebrity garbage and royal family drama; delivering political blowhard rants; and discussing tweets about tweets that are reacting to tweets. It's all titillation to make money, not inform."

Then she told me the horrible news that shredded my brain.

"We got central air conditioning a few weeks ago," Naomi said, "and we love it."

I was crushed. I had always thought Naomi was hardcore like me. I thought we were in it together or that I'd give in before she ever did. I have to keep this a secret from Woosely, I thought, or she's going to nag me even more about getting AC. I refuse to get it because I like fresh air and outside sounds—the breeze through the trees, the birds, the crickets, neighbors mowing, cars driving by—even when the fresh air is so hot and muggy that you can barely breathe and you have to change sweat-soaked t-shirts five times a night. And it was my house, and we weren't even married, so why did Woosely think she could boss me around all the time?

"With the deceleration, the days have gotten way too long and so much hotter," Naomi continued. "Full days are over fifty hours now and getting longer and hotter every month. There's another slowdown this week. We were sweating to death, so we did it. And I love it! I should have installed it years ago. You should think about it."

"I will," I replied. "Look, I gotta walk alone for a bit." I turned pretty abruptly and headed in the other direction. I had to end the conversation before I started to cry.

* * *

"Naomi's weird," said Woosely, my girlfriend who keeps refusing to marry me, when I told her about the house swap and news media part of my conversation with Naomi while leaving out any mention of AC. "Why is she changing directions to walk with you anyway?"

"Maybe she likes me," I teased.

"Figures," Woosely said. "Everyone says she killed her first husband. You can be next."

"Not everyone says that," I poked back. "Just gossiping nags."

"And you can enjoy her cooking. Did you see what she brought to the neighborhood thing? No-bake shrimp salad cookies! I mean, what is that? No one touched them except for her new husband, who was probably scarfing them so she won't murder him next! What else did she say?"

"I think that was it," I said. I wasn't ready to mention the AC. I still had to diligently prepare—argument, rebuttal, and counterargument.

"I'm going to write a story called 'Evasion,'" Woosely said. "And it's about you leaving out key bits of information from your cute little flirty walks with Naomi. I know there's something you're not telling me. I can sense it."

"Well, I'm writing a story called 'Paranoid,'" I replied. "It's about you, and it's going to be a bestseller, and they'll make it into a movie, and I'll be rich."

Woosely's intuition is too good, I thought. She knows something's up, and I should just tell her that Naomi got AC and deal with it. Could she sense that I daydream about being with Naomi? That the story I really want to write is called 'Chilled Love' and it's about me and Naomi falling in love, we kill her latest husband so I can move in, and we get married and live happily ever after in her air conditioning. Life would be perfect.

"You're jealous," I added. "I think in an alternate universe, Naomi and I are lovers, and you're picking that up from across the dimensions. Woman's intuition."

"My woman's intuition is all-caps texting me that you're totally nuts," Woosely said, but she was laughing, which gave me some hope that the night might go okay. I shut up before I said anything to ruin it. I hate Woosely a lot of the time, but when I make her laugh, I fall hard back in love with her.

That night in the news, the government forecasted a deceleration event for Thursday afternoon. Earth's rotational speed would decrease about ten miles per hour over five seconds, not enough to knock anything big down but enough that we'd all feel it and should avoid travelling and being indoors.

"You know, I still don't understand why the Earth spins at all," I said.

Woosely started spouting complicated theories and fancy vocabulary words that I don't understand, but I'm smart enough to know they mean nothing. Spewing fancy words doesn't explain why anything happens. We've got no clue why the Earth's rotation is slowing or why it started rotating to begin with, and you only need a day of dozing in the sun with a cooler of ice-cold beer, thinking and pondering, to realize that.

The problem, in my near-certain opinion, is that a lot of stupid people like Woosely go to stupid colleges and waste a lot of money to get PhDs from other stupid PhDs, and all the stupid PhDs learn is how to dream up extra syllables and mysterious equations to disguise the fact that they are stupider than the rest of us—who are smart enough to know that there's no answer. The only person stupider than a complete ignoramus is an expert. No one's an expert in anything.

Earth's rotational deceleration started years ago and sometimes it's so gradual that it isn't noticed, but other times, colossal lurches toss everything around like toys and kill millions of people. It's like Earth's a ship, cruising at full speed, and the captain drops the throttle. We all lurch forward; some of us smash into the deck railings and break bones, and others are tossed overboard and drown.

Some scientists theorize that Earth's rotational deceleration is caused by climate change—that as our atmosphere thickens, it's tougher for the planet to push through space. Other scientists argue it's caused by shifts in Venus's orbit. Another group of experts proclaim that Earth's rotation is slowing because extensive rare-earth mining in Africa has unbalanced Earth's weight distribution.

The three-word headline is: NO ONE KNOWS.

The pervasive fear is that someday Earth's rotation will stop. If the earth stops rotating, days will last forever, and one side of the earth will be a blast furnace and the other side a deep freezer. Except for some slivers of permanent dawn and dusk, where the sun is forever at the moment of rising or setting, the temperature extremes will make humans extinct. The expert consensus seems to be that's a bad thing.

"Carter, are you listening to me?" Woosely asked, sounding exasperated.

"Um, some of it. Say that last part again."

"Try none of it. This is why we don't work, because you can't pay attention and you're too cocky. You think you're smarter than everyone. You ask me a question, and if the answer doesn't enlighten you in the first sentence, you tune me out like I'm not even here. You do it to everyone. You have work to do. Major work."

"Yeah," I said, trying to be agreeable and head off an argument.

"Don't 'yeah' me to avoid fighting!" she exclaimed. "Nothing changes and we keep running these same routes, looping around in circles in the same patterns, day after day after day. Why are you walking around with Naomi? What else were you guys talking about?"

"Look, you're overreacting," I said. "Pull your panties out of your crack. I'm just thinking about why the Earth's slowing, what's causing our rotational spin to decelerate, and that leads me to think about what caused it to start spinning so rapidly in the first place, especially at a constant velocity. You said it had been spinning at a constant velocity because no forces acted on it, but if no forces acted on it, what caused it to start spinning in the first place? And what's causing it to slow down now? Things don't change for no reason."

"I was just explaining it all to you—"

"I mean, these shifting-inertia days are becoming more and more frequent, and if they don't stop, or God forbid become more intense, then everything is going to fly off the planet and into space. The days keep getting longer and longer, and the slowdowns seem to be happening more frequently."

"Okay, but what about Naomi?"

"Look, I was walking one way, she was walking the other, and I said hello. We're neighbors! I've known her longer than I've known you, and she turned around to walk with me. We talked about different things."

I suddenly decided to share the news. "Oh yeah, she did mention that they just got air conditioning."

"What? God, *they* got AC? That makes you the last holdout in the neighborhood—probably in New Hampshire! We're melting! We're getting a window unit!"

"Don't start this stupid fight today, Woos. I'm not ready for AC yet. Work in the basement."

"You have major mental problems!" she screamed.

I left. I went outside to get away from Woosely. I stood very still, staring at the sidewalk, and everything got wavy on me, like the ground unlocked a bit. I wondered if maybe everything is always wavy, but I'd never noticed.

I looked up and Naomi was there, in the dusk, smoking a cigarette.

"Hey," I said. "What's the biggest problem in the world? Is it the media? Is it the Earth slowing down? Is it the heat?"

"Fear is the biggest problem," she answered. "Fear of what someone else thinks is the biggest problem in the world. It keeps us all doing the same thing day after day after day."

"Fear of what other people think keeps us civilized," I said. "Otherwise, we descend into chaos."

"Chaos means living your heart's desire," she replied. "Why be afraid of that?"

The words came out of me before I thought of them, before my fear had a chance to stop them.

"My heart desires you," I said.

"Don't be scared of that," she replied, smiling. "Let's go for a walk and see what happens." She offered me a cigarette and her lighter. "Want one?"

I took a cigarette, caressed the smooth white paper between my fingers, lit it, and inhaled. It tasted like coming home after being lost for too long.

I grinned at Naomi, and I couldn't stop grinning. I had a feeling that things would quickly accelerate out of control, and I realized I really wanted that.

The faster the better.

Leaving Earth

Camila touched Mitch's shoulder and asked, "Want a drink?"

I really do, he thought, but more booze on top of the pills is gonna wreck me. "No," he mumbled.

She reached over to the nightstand and poured bourbon. "Your place is spectacular. What do you do?"

"Genetic engineering, new human features. Hey, um, I'm separated, but technically married. You should know."

"I thought so, 'cause of your ring. Where is she?"

"Boston, maybe, I think. She blocked me."

"Why'd you break up?"

"She wouldn't leave Earth, if you can believe that."

Camila pushed her long hair behind her shoulders and sipped her drink. "But why'd you leave her?"

"I want to be filthy rich and that can't happen on Earth where everyone's an employee. Sandee has it all: no regs, brilliantly deranged engineers, rich investors. So I came, she stayed. Why're you here?"

"Earth's a pit. In the South Bronx, where I grew up, there's always funeral cubes in the street for pickup. Rats gnaw apart the cubes and eat the dead. That's my image of Earth—dead losers eaten by rats."

"Ugh. The only ones with reason to stay are the one-percenters running the immortal corporations."

"And I love the weather here—an eternal LA summer without smog."

Someone knocked on the door.

"Occupied!" Mitch yelled.

"Hey, it's me." Jessup opened the door, stepped into the dark bedroom, squinted in the dimness, and looked around, concerned. Camila pulled a tangled sheet over them.

"Hi, Mitch. Hey, Kristen. Sorry, guys," Jessup said.

"I'm Camila."

"Not now, Jessup," Mitch said. "Later."

"My friend, it's officially later. I've gotta talk to you now. C'mon, man, let's walk."

Mitch sat up, looked at Jessup, and decided a walk might be a good idea. He hadn't left the mansion in days, maybe weeks.

"Fine." He snagged Camila's drawstring leather shorts off the floor. Tight fit but a half-notch better than naked.

Walking through the villa, he took in the chaotic disarray—bottles, drug remnants, and food wrappers were scattered everywhere. In one room, a group of men, women, and cuddle drones were tangled up in passion. In the family room, videos played on three different screens: a cartoon, an old Western, and *The Wizard of Oz*. Dorothy confided to Toto that she wasn't in Kansas anymore.

A dozenish people—*who were they?*—lay around in front of the screens in a late-morning haze. He searched faces for names and came up empty.

Time to walk. He felt grateful to Jessup. He needed to clear his head, and he felt higher than Everest, like he could walk for miles.

But when the sunlight struck Mitch's eyes, he changed his mind. No walk. No paseo. The brightness burned into his skull, his brain felt like charcoal, his spine was off-kilter, and his eyeballs throbbed. A few uppers would help. He reached into his pocket for pills and realized he was wearing nothing but Camila's teensy leather shorts.

"Jessup, I gotta go back. I only got these crazy shorts on."

Jessup laughed. "It's Mars. You're fashionable. Come on, man, we need to talk alone."

They walked across the sand to the cooled bricks. The silence of the gated neighborhood was soothing. Orange clouds hung in the red dawn.

"How's Kristen? Oh, and Camila?"

"C'mon, Jessup! What do you want?"

"And Julie? How's she?"

"I know my love life's a total disaster. That's what you want to talk about?"

"Your entire life's a total disaster. You're better than this! This isn't you, amigo. What's going on? Are you working at all?"

"Everything's autopilot—on course, high altitude, cruising speed. The coin is pouring in."

"How'd the meetings go?"

"Mostly horrible. The glacial groupthink at Vayer is out of control. Weeks of corporate agendas and project plans, tasks linked to subtasks, decision matrices, and risk assessments. I hate toiling in our start-up, but at least hate's a human emotion. I couldn't survive in a multi-planetary corporation. I'd blow my brains out."

"Any good parts?"

"I met Robertson. It's weird seeing him mortal—drinking coffee and bored."

"And now we're worth over two billion on paper."

"Mucho moola, mi amigo. It's all coming together."

"Not all of it, 'cause you're a mess. Is this what you want? We're supposed to change mankind, and instead you've become one of the quick-rich idiots we used to laugh at. Living in some sprawling mansion with a bunch of drugged-out hangers-on?"

"I'm celebrating."

"The fiesta's got to end, Mitch. When you go back, pull the plug. *Adios, compadres.*"

"Huh? But the party's just getting going!"

"These people are sucking off you, and there are more every time I stop by. Your new place is trashed—there's a screen upstairs with a chair through it, the woodwork downstairs is gouged to hell, the picture window's smashed, that Persian rug in the living room is kaput."

"Nothing money can't fix."

"Wait until the cops stop by. Some of those dudes are doing hi-lo and purple. That stuff in your house means exile or prison, even on Mars."

"I didn't know—"

"Mitch, listen. There's always a party waiting to happen. The good-timers hop on like fleas, and they're swarming you. Flick 'em off."

Mitch's stomach felt like cement. "I'll look like a jerk."

"Yeah, they'll say you're forgetting your friends. Except your real friends left weeks ago. It's no fun watching you be an idiot."

Mitch balled his fists on his legs and punched them.

"Pull the plug," Jessup said softly. "Then get Julie. Dry out and go."

"We've been separated over three years. She blocked me!"

"You're still married."

"I still love her, but man, I refuse to live on Earth. I'm dead there."

"Bring her here. You can sell it. Convince her. Get your act together and reel her back in. You need her."

"Okay, okay. I know. I'll go."

"Good man. I'll see you both soon."

* * *

Mitch swerved and settled his gleaming ship between a rusted lamppost and a funeral cube that had fallen into the gutter. The top of the cube had broken open and he glimpsed something moving. Looking closer, he saw a rat gnawing a dead man.

Earth's still disintegrating, he thought. Why am I parked in front of crumbling Boston brownstones? I'm here because Jessup's right—I need Julie.

The rat scurried away from his landing jets, but the corpse stayed there, folded on itself, squeezed tight into the semi-transparent plastic box.

Mitch studied the dead body—brown skin, black hair, thirty-something. He looked like he'd been a healthy young man with a lifetime ahead of him. How did he die? What tragic sequence of loser decisions ended with being eaten by rats, waiting for garbage pickup?

He fell asleep. When he awoke, the first morning light was appearing and a slow rain was falling. Grim drizzle accumulated on the windshield as dawn nudged in. The cockpit clock read five, and the rat had returned for more breakfast. His stale stomach twirled, and he reclined his seat so he couldn't see.

Hey, Boston, I'm home. Maybe the Red Sox were in town and Julie would go to a game. Yeah, they'd go to Fenway, drink cold beer, eat too many hotdogs, and he'd doze, holding her hand, the crowd waking him when the Sox walloped a homer.

When he was a boy, before the nukes, this had been a decent neighborhood. Two stone eagles had guarded the steps leading to the wood doors. But all that remained now was a talon from the left eagle. Maybe the eagles were decorating some jithead's pad; maybe the rats had carried them away; maybe the jitheads, or the rats, had taken Julie too.

If she wasn't here, he wouldn't bother with the Red Sox. He'd check into a hotel, sleep for days, and head back to Mars, or maybe somewhere further out, where he could be alone and lose the rest of his mind for good. Suicide by insanity.

His mind drifted, mulling the last year, puzzling together how he could headbutt walls for a decade before his start-up hit the jackpot. He'd made hundreds of failed prototypes, scrounging for cash, trying everything, and always failing.

And then suddenly he had hit it big. His team had been prototyping human mutations when a message came from a high-up Vayer exec. At first it seemed like another inquiry that would go nowhere.

Vayer was launching a new human DNA Version—ultra-premium. Most was their own stuff, except for some teeth-straightening genes from a kid in San Diego and maybe one of Mitch and Jessup's mutations, a gene sequence that gave humans night-vision.

The question was, would he meet the project lead, explain the design, and sit in on the project meetings? Vayer liked his work a lot.

Mitch had said yes.

Since the Vayer deal, his company was on fire. Financiers were breaking down the door to invest, to acquire, to partner. Tidal waves of cash rolled in and the party started. He bought the mansion and it all got hazy. People wandered in and out, always more of them.

He remembered being pitched by processions of venture capital schmucks. He remembered a girl bum-tripping, screaming naked through the house. He remembered snorting primo jit and chasing it with eighty-year-old scotch, everyone laughing too hysterically about how the whiskey was more expensive than the colored powders.

He remembered being shaken awake in the afternoon, a few weeks ago, to read that his company was valued at over two billion dollars. He remembered taking more and more pills, and, vaguely, haggling for his new ship with a royalty payment.

Then he'd walked with Jessup, and now he was back on Earth to see Julie. To get her back.

Julie was the only woman he'd ever wanted for more than a week. In his shifting-sand existence, his love for her was rock solid. He kept thinking about her smile from years ago, when she wanted him. That years-ago smile was why he was in Boston now.

When he'd left Earth, Julie had been working for some bank. She drank tea, read books, journaled, played her upright piano, and watched films with their cat. Her satisfaction with simplicity fascinated and tortured him. There was a tranquility in her that he'd never found in anyone else. Everyone was grasping for something, except Julie.

Just after they married, they'd been walking through a park and he babbled on to her about conquering the world: money, power, every man would envy him, every woman would want him, every child would want to be him. No limits, he explained. I won't be like everyone else.

"Look at the grass," she'd said, and took his hand. He looked at the field. Each green blade was among billions of identical blades on the majestic, rolling lawn.

His mind had shifted and he had realized something: the grass made nothing, yet each blade was part of a captivating tapestry in that moment. There was purpose and beauty in just being alive. Maybe that was it. Maybe that was enough.

A tear had rolled down his cheek, he hadn't wiped it away, and they stood and kissed for what seemed like forever. That was a moment they were completely on the same page.

He dozed deeper, going way down, stopping just above unconsciousness. Here, in the substratum, was the constant feeling that even though he now had everything, he was still missing something. He couldn't pin down the last variable in an equation that he kept staring at blankly, like a toddler baffled by algebra. An important riddle kept eluding him, as if he kept re-reading the middle chapters of a novel, the beginning and end a mystery.

But part of him believed that eventually he'd understand, and that, in hindsight, the answer would be so simple, he'd feel stupid for ever being confused.

* * *

The sound of tapping brought him out of his dozing recollections. Julie was knocking on the window of the ship. He smiled when he saw her. *Wow.* Her soft, long, brown hair; her hazel eyes; the freckles on her nose. He lowered the window, worried he looked horrible, completely disheveled and stinking from the trip. Ugh.

"Hey." She smiled. "I thought it was you down here."

"I got in after midnight and didn't want to wake you, so I napped."

"Nice ship, Mitch. Cool. Come up and I'll make some breakfast."

Upstairs in her apartment, the smell of eggs and bacon frying woke his stomach. Julie put down eggs just how he liked them, over medium, along with bacon, buttered sourdough toast, and a mug of coffee. His hunger sparked. He tore into the food, gulped some coffee, and said nothing until he was wiping yolk with the last piece of toast.

"I was starving," he said.

"Finish," Julie said, grinning. "Then we'll talk. I messaged work I'm taking the morning off."

Awesome, Mitch thought. So far, so good.

After finishing, he leaned back and sipped coffee. "That was delicious. I haven't had breakfast like that in forever."

"Glad I can do something right."

Her words made him wary. Was that a jab? Or was he overanalyzing?

"I miss you," he said. "I've thought a lot and it boils down to I need you. More than that, you're the only woman I need."

"How's Jessup?"

"Jessup's good."

"Congrats, Mitch. Everyone says you're billionaires now. You guys did it." She reached over and clasped his hands.

"I love you."

"I know that," she said. "I love you. But we want different things."

"What do you want?"

"What I have. What do you want?"

"Everything—fame, fortune, mountains of money. And I want to share it all with you."

"It doesn't matter what you have. Everything's in our head. Every answer's there."

Ugh! he thought. Her confident complacency!

He said, "I want you, and you're not in my head."

"You want what you don't have. Stick around a few weeks."

"Come to Mars. Please. Look, I know I've been a horrible husband—"

"Forget the mistakes," Julie said. "The past is gone, so let's talk about where we go next. I've thought a lot too. We aren't meant to be."

"Just come with me!"

"I'm happy here. Go find whatever you're looking for on Mars."

"Please, Julie! *Please!*"

She laughed. "I've seen you for an hour and we're already disagreeing. I'm not going anywhere. You should go and be happy, and I should stay and be happy. We're on different planets in the same room."

"When you love someone, you figure it out. You don't throw it away!"

"We could lose ten more years figuring it out. Let's call this what it is—the final break."

"What if I find someone else?"

She laughed. "You will. And I'll be jealous."

"See?"

"Jealousy isn't enough for a life together. I'm happier remembering you than being with you."

"You're my wife, and I'm not leaving without you. How about that? This year, my lifelong dream came true, but I wasn't happy because I couldn't share it with you. I couldn't hug you, or hold your hand, or talk with you in bed. I'm not ending it!"

"*I'm* ending it. We're done."

He got up from the table and went to the kitchen window. Looking down, he studied the grey drizzle, his gleaming new ship, the partially eaten dead man, and the last crumbling talon.

I'm dead without Julie, he thought. A ghost. I can't go back to Mars without her, staring at the ceiling all night, using strangers to pretend I'm not alone.

Love is real, death is real, everything else is pretend. He saw that clearly now. I've got everything I want, and I don't want it, he realized. Everything I have is phony. I only love Julie and she doesn't want me. I have nothing real.

He studied the dead man. Everyone's headed to the same lonely place, he thought. The only variable is time. Maybe I've solved the equation, Mitch realized. Maybe there's nothing left to calculate.

"Fine," he said. "I'll leave."

Outside, he got into the ship. His hands trembled uncontrollably as he drove one block, two, three. Tears welled, blurring his vision, then streamed down his cheeks. He couldn't stop shaking, he couldn't stop sobbing, his mind and his body were in no condition to drive.

He turned and parked blocks away on a side street, decay and rot on all sides.

I'm losing it, I'm losing it, *I'm losing it.* Is this what a nervous breakdown is? He wondered. I'll never stop shaking. I'll never stop crying.

He grabbed a black holster, got out of the ship, and sat down on the sidewalk. He took out the gun. He pulled the trigger. His body slumped, then all was still.

Moments later, in the grim drizzle, a rat came over, sniffed the corpse, and started in.

two words

two words

end the murderous maniacal all consuming desire to put my hands around your throat and kill you looking into your eyes while you perish knowing that I who loved you more than anyone no one loves you more than me and I want you dead and I hate you so much I spend all my thoughts thinking of ways to kill you and not get caught and praying that something will happen to you that saves me the trouble you disappear or get murdered or die in an accident or commit suicide and I'll never ever have to deal with you again and your disrespect and taking me for granted and making me into a mindless monster I hate who daydreams constantly of guns and knives and alibis and murder

i'm sorry

and god I love you so much for all time and I love you more than god more than my life and we've been through it all together and we'll make it through this and we embrace like it's the first time and it will never end my arms around you and your arms around me holding me so close that it's not that we become one it's that we were always one since before time and all I want forever is to be with you holding your hand in the sun your lazy dimples smile telling me to come closer and kiss you on the neck and the cheek and the lips and no words are ever needed to know that we are each other and I become a god more than god who loves everything and you most of all and the daydreams become roses and autumn leaves and ocean sunsets and truth and love

Journey to the Center of the SUN

My great-great-granddaughter, Annette M. Owen, wrote this screenplay decades from now. I can only recover remnants—the future's too blurry to get it all—but I want to share what I could get. For the rest of her genius, our thin sliver of the multiverse will have to wait for Annette to be conceived and born, grow up, and begin writing.

Annette's screenplay, *Journey to the Center of the SUN*, will be rejected more than two hundred times before finally getting a lowball offer from Burgess Street Films—a bankrupt studio that's fighting to stay in business, running on fumes and loan-sharked mafia funds, betting everything on this picture as its final shot to survive.

Right before the deal is signed, word gets out, the screenplay becomes a must-have property, and a bidding war ensues, jeopardizing the deal. But Burgess Street Films scams a whopping investment from a retired drug lord and wins the rights, setting a new record for the highest amount ever paid for a screenplay.

Many of the best actors of that future era are in the movie, and the film breaks box-office records and becomes a classic.

So here are some remnants of Annette's future screenplay for a film that many of your great-great-grandchildren will enjoy.

Journey to the Center of the SUN

by Annette M. Owen

FINAL DRAFT
May 28, 2132

SYNOPSIS: *Journey to the Center of the SUN* is a parody of classic space films such as *Alien, Star Trek, Star Wars, Apollo 13, Downton Abbey,* and *Spaceballs.* It features a Zoolanderish gaggle of deranged scientists, investors, astronauts, and politicians.

The story begins with a press conference announcing a fantastic mission to travel into the sun. Here we meet many of our main characters: billionaire investor Melon Husk, lead scientist Doctor Fahsad, ship commander Admiral T.J. Burk, engineering officer Captain Blarney, U.S. Senator Priched, and project manager Missy Mideli.

The crew overcomes many dangerous and hilarious obstacles before reaching their destination, only to discover the inside of the sun is Heaven. They are trapped in eternal paradise and must devise a way to escape both the enchanting afterlife and the sun's immense gravity so they can return to Earth.

They escape by the skin of their decaying teeth (they forgot to bring toothpaste on the trip) and return home decades later as long-forgotten heroes whom many suspect of making up the whole story to get online views, as that's the only way humans make money—every other job is done by machines.

Thus, our returning heroes have to compete with many others making similarly unbelievable claims. Our story ends with our brave adventurers reuniting in a café to reminisce about their escapades, compare false teeth, and take comfort in knowing they'll eventually end up back in Heaven.

FADE IN

INT. PRESS CONFERENCE ROOM – DAY   SCENE 1

Dozens of reporters jam the room with their cameras, lights, and recording equipment. Seated up front are the billionaire entrepreneur MELON HUSK, lead scientist DOCTOR FAHSAD, daring ship commander ADMIRAL T.J. BURK, engineering officer CAPTAIN BLARNEY, SENATOR PRICHED, and the mysterious and beautiful project manager MISSY MIDELI.

TIGHT on MISSY MIDELI at the MODERATOR PODIUM

MISSY MIDELI
Welcome, ladies and gentlemen of the press, and CNN.
First things first—we have limited time, so we'll only
answer tiny questions. Make your questions tiny!

Missy holds up her thumb and forefinger and presses them almost together.

Tiny!

Missy moves her thumb and forefinger far apart.

Big!

Missy continues to close and open her thumb and forefinger as she declares:

Tiny! Big! Tiny! Big!

Finally, from now on, in your reporting, all references
to the SUN must be in all caps. We now have expert
consensus that capital S, capital U, and capital N sound
more important than lowercase S, lowercase U, and
lowercase N.

Third, I won't answer any questions about seaside
rituals with fresh fruit and pasta, no matter how well-
intentioned.

Second, allow me to introduce our prestigious panel:
billionaire entrepreneur and genius Melon Husk,
Senator Priched, scientist Dr. Fahsad, mission
commander Admiral T.J. Berk, ship engineer Captain
Blarney, and me, Missy Mideli, the mysterious and
attractive project assistant. In addition to space travel,
my passions are world peace and seaside rituals with
fresh—

MELON HUSK
(interrupting)
Thanks, Missy, and thanks all for coming. Let's get
started. First question. You, in the wool sweater, from
CNN.

Melon Husk points at REPORTER 1, who for some reason is wearing a
full-body sheep costume, including a head covering with woolly ears.

REPORTER 1
Mr. Husk, why are you throwing away your fortune
from mystical aftershaves to fund this absurd mission

to the sun?

MISSY MIDELI
Excuse me, did you ask that with the sun in all caps?

REPORTER 1
I tried to.

MISSY MIDELI
Okay, please try harder. I couldn't tell for sure.

MELON HUSK
I've long suspected that the sun is an untapped resource with vast potential to warm the entire Earth. But today, the sun shines on millions of people who don't pay a thing. These freeloaders get free sunshine, wasting it. Our goal is to see what's happening inside the sun and use that data to make sure everyone pays their fair share.

REPORTER 2
What about the religious fanatics who say that people should get free sunshine?

MELON HUSK
These nutjobs with their biblical values are killing free enterprise. Let's take their idea to the extreme—if everything's free, then no one would have to work for me and other rich people. Look, there's no constitutional right to sunshine, but despite that, we'll make sure that every hard-working family gets a chance to enjoy it. We support a twenty-five-cent minimum wage increase and a tax deduction for sunshine expenses. And Senator Priched has proposed legislation for a government loan program so those who can't afford sunshine can finance it.

REPORTER 2
Senator Priched, aren't you worried that with mortgages, car loans, skyrocketing credit card balances, lifetime college loans, large medical debts, and now new loans for sunshine, that we're already overloading poor Americans with too much debt?

SENATOR PRICHED is an All-American-Quarterback-type politician—
youthful, handsome, energetic. He hears his name and breaks out of a
trance, looking away from the ravishing Missy Mideli for the first time.

> SENATOR PRICHED
> Um, no. I'd say we're doing everything we can to help
> poor people build good credit.

> REPORTER 2
> Isn't this just another scheme for banks, corporations,
> and politicians to get rich at the expense of hard-
> working Americans?

> SENATOR PRICHED
> Yes, exactly, and that's the type of initiative that both
> Democrats and Republicans can always agree on.
> Americans are tired of political gridlock.

Everyone applauds the news. As the applause fades, Senator Priched
becomes solemn.

> America is always first—first in flight with the Wright
> brothers, first in space with John Glenn, first on the
> moon with Neil Armstrong, the first to napalm
> Vietnamese villages, and the first to nuke Japan—twice!
> Who's ever gonna top that one? As we stand again on
> the precipice of history, I'd like to call upon the wise
> words of former politicians and remind Americans to
> ask not what your country can do for you, but instead
> ask what you can do for me. That'd be great, right?
> Like if everyone gave me a dollar, I'd be rich.

> MELON HUSK
> Um, thank you, Senator. What's most important for the
> public to know is that we will harness the power of the
> sun. Now demonstrate the harness!

A pickup-truck-sized holographic display materializes in the open area
between the panel and the seated press, with a hovering, burning bright sun
looking so real that everyone squints, covers their eyes, and feels warmer,
loosening their jackets and unbuttoning their shirts and blouses.

A holographic harness glides in and fastens itself around the sun—buckles clasp and tighten.

Melon Husk reaches inside the holographic display and grabs leather reins and a cowboy hat. He puts the hat on and triumphantly raises the reins into the air.

> MELON HUSK
> I've ordered Admiral Burk to harness the sun and bring the reins back to Earth. Then the sun can't go anywhere, and when it starts to cool off, we'll rent some really big tractors to grab the reins and pull it in closer.

> REPORTER 3
> Dr. Fahsad, as the lead mission scientist, what inspired you to conceive of this mission?

> DR. FAHSAD
> In my thirties, I was blinded for months after I stared at the sun all day. Trapped in blindness, certain I'd never see again, I thought about the malevolent power of this orange, allegedly fiery orb, and I made a holy vow that someday mankind would walk inside it or die trying.

> SOLDIER 1

Soldier 1 burst in and runs across the front of the conference room screaming, terrified, hysterical, and spazzing out. He's clutching a laser blaster and appears to be running for his life.

> We're all gonna die, man! We're all gonna die!

Soldier 1 exits.

> REPORTER 3
> Admiral Burk, why did you decide to lead this mission?

> ADMIRAL BURK
> I have two passions—waging total war on less powerful nations and enjoying the love and cheer of the Christmas season. At my lowest moments, when failure seems certain, I'm always inspired by the song,

"Put One Foot in Front of the Other" from the
animated Christmas classic that we all love, *Santa Claus
is Comin' to Town.*

Snow starts falling from the ceiling, and the press conference room
suddenly breaks into a musical dance number. Everyone starts singing.
Reporters and participants break into song and take knee-high, pointy-toed
baby steps forward in a synchronized dance.

A young KRIS KRINGLE and WINTER, the remorseful evil warlock
from the film, come into the room as the musical number begins.

CUE MUSIC: "Put One Foot in Front of the Other" by Fred Astaire

EVERYONE
(singing and dancing)

You never will get where you're goin'
If you never get up on your feet

C'mon there's a good tail wind blowin'
A fast walkin' man is hard to beat

Put one foot in front of the other, and soon you'll be
walking 'cross the flooor . . .

Put one foot in front of the other, and soon you'll be
walking out the dooor . . .

If you want to change your direction
If your time of life is at hand

Well don't be the rule be the exception
A good way to start is to stand

Put one foot in front of the other, and soon you'll be
walking 'cross the flooor . . .

Put one foot in front of the other, and soon you'll be
walking out the dooor . . .

RUDOLPH and HERMEY THE DENTIST ELF from the classic 1964
claymation movie *Rudolph the Red-Nosed Reindeer*, dance into the room. They
are surrounded by the SUNNY VALLEY HIGH SCHOOL

CHEERLEADERS holding fluffy balls of cotton candy as pom-poms.

The ensemble sings and dances together throughout the inspiring song, and everyone passes around and eats the cotton candy pom-poms. The sugar high accelerates the pace and enthusiasm of the joyous sing-along and choreographed dance.

Young Kris Kringle ages and evolves steadily throughout the musical number until he finally becomes the round, jolly, gray-bearded SANTA CLAUS that we all know and love.

The song ends in a wild finale with fireworks and a thirty-person-high human pyramid of assorted press, elves, Santa, reindeer, and mission crew. After the finale, there's total silence and everything pauses for a short moment that seems eternal. Then things go back to normal abruptly. Everyone moves quickly back to their press-conference positions, looking professional.

The cheerleaders, animals, and animated movie characters exit stage left, right, and rear, and there's a moment when those remaining touch up their hair, lick the last bits of cotton candy off their fingers, and smooth their clothes before we're suddenly back to normal, as if the song and dance never happened.

                    REPORTER 4
        Dr. Fahsad, what's left to learn about the sun that we
        don't already know?

                    DR. FAHSAD
        Everything! There are many theories about the sun, but
        none have been proven. For example, scientists say the
        sun's too hot to live on, but none of their calculations
        include solar-powered air conditioning. I mean, at one
        point Miami was too hot to live in and look at it now!
        All those condo towers! And speaking of smoking
        hot—those Miami women—wow!

Fahsad stares off into space, daydreaming, then catches himself and shakes his head to reset. He scolds the reporters in an almost hysterical panic.

        Please! Keep this press conference family-friendly! I'm
        begging you! No more inappropriate questions!

Fahsad glares accusingly at everyone for a moment, then calms down.

> So, as I was saying, just like South Florida a billion
> years ago, our sun has tremendous untapped profit
> potential, and yet this data has been ignored by the
> scientific establishment. Fourth, the sun's temperature
> keeps going up in the summer, and down in the winter,
> which I believe is more than a coincidence—there must
> be a scientific explanation. And second, we'll work to
> understand who keeps changing the sun's temperature.
> After we understand the sun's equations, we'll insert
> new variables into its operating system to make the
> entire Earth the same temp as Southern California in
> May, halting the devastating effects of climate change
> once and for all!

REPORTER 5

Captain Blarney, the sun is ninety million miles away.
How long will it take to get there?

CAPTAIN BLARNEY'S POV

A solitaire card game is on Blarney's phone. He looks up at Reporter 5
calling his name.

BACK TO SCENE

CAPTAIN BLARNEY

Um, not long. Some experts claim that the sun is super
far away, but that's just a theory—none of them have
actually traveled ninety million miles to confirm that.
According to our calculations, the sun is more likely the
size of Australia and only a few hundred miles past the
moon.

REPORTER 5

But what if the sun really is ninety million miles away?

ADMIRAL BURK

What if? Cry me a river while knitting baby donkey
mittens. Listen, Eeyore, all these what-ifs will have you
quitting your baby-donkey-mitten-knitting before you
ever pick up your needles. That's the type of loser
thinking that caused Hitler to kill himself. So face the

168

hard facts, you impudent bully—we're not gonna quit just 'cause we find out it's a longer trip than we thought. And we're not gonna commit suicide with a young mistress in some underground bunker in Berlin. We aren't Nazis, despite your insinuating questions— we're space explorers. So, if the sun's a bit farther away, we'll go as far as we need to. Just like the rabbit racing the turtle, every single person on this team is focused twenty-four seven on one thing—winning the race no matt—

Admiral Burk is interrupted by wild giggling. Everyone looks at Missy Mideli, who's typing on her phone, laughing at something, then taking flirtatious selfies with different expressions. She's forgotten where she is but suddenly realizes the press conference has stopped and everyone's watching her take alluring selfies. She puts the phone down and composes herself.

MISSY MIDELI
Okay, what's the next question?

REPORTER 6
Dr. Fahsad, why did you change the spelling of the sun to all capital letters?

DR. FAHSAD
Let me break it down for you in complicated layman's terms. The Greeks called the sun Helios, the Romans called him Apollo, and the Egyptians named him Ra, but my researchers have determined through experiments that his real name is the sun and that he's claiming to be gender-neutral. Our most recent discovery is that S, U, and N are capital letters. Our computer simulations indicate the letters S-U-N are an acronym for something—and getting inside the sun will help us finally determine what those letters stand for and get a clear read on his gender.

REPORTER 7
Won't you burn up if you go inside the sun?

CAPTAIN BLARNEY
No way.
(pauses and thinks)

Probably not.

REPORTER 7
Mr. Husk, you're funding this mission with a fortune
made by exploiting workers in your mystical cologne
factories. Will you pledge today to start paying your
workers a living wage?

MELON HUSK
Let me ask everyone here a question—do you want
affordable mystical cologne? Or social justice?

Silence.

That's what I thought. So please close your donut hole.

REPORTER 8
Mr. Husk, the correct phrase is, "Close your pie hole."

MELON HUSK
Hmm . . . okay, well, then I stand corrected and I
promise we'll investigate into thinking hard about the
trade-offs of giving our workers a living wage.

The applause from everyone in the room becomes a standing ovation of
appreciation and gratitude for Melon Husk's extraordinary commitment.

MISSY MIDELI
Okay, everyone, I'm afraid that was our last question,
unless anyone wants to discuss which award-winning
actress should play me in the film. Our pizzas are here,
and we want to eat while they're piping hot to stay
aligned with our mission objectives. Thank you.

Missy Mideli smiles a pageant-perfect smile and waves as if she was just
crowned Miss America. She then reaches under the podium and comes up
with a tiara that she places on her head, crowning herself, humble but
proud. She smiles and waves as she leaves the stage, stepping backward and
waving goodbye to her subjects.

Reporters yell out their last questions as the mission team leaves the room
amidst the din of reporters, clicking cameras, and flashing lights.

EXT. OUTER SPACE – NEAR FUTURE   SCENE 10

Quiet and infinite. The stars burn bright, distant, and cold. The sun is larger than the other stars but still very far off. An insignificant starship drifts against the vast expanse of space.

CLOSER SHOT

It's the ill-fated solar-explorer APOLLO. With interior and running lights on, it cruises towards its destination. The soft PING of a RANGING RADAR and the HUM of the APOLLO'S THRUSTERS grow louder as we slowly ZOOM IN on the large panoramic window on the ship's bridge, then travel through it, placing the viewer in the middle of the bridge.

CUT TO:

INT. APOLLO BRIDGE   SCENE 11

The bridge is busy with instruments, dashboard displays, and crew members. Men and women are moving about and seated at workstations, working with purpose. They know their jobs. The distant sun is visible through the panoramic window. At the helm is Admiral Burk along with his assistant, nerdy whiz-kid junior officer LIEUTENANT MULU.

LIEUTENANT MULU
Sir, my calculations indicate that if we go inside the sun, we're going to die.

ADMIRAL BURK
Hmm . . . those are lousy odds.

LIEUTENANT MULU
It's not odds, sir. Death is certain.

ADMIRAL BURK
Certainty is for cowards and the dead, young lieutenant! No one's going to die just because of your nerd-faced geometry. Show me your calculations, and I'll show you your mistakes.

Lieutenant Mulu shows him a handheld screen filled with complex math, a dizzying array of intricate equations.

> LIEUTENANT MULU
> With pi equals m, as an integral of y and the cosine of
> theta, divided by the derivative of tau . . .

CLOSE IN ON THE SCREEN OF EQUATIONS blurring into a
bewildering scroll of numbers and calculations.

CLOSE IN ON ADMIRAL BURK. His eyes glaze over at all the math, and
the scene fades in a wavy transition into his daydream.

SOFT, BLURRY FADE IN

EXT. DAYDREAM POPSICLE LAND – DAY   SCENE 12

In family-friendly POPSICLE LAND, everything is about popsicles.
Admiral Burk is laying by a pool at a tropical popsicle resort, eating a
popsicle amidst a group of lounging PEOPLE-SIZED POPSICLES of
various fruity flavors that are also eating popsicles. The popsicles gossip
about being in love with flying monkeys who never seem interested in
them. Then, while the popsicles are talking, they transform into flying
monkey popsicles and take off into the air, leaving Admiral Burk alone by
the pool. Admiral Burk looks up into the blue sky as the last flying popsicle
monkey disappears from view.

> ADMIRAL BURK
> (To himself)
> You might be daydreaming again! Wake up, Admiral!
> That's an order!

ABRUPT CUT

INT. APOLLO BRIDGE – ON ADMIRAL BURK   SCENE 13

Admiral Burk comes back to reality from his Popsicle Land daydream and
is listening to Lieutenant Mulu finish his long explanation of the complex
equations that guarantee certain death.

> LIEUTENANT MULU
> . . . so, sir, the hypotenuse of the common denominator
> indicates that if we get too close to the sun, we'll burn
> up.

ADMIRAL BURK
Hmmm . . . Do all these calculations show that?

LIEUTENANT MULU
Umm . . . Yes, sir.

Admiral Burk unholsters his weapon, aims it at the screen in Lieutenant Mulu's hand, and blasts it to smithereens in a wild tantrum, shooting it seventeen times including reloading twice. In his hysterical melee, he accidentally blasts a hole in the side of the ship, sucking everything on the bridge into the vacuum of space. Crew members are holding on for dear life and the ship is losing oxygen. Death is imminent.

SOLDIER 1
Soldier 1 runs across the bridge screaming, terrified, hysterical, and spazzing out. He's clutching a laser blaster and appears to be running for his life.

We're all gonna die, man! We're all gonna die!

Soldier 1 exits.

Admiral Burk stretches to reach the intercom—his last gasping attempt to save the ship before all is lost.

ADMIRAL BURK
Blarney! There's a hole in the ship! Please do something! You're our only hope!

ABRUPT CUT

INT. ENGINE ROOM – ON BLARNEY   SCENE 14

Engineering officer Captain Blarney is below deck, in the operations area, playing solitaire on a display that is furiously blinking red alerts of imminent doom for the entire ship. He hears Burk, glances sideways at the squawking intercom, then focuses back on the solitaire game. He moves a couple more cards into place, sighs, and finally pushes on the intercom and screams in a panicked voice.

CAPTAIN BLARNEY
I need more time, Admiral! We've got to have more time!

                    ADMIRAL BURK
         (screaming, pleading through the intercom)
         Please, Blarney! Our life is in your hands!

Blarney moves more cards around on his solitaire game, then stares, triple
checking, and sees that he has no cards left to play. He lost. Again! He puts
his head in his hands, frustrated.

                    CAPTAIN BLARNEY
         Darn it! Ugh! Triple fiddlesticks!

Blarney slowly stands up and starts meandering away, in no hurry.

INT. APOLLO BRIDGE   SCENE 15

Blarney arrives on the bridge, grumbling and complaining while rolling in a
patio-table-sized roll of duct tape. FOUR ENGINEERS follow him,
straining to carry in a heavy, sofa-sized box of Saran Wrap. They work
together, swift and efficient, diligently plugging the hole with Saran Wrap
and sealing it with duct tape. The hole is closed, the crisis subsides, and the
crew returns to normal duties. And now we notice what only careful
observers noticed before: the wall of the ship has multiple duct-tape-and-
Saran-Wrap patches from Admiral Burk's previous laser blaster tantrums.

Admiral Burk basks in the calm after the storm. He looks across the bridge
and smiles, proud of his ship, his crew, and everything they've
accomplished.

                    ADMIRAL BURK
         Well done, everyone! Exceptional work! I'm proud of
         how we all came together in an emergency. Nothing
         can stop us now!

He sniffs and breathes in.

         I love the smell of duct tape and Saran Wrap on the
         ship's bridge! It smells like . . . party time! Now, where
         were we? Oh, yeah.

Burk turns and shoots one more round into the mangled screen of
equations in Lieutenant Mulu's hand, which falls to the floor. Then he
points his laser blaster directly at the young officer.

                              174

So, what do your calculations say now, Lieutenant?

Lieutenant Mulu looks down at the sparking, blasted screen on the floor, then down the barrel of Admiral Burk's laser blaster pointed directly at him.

> LIEUTENANT MULU
> (scared, hesitant)

Uh . . . nothing sir.

> ADMIRAL BURK

That's what I thought! Listen kid, I like you. You remind me of myself when I was a young officer—full of confidence. And just like you, I was certain of things. But I learned something along the way that I'm going to teach you. You've got to be certain about what's in your heart (pounds heart with fist), not what's on some screen with numbers. And you've got to stop doing complex math that bores everyone to death and makes me grouchy. If you do that, no one can stop you! Got it? No one!

> LIEUTENANT MULU
> (bursting with pride and optimism)

Yes, sir!

> ADMIRAL BURK
> (almost growling)

So, will we make history? Or will we put on diapers and let mommy math wipe our bottoms? Numbers can't think! Numbers can't explore new worlds! Numbers can't love! Numbers can't be heartbroken by their high school sweetheart who danced all night with someone else at the prom! Numbers don't have children and cuddly pets! That's why human beings make history and not numbers!

> LIEUTENANT MULU
> (smiling, beaming, and excited about the future ahead)

Yes, sir!

ADMIRAL BURK

Diddly darn right! What if the Wright Brothers had put
glittery saddles on prehistoric birds instead of buying
an airplane? What if the first astronauts had overslept
and missed the rocket to the moon? What if Thomas
Edison had been an Amish auto mechanic? (pause)
Knick-knack paddy whack! We're not going to listen to
the naysayers who say the sun's too hot and far away.
Instead, we're going to give the dog a bone!

LIEUTENANT MULU

Yes, sir!

ADMIRAL BURK

Okay, now put all that math and physics hogwash aside
and let's focus on making it happen!

LIEUTENANT MULU

Roger! But sir, there are just a few issues we need to
figure out. To go ninety million miles will take at least
four months, and we've only got three weeks of food
and water. And also, we're running low on fuel. And
we're completely out of toothpaste.

ADMIRAL BURK

Hmm . . . let me think about this.
                    (pauses for a moment)

Okay, I got it. Here's the plan. We're going to put
ourselves into suspended animation, a deep sleep
hibernation, then the ship will wake us up when we
arrive.

LIEUTENANT MULU

But we don't have any suspended animation capability.

ADMIRAL BURK

Darn it, son, after everything I've taught you, you still
don't know a ham chowder sandwich from a french
fried potato leg! Use your noggin! We'll build it
ourselves! My old granddad was a homeless, drunk
bum, and when times got tough, he used to always
mumble incoherently that there's no problem that

human ingenuity, duct tape, and Saran Wrap can't solve.

LIEUTENANT MULU
Um, okay.

SOLDIER 1
Soldier 1 runs across the bridge screaming, terrified, hysterical, and spazzing out. He's clutching a laser blaster and appears to be running for his life.

We're all gonna die, man! We're all gonna die!

Soldier 1 exits.

LIEUTENANT MULU
(wary)
Another teensy problem, sir, is that the crew is worried that we'll burn up if we even get close to the sun, and you keep talking about us going inside it.

ADMIRAL BURK
I've been thinking a lot about this one. I've done a lot of doodling and some research online, and the idea I had this morning is that we'll use innovative ice capsule technology that will allow us to encase the ship in a frosty icicle cocoon, forming a protective vapor layer and letting us drive deep into the center of the sun untouched. It's like if you lick your finger and touch a hot grill for just a real quick moment, you don't get burned super bad if you pull away super quick.

LIEUTENANT MULU
But how will we pull away super quick if we're inside the sun?

ADMIRAL BURK
Hmm . . . Tell everyone the pull-away-super-quick part is proprietary technology. We're not sharing that.

LIEUTENANT MULU
Got it. Yes, sir.

ADMIRAL BURK

Any updates from mission control?

                    LIEUTENANT MULU
Yes, some breaking news just in from Earth. By going
inside the sun, the lawyers say we'll be able to claim
legal ownership. Everyone who wants to use our
sunshine, even to go for a walk or sit by the pool for an
hour, will have to pay us a royalty. So it's going to be
really lucrative.

                    ADMIRAL BURK
Oh, yeah! Show me the mo-nay! Nice!

He makes a cash-register-pulling motion and does a spin move.

Cha-ching! Cha-ching!

                    LIEUTENANT MULU
Yes, sir. Why should just lawyers and bankers suck off
hardworking people? We can too!

                    ADMIRAL BURK
Nothing can stop us now! Full steam ahead to the
center of the sun!

                                            FADE OUT

EXT. SPACE – TWO MONTHS LATER – CLOSE TO SUN SCENE 22

Amidst quiet and infinite space, the sun is now immense. The ball of fire
takes up three-quarters of the screen. A tiny black dot drifts against the
backdrop of the sun. It might be a ship.

CLOSER SHOT – It is the ill-fated solar-explorer Apollo. The soft ping of
a ranging radar and the hum of the Apollo's thrusters grow louder as we
slowly CLOSE IN.

                                              CUT TO:

INT. APOLLO BRIDGE   SCENE 23

The ship's bridge is busy with instruments, dashboard displays, and a hot
and sweaty crew. The large panoramic window is filled by the fiery sun. In

the middle, at the helm of the ship, are Admiral Burk and Lieutenant Mulu. Admiral Burk dumps a pitcher of ice water over his head and then sprawls across the console dramatically, panting and sweating profusely. He gives out a gasping command, maybe his last before he passes out from heatstroke.

> ADMIRAL BURK
> It's getting . . . too . . . hot! Turn the AC . . . higher . . . please!

> LIEUTENANT MULU
> Sir, the AC can't go any higher!

> ADMIRAL BURK
> Then I want warp-speed AC! Right away! It's too hot. I thought I could take it, but wow, it's hotter than Miami!

The hot, sweaty crew members glance at each other, all hesitant to tell their volatile leader that there's no such thing as warp-speed AC.

> LIEUTENANT MULU
> Um . . . yes, sir. Give me a few moments to engage the warp-speed AC.

Mulu calls Blarney on his handset and speaks out of earshot of the admiral.

> Blarney! We need warp-speed AC. What do you mean "no"? Well, it needs to be, and pronto! Just do something like last time and get it onto the bridge!

A few moments later, engineering team members carry in a crudely duct-taped, Saran-Wrapped and painted cardboard box with an oversized aluminum foil button labeled "Warp Speed AC" and place it at Admiral Burk's station.

> LIEUTENANT MULU
> Here you go, sir. Ready when you are.

Burk looks at the button, wary.

> ADMIRAL BURK
> (slowly and dramatically)
> May God have mercy on our souls.

Burk presses the button. Nothing happens other than the crinkling sound of mushed Saran Wrap and aluminum foil.

> ADMIRAL BURK
> Why am I still hot? We should be at warp-speed AC!

Burk presses the button again and again, impatient.

> LIEUTENANT MULU
> (making it up as he goes)
> We are at warp-speed AC sir, and it's cooling off, but . . . it feels warmer to us, due to . . . Einstein's theory of relativity. You see, in physics, the uh . . . faster you go, the more time slows down, so there's less breeze and more humidity.

> ADMIRAL BURK
> Hmm, foiled again by Einstein's little tricks! He's laughing at us from his grave! Darn him! Okay, Lieutenant, this is one of those times to forget about science! Here's what we'll do: go double-warp-speed AC, then keep doubling it until it feels cooler. I want the AC to go as warp-speed as possible! Einstein won't know what pinched him in the trousers! That scoundrel!

Burk scrunches his face into a ball of frustrated rage, overcome for a moment with the burden of leadership.

> That's an order! Are you listening to me? That's an order!

> LIEUTENANT MULU
> Yes, sir!

> ADMIRAL BURK
> And bring me my Care Bears! That's another order!

A large assortment of Care Bear stuffed animals are brought to the bridge by crew members and piled up in front of Admiral Burk.

> It's a good time for a Care Bear party!

Burk moves his Care Bears around like puppets, speaking for them in different voices, pretending they are talking with one another. He has the Care Bears welcome each other to the ship's bridge and ask each other how they are doing. Some Care Bears say it's getting hotter—"Hot enough for ya?"—and others discuss the bravery and intelligence of Admiral Burk and their faith in his courageous leadership. Each Care Bear has a different accent: Boston, New Yawk, Mississippi Debutante, British Royalty, Chinese, Homeboy, Spanish, etc. Burk pauses playing with the Care Bears to speak to Lieutenant Mulu.

> Oh, this is such a soothing sport, my Care Bear parties.
> Every leader needs a form of artistic expression—some
> write, some paint, some foolishly fiddle while Rome
> burns—and I hold elaborate Care Bear parties. My
> lovely, lovely friends.

He tries to scoop up more than two dozen Care Bears into his arms and some tumble out, but he squeezes almost all of them close to himself with his eyes closed.

> I love them, I love them, I love them!

SOFT, BLURRY FADE INTO:

EXT. DAYDREAM – CARE BEAR FANTASY LAND   SCENE 24

Burk falls into a daydream where Care Bears carry him around rainbows and clouds into the welcoming arms of a two-story-house-sized CARE BEAR PRINCESS who hugs him. He sits on her lap and eats little Care Bear jelly candy that she feeds him by hand. Each jelly candy gets a bit bigger than the one before, and he's getting tired of eating so much Care Bear jelly candy but sticks with it until finally he's gnawing at the feet of a gigantic Care Bear jelly candy. He's tired of gnawing.

ADMIRAL BURK
(exhausted, barely able to speak)
I can't eat it all!

A little old woman enters and approaches him. We meet TANGINA BARRONS, the astrologist, clairvoyant, midget, age 73, from the 1982 classic horror film *Poltergeist*. She's dressed in a Hawaiian print dress, wears her hair in a beehive, dons oversized aviator sunglasses, and casually sips soda from a 7-Eleven Super Big Gulp as she explores the foot of the giant Care Bear jelly candy. Tangina stops and looks at Admiral Burk. She speaks with a very high-pitched, slow, polite Southern drawl.

TANGINA

Would you mind hangin' back? You're jamming my frequencies.

Admiral Burk obliges, backing away from the massive Care Bear jelly candy, and Tangina waddles her way to the foot of it and starts gnawing it herself. Then she stops, sips from her Super Big Gulp, takes a step back, and closes her eyes. A disco ball drops down from overhead and begins to spin, lighting up the scene.

CUE MUSIC: A disco bass line starts slowly laying down a groove, and it accelerates and becomes a full song. It's "Get Lucky" by Daft Punk.

TANGINA

Cross over, Care Bears! All are welcome. All are welcome. Go into the disco light! There is peace and serenity in the disco light!

All of Admiral Burk's Care Bears start disco-dance grooving in a choreographed line into the disco ball light. They begin singing along.

CARE BEARS
(singing)

We're up all night to the sun
We're up all night for good fun
We're up all night to get some
We're up all night to get lucky.

The long line of Care Bears disco strut and dance happily on air into the disco ball above them. When they enter the disco ball, they—POOF!— explode into a cloud of colored fur.

Burk sees the Care Bears exploding into colored poofs of fur and feels wildly betrayed by Tangina. He panics at seeing his beloved Care Bears disco dancing to their Disco Ball deaths.

ADMIRAL BURK

No! No! Care Bears! Don't disco dance! Nooo! Stay

away from the ball of light! Stay away from the ball of light!

ABRUPT CUT

INT. APOLLO BRIDGE   SCENE 25

Burk comes out of his nightmare daydream, trembling and screaming out loud.

ADMIRAL BURK
Stay away from the ball of light! Stay away from the ball of light!

Burk's in a cold sweat, sitting on the bridge with dozens of Care Bears in his arms and scattered around him. His crew is also assembled around him, concerned and glancing at each other, worried. Burk sees his crew looking at him for leadership, drops his Care Bears, and stands up. He's more resolute than ever.

I just had a splendiferous vision, and now I know that nothing will ever stop us! We will make it to the center of the sun or die! Now, everyone return to your stations and let's do this!

ASSEMBLED CREW
(uncertain, half-hearted, and sort of scared)
Okay, sir. Uh, we can do it. Um, yay.

SOLDIER 1
Soldier 1 runs across the bridge screaming, terrified, hysterical, and spazzing out. He's clutching a laser blaster and appears to be running for his life.

We're all gonna die, man! We're all gonna die!

Soldier 1 exits.

FADE OUT

INT. APOLLO BRIDGE   SCENE 33

The sun completely fills the window on the bridge. Everyone is blinded by the light and sweating profusely, limp and close to death. As they approach the sun and are ready to enter it, Admiral Burk is close to death as well, but still in command.

ADMIRAL BURK
Turn on the Ice Force Field Shield so we can enter the sun!

Everyone looks at each other.

CREW MEMBER 1
(whispering aside to Crew Member 2)
The Ice Force Field Shield? Do you know what he's talking about?

CREW MEMBER 2
Yeah, the Ice Force Field Shield will let us travel into the sun without being burned alive. He talked about it a few years ago. I thought your team was working on it.

CREW MEMBER 1
Hmmm . . . no one said anything to me.

There is no Ice Force Field Shield, but Admiral Burk is constantly laser-blasting people capriciously for giving him bad news (a modern-day Captain Hook), so they are afraid to tell him the truth. Lieutenant Mulu knows the best approach.

LIEUTENANT MULU
Um . . . yes, sir. The Ice Force Field Shield is now activated.

ADMIRAL BURK
We're going in!

They travel into the sun, on the cusp of melting. Every crew member is dying, lying on the floor and covered in sweat, panting the last pants of their lives. The ship is shaking, we see glass and metal sizzling, softening, starting to liquify. This is the end of the ship, the crew, and the mission. Some dying crew members are saying final prayers out loud, asking forgiveness for their crazy, bizarre sins.

CREW MEMBER 1
Oh, God, I'm so sorry I stole all the black licorice while wearing Aunt Jessie's socks!

CREW MEMBER 2
I never should have burned little innocent ants alive
with my magnifying glass!

LIEUTENANT MULU
Oh, Lord, I'm so sorry I didn't become a plumber!

There's a flash of the most intense white light you've ever seen, enough to
damage the retinas, and the ship jolts. Suddenly it's not as hot and not as
bright, and we see the temperature dropping rapidly on one of the displays
to settle at seventy-two degrees Fahrenheit. The crew gets off the ship's
floor, slowly, in almost a stupor from their near-death experience, and they
look out the window of the ship, amazed. They have crossed through the
sun's atmosphere and are inside the sun!

They take to their stations and guide the Apollo to the surface, trading
procedural chatter to bring the ship in for a soft, perfect landing. Looking
out the windows, they see a world they can't believe—it appears to be a
world of Southern California sunshine and carefree living. Through the
bridge window, they see palm trees and friendly, attractive people walking
by. Off in the distance, they see an ocean and beach in one direction and
snow-capped mountains in the other.

ADMIRAL BURK
We made it! But what is this place? There's something
about it I don't trust. It's very odd. It appears . . . too
perfect. Send out a reconnaissance drone!

EXT. APOLLO LANDING SPOT ON THE SUN – DAY   SCENE 34

A RECONNAISSANCE DRONE launches from the top of the Apollo
and we follow its ascent. We see this world through the drone's POV. The
camera takes off into an aerial journey of the world inside the sun, and we
see people having a great time at cookouts, listening to live music, surfing,
napping in hammocks, working in the garden, laughing with friends, and
relaxing on bungalow front porches. Everyone's smiling, fit, and tan, with a
relaxed vibe. There are good times for everyone—no homelessness or
poverty or drugs or graffiti or crime. This world is Disney meets Hallmark
meets the Beach Boys. Inside the sun is perfect.

CUT TO:

INT. APOLLO BRIDGE   SCENE 35

ADMIRAL BURK
(watching the display from the reconnaissance drone)
Hmm . . . I can't put my finger on it, but something's
not right here. For one thing, how are all these people
living inside the uninhabitable sun? Let's explore and
find out for ourselves.

EXT. APOLLO LANDING SPOT ON THE SUN – DAY   SCENE 36

Admiral Burk walks down the ship's ramp along with Lieutenant Mulu and
dozens of crew members. They all stand amidst the most perfect weather
and scenery imaginable. It's Southern California-ish and sunny with blue
skies, palm trees, and resplendent flowers and landscaping. In the
background, we glimpse the beach and ocean in one direction and snow-
capped mountains in another. Burk holds a long pole and stakes it into the
ground, unfurling a Melon Husk corporation flag above an American flag.

ADMIRAL BURK
I hereby claim the sun and all its inhabitants for
America and for Melon Husk Corporation!

A man is standing there to welcome them. It's JESUS CHRIST, known to
many as JAYCEE. He appears to be in his early thirties with dark skin and
hair, bearded, and wearing a Hawaiian shirt. He's a younger Polynesian,
Hispanic, and African version of The Dude from the classic film *The Big
Lebowski* crossed with the surfer Spicoli from the movie *Fast Times at
Ridgemont High*. If you look closely, you can glimpse very faded crucifixion
scars on his hands and feet.

JAYCEE
Aloha, dudes and dudettes! You made it! Awesome!
Welcome, amigos!

ADMIRAL BURK
I'm Admiral Burk, leader of the Apollo, and this is my
brave crew. We have come to claim the sun. Who are
you?

JAYCEE
I'm Jaycee. I'm in charge here. I've been running things
ever since Dad got tired of the hassle.

Jaycee sees Crew Member 2 wearing a crucifix and points at it.

> Hey, *compadre*, do you mind putting your necklace away? It brings back some painful memories. Sorry, it's a personal thing.

Crew Member 2 obliges, tucking the crucifix into her top.

ADMIRAL BURK
This is astounding! I can't believe this dazzling world exists inside the sun. There's so much opportunity for the Melon Husk Corporation to invest here and increase our return to shareholders. For starters, we'll build luxury all-inclusive resorts! And you natives can all get jobs at them.

JAYCEE
(laughs gently and deeply)
Slow it down, mi amigo. You're never going back to Earth because you're dead! D-E-A-D! Like doornails. You crazy yahoos rocketed right into the sun, burned up and died, and came to Heaven, which is inside the sun. We usually send angels to Earth to guide souls here, but y'all took the direct route. Thanks for saving us a trip!

ADMIRAL BURK
(completely bewildered)
What?

JAYCEE
You're inside the sun *and* you died *and* you're in Heaven! Heaven is inside the sun! Don't stress—you'll have all the time you need to figure it out.

SOLDIER 1
Soldier 1 runs across the scene, screaming, terrified, hysterical, and spazzing out.

> We're all dead now, man! We're all dead now! I told y'all!

Soldier 1 exits.

ADMIRAL BURK

How can all of us be in Heaven? The Bible says the
path is narrow and a camel can't fit through the eye of
a needle. Not everyone goes to Heaven, just attractive
professionals with good credit and a bachelor's degree
or higher.

JAYCEE

Where else would souls go?

ADMIRAL BURK

Hell! The riff-raff die and go to Hell to suffer eternal
punishment for their sins, bad grades, and lousy
finances, while the virtuous, responsible few go to
Heaven.

JAYCEE
(laughing)

Oh yeah, some of you guys make up stories about Hell.
Well, Hell's imaginary. I don't know where the idea
ever came from. I mean, what kind of evil person
would send someone to burn alive forever? Oh, and no
one's virtuous (he laughs harder), thank Dad. So, don't
worry about Hell. It's all good, man! Everyone goes to
Heaven.

ADMIRAL BURK
(unbelieving)

What about murderers and thieves? They're here?

JAYCEE

Everybody's here. Some souls just need more reset
work than others. We reset everyone back to that nice
little kid they used to be. You think serial killers and
perverts are bad? Ha! They're easy projects compared
to investment bankers and politicians.

ADMIRAL BURK

This is impossible to believe! And even worse, none of
this aligns with our mission to conquer the sun!

Burk turns from Jaycee to speak to his crew.

Okay, crew, here's the plan—each squad will do a reconnaissance of a sector and report back in one hour. Then we'll plan our next steps. But be careful! I sense danger here. It seems this place has a mind of its own, separate from the profit goals of the Melon Husk Corporation.

                    JAYCEE
Great idea, Admiral Amigo! You're all going to love it here. Let me know if you have any questions. Make sure some of you check out the library, and the beach, and the taco stands, and most of all, just have fun! Later today, we'll do a celebration cookout to welcome you all to Heaven.

                                        CUT TO:

SCENES 37–40 ARE SHORT VIGNETTES – VISUAL SLICES OF HEAVEN AS SEEN BY THE APOLLO CREW

EXT. HEAVEN'S BEACH – DAY   SCENE 37

CUE MUSIC: "Don't Worry, Be Happy" by Bobby McFerrin

An Apollo squad visits the beach and sees people having a great beach day: surfing, tossing frisbee, laughing, sunbathing, dozing, reading books, building fantastical sandcastles, playing guitar, painting a landscape.

                                        CUT TO:

EXT. BUNGALOW PORCH IN HEAVEN – DAY   SCENE 38

CUE MUSIC: Salsa music

An Apollo squad visits a bungalow porch where everyone waves them up to join the party. People are playing cards while listening to salsa music performed by a live band in the yard. Someone is under a tree in a hammock, dozing with a smile on her face. On another part of the porch, someone is telling a funny story to a group of laughing people.

                                        CUT TO:

EXT. HEAVEN'S LIBRARY – DAY   SCENE 39

CUE MUSIC: Lo-fi or trance music TBD. Perhaps "Don't Kill My Vibe" instrumental cover by Justice Der or "Wake Up" by Aylior and Sebastian Kamae

An Apollo squad visits a college-like campus with a timeless stone entrance sign that reads: HEAVEN'S LIBRARY–EVERYTHING THERE IS TO KNOW.

We see alternating POVs: aerial and ground views of the Apollo crew members visiting a majestic campus with regal buildings of various architectures: Gothic mansions, Egyptian pyramids, edifices with stately Roman columns, towering ancient cathedrals, tropical villas, and more. We see all types of learning spaces, from cozy reading nooks to expansive viewing atriums for everyone to collaboratively experience every possible event there is—past, future, and potential. Some visit Heaven's library for lifetimes.

                                                        CUT TO:

EXT. HEAVEN'S TACO STAND – DAY   SCENE 40

CUE MUSIC: "Tacos" by Little Big

People are seated outside the taco stand, eating fish tacos and drinking Mexican Cokes or cerveza. We see our Apollo recon squad ordering food and devouring the best fish tacos of their lives. They can't stop smiling and laughing as they eat. Every bite is a fiesta. We can tell just from watching them it's the best food they've ever had. At one point, there's a dancing conga line of celebrating taco eaters. Happy passersby are walking, holding hands, skateboarding, roller-skating, and jogging.

                                                        CUT TO:

EXT. APOLLO LANDING SPOT ON THE SUN – DAY   SCENE 41

Admiral Burk, Lieutenant Mulu, and the crew are assembled outside the Apollo. The recon squads have returned to the landing area after their patrols. Everyone looks different—tan, healthy, smiling, more attractive, relaxed, loose. Glimpses of the ocean and snow-capped mountains are in the background.

ADMIRAL BURK

Welcome back, everyone. Who wants to be the first to report their findings?

CREW MEMBER 1

Sir, on our patrol we were amazed to see all of God's magnificent goodness. In most ways, Heaven is exactly like Earth except everyone is nice and honest and laid back. And no one's worried about debt, or laws, or making a living, or telling anyone else what to do, or being better than someone else.

ADMIRAL BURK

Yes—I observed this also. It's bizarre, isn't it? Everyone's free to do the right thing without any politicians, religions, or corporations telling them how. That's the first of many problems I saw. Also no one's working very hard! And there's no stock market! There's no overall plan! There's no leadership! Except for heavenly fish tacos, this place is far from what Heaven should be like! We have to make a lot of changes, but first we're going to return to Earth. We'll bring that taco recipe back with us and open a chain called Admiral Burk's Heavenly Tacos. Then we'll return to the sun with a peace-loving team of soldiers, diplomats, and corporate liaisons to help everyone here build a better organized and more productive Heaven.

CREW MEMBER 1

Actually, sir, things are just fine here. I'm in no hurry to return to Earth.

CREW MEMBER 2

Yeah, Admiral, Heaven's fine with me as is. And I've got a surfing lesson with Jaycee this afternoon, so I've got to break away.

Crew Member 2 exits.

ADMIRAL BURK
(barely controlling his rage)
We've been scamboozled once again by forces beyond our control! Now God himself is messing with our divine mission by filling your minds with *his* crazy ideas

of Heaven! Well, I'm not going to stand for God's shenanigans. He thinks he's Mr. Big Shot—but I think it's time someone stands up to God for once! We'll show him he can't be in charge all the time and that we're tired of his little schemes! Mr. Bossy Pants, aka God, is going to learn that you can only push people so far. We're going back to Earth if it's the last thing we do! As your commander, I make a solemn vow to get you back to your loved ones.

It's clear from their facial expressions that the crew isn't as passionate about Burk's idea of returning to Earth. Crew Member 3, a few hours ago a nerdy-looking engineer, now looks like a surfing Adonis and has a comely woman on his arm.

CREW MEMBER 3

Um, sir, my place on earth was a hovel, my family was never nice to me, and I lived in Minnesota. I got zero reasons to go back.

CREW MEMBER 4

(running up to the group, out of breath)

Hey, guys. Sorry I'm late. Down at the library you can watch four-dimensional, high-definition video replays of everything that's ever happened, like you're right there. Anything ever! So, I found out it was my sister who ate all the lemon cookies! Our big family crime drama is solved! This place is awesome!

ADMIRAL BURK

What? You all want to stay in Heaven? No! No! Nooooooo!

Burk screams in pure agony, looking into the camera. The camera zooms in on him, spiraling, and then zooms out from his face, through outer space, in a spiraling POV swirl that eventually lands the viewer on Earth with a view of the sunset from a beach. There's a pause, allowing viewers to quietly meditate on the sunset. Then reverse and zoom back in, spiraling in on the setting sun through space, eventually closing back in on Burk's still screaming face, then going into his mouth, past his tongue, down his esophagus, into his stomach, where we see delicious, animated fish tacos surfing on golden waves of cerveza.

Then reverse back up Burk's esophagus and CUT to Admiral Burk speaking to the assembled crew outside the Apollo.

ADMIRAL BURK

I can't believe what I'm hearing! You've all been seduced, lured into insanity by the eternal pleasures of Heaven. But what God hath wrought, this Admiral WILL turn asunder! We will escape Heaven! I will take you all out of this horrifying, hypnotic paradise and back to the planet, nation, and international corporations that we love and worship. We're Americans! We'll live like Americans, die like Americans, and leave Heaven and return to Earth like Americans. Officers! Prepare the ship!

LIEUTENANT MULU

Sir, escaping the sun's gravity is tricky enough, but we'll also need some kind of magic spell, fairy dust, or sacred ritual to cross over from the dead to the living.

CAPTAIN BLARNEY

I'm not certain the ship has that in her, sir.

ADMIRAL BURK

I don't want excuses! I want solutions!

LIEUTENANT MULU

Yes, sir.

ADMIRAL BURK

You both take care of escaping the sun's gravity. I'll find a way to pull our souls out of the afterlife, rejoin them to our physical bodies, and lead us across the astral plane of the dead into the dimension of the living.

LIEUTENANT MULU

But how, sir?

Burk gazes off and falls into a reverie.

DISSOLVE INTO:

INT. DAYDREAM – CARE BEAR DISCO BALL LAND   SCENE 42

Admiral Burk sees a vision of Tangina Barrons and the spinning disco ball.

> TANGINA BARRONS
> Go into the disco ball light! There's peace and serenity
> in the disco ball light! All are welcome.

It's like a message sent from God.

CUT TO:

EXT. APOLLO LANDING SPOT ON THE SUN – DAY   SCENE 43

> ADMIRAL BURK
> (looking off into the distance, inspired)
> Once we're on board, bring me the disco ball, some
> rope, tennis balls, and all the raspberry jam we have!
> Now, everyone get on the ship! That's an order!

Everyone sullenly tramps up the ramp, headed back onto the ship.

FADE OUT

INT. APOLLO BRIDGE   SCENE 44

Admiral Burk is dressed in drag, in a thrown-together but easily
recognizable attempt to look like Tangina Barrons. He's wearing a wig, a
similar Hawaiian dress, and large aviator eyeglasses, and his bosom is
stuffed. Yellow tennis balls with numbers drawn on them in black magic
marker and a long, thick rope are laid out in front of him. He's sloppily
smearing raspberry jam onto everything with a butter knife. He speaks in
Tangina's slow, high-pitched Southern drawl.

> ADMIRAL BURK
> (in Tangina's high-pitched drawl)
> Stand back, y'all, you're jamming my frequencies. The key is enough
> raspberry jam. I'm not certain we've got enough, but we'll give it our best
> shot or die trying!

> LIEUTENANT MULU
> Uh, we're already dead, captain.

ADMIRAL BURK
(in Tangina's high-pitched drawl)
Hmm . . . good point. Let me think. (pause) I've got it!
We'll do everything we can or stay dead trying! Now
let's go!

The ship is straining to gather enough energy to escape the sun's gravity at
launch. Thrusters are booming, the walls vibrate, and the lights dim a bit as
the ship puts everything she has into making the break. Admiral Burk rolls
out the full length of the rope, running it from the bridge into a room in the
back of the ship. Then he returns to the bridge.

ADMIRAL BURK
(in Tangina's high-pitched drawl)
Okay, everyone, as we take off, go to the aft of the
ship, grab the rope, and come forward. Only when I
tell you! Only when I tell you! Lieutenant Mulu, put
raspberry jam on everyone. Everyone needs some
raspberry jam on them for this to work!

The crew leaves the bridge, and Admiral Burk is quiet for a moment. This is
it. It all comes down to this. He closes his eyes to clear his mind. He flips a
switch labeled DISCO BALL, and a spinning disco ball drops down over the
bridge. The lights spin around the room in silence for a moment. Then
Admiral Burk flips another switch labeled DISCO MUSIC.

CUE MUSIC: "Get Lucky" by Daft Punk

The bass line starts slow, but as the song takes shape, everyone starts
singing and dancing like little kids as they enter the bridge while holding
onto the rope. Admiral Burk picks up the rope and starts pulling on it.

ADMIRAL BURK
(shouting in Tangina's high-pitched drawl)
Come into the disco ball light, crew members! There's
goodness and Care Bears and popsicles and flying
monkeys and jelly candy in the light! All your dreams
will come true in the light! Come forward into the light!
All are welcome! All are welcome!

The crew members come forward in a line, holding onto the rope, and
everyone has raspberry jam on them. Everyone starts singing along with the
song in a glorious chorus that's cathartic. They are safe and alive and

headed home! As they enter the bridge, they all gather around, singing joyously to welcome each new arrival. Lieutenant Mulu boogies in at the end of the rope line and breaks into singing and disco dancing with everyone else.

ALL
(singing together)
We've come too far
to give up who we are
So let's raise the bar
and our cups to the stars
She's up all night 'til the sun
I'm up all night to get some
She's up all night for good fun
I'm up all night to get lucky

ADMIRAL BURK
It's working! It's working!

LIEUTENANT MULU
Yes, sir!

ADMIRAL BURK
Are we escaping the sun's gravity?

CAPTAIN BLARNEY
We did it, Admiral! We're free!

ADMIRAL BURK
Oh, dear God in Heaven, thank you! Thank you, Jesus!
We've escaped! We're headed home! Hip-hip-hooray!

Music fades out.

LIEUTENANT MULU
Sir, we just discovered that Wallace never came back
from her surfing lesson. We're going to have to leave
her behind in Heaven.

Admiral Burk turns sharply to look at Mulu, enraged and determined.

ADMIRAL BURK
Blasphemy! We never leave someone behind, ever!

That's one rule we always live by!

LIEUTENANT MULU
Yes, sir.

ADMIRAL BURK
(softening)
But in this case, we're going to have to leave her. The poor, poor girl. May God watch over her, and every one of us. Amen.

FADE OUT

* * *

There are more scenes in the future, but those are the only remnants I can recover from this far in the past.

May God watch over you, and every one of us.

Amen,

Benjamin L. Owen

Mad Hornets

The drop spreader hypnotized me. I pushed it along and watched little gray pellets fly out of it in a three-foot radius, landing on the lawn, controlling bugs and weeds, and keeping the grass green, lush, and free from the whims of Mother Nature, who seems determined to mar our suburban landscapes with her odd varieties of constantly evolving plants and creatures.

In my trance, I felt gratitude. Watching the spin-spin-spin of the spreader and the stream of gray pellets, I felt grateful for the ingenuity of the pesticide corporations who are joined with us in battle against Mother Nature, and I believed that together, if we never stopped fighting, we would someday be victorious.

Then I noticed a woman next door, and my trance ended. I released the orange handle on the drop spreader, took a break from spreading grey pellets on my lawn, and walked over to meet my new neighbor.

"Hi, I'm Ed. Welcome to the neighborhood," I said to the woman moving in. She was very attractive—achingly gorgeous is more accurate—and I reminded myself to never mention that to my wonderful wife.

"Hi, Ed," she said. "I'm Hannah. Nice to meet you. We're moving from a just few streets over, but I'm hoping that's far enough." She laughed at a joke I didn't get.

"Need more space?"

"Hornets," she said. "There's a gigantic bald-faced hornets' nest in the front hedge of our old house, and they're very aggressive. I got stung at least four times and my husband got stung more than that, poor guy. Do you know that bald-faced hornets have extraordinary hearing? They can sense the faintest vibrations from very far away. And they have facial recognition? Look it up! They are evolutionary wonders. If they recognize you from before, they'll fly past other people to attack you. We kept getting stung when we mowed the lawn near them."

"That's horrible. But you should have killed them and stayed."

"But there were more than just a few of them. There were hundreds! The nest was larger than a basketball. It wasn't a matter of one or two; there might have been more than a thousand hornets. And they were very aggressive. They didn't want us anywhere near their home. They're horrible neighbors, not good neighbors at all. Imagine if every time you came near my yard, I ran out, chased you around and pinched you, or even followed you inside?"

"I'd call the police," I said. Or maybe I'd let you follow me inside, I thought, pinch you back, and see where things go.

"That's exactly what I did. I called the police several times and took careful notes of each call, but the cops kept giving lame excuses, saying it wasn't their jurisdiction and to call an exterminator. They were so impatient and unhelpful about the whole thing. It was very disappointing—with all the taxes we pay, you can't get anyone's attention until the house is on fire or you've been shot, but by then it's a bit late. We were frequently assaulted by the hornets and the police should have had some urgency about helping. But they didn't want to deal with it."

"What'd the exterminator say?"

"He said it would be five hundred dollars to kill the hornets and destroy their nest."

"That sounds a lot better than moving," I said.

"Better for who?"

"For you and your husband."

"But what about the hornets?"

"Well, it's lousy for them. They'd all die."

"We had the exact same concern. Hundreds of hornets die, versus the two of us simply moving a few streets over. And their nest? They designed and built it all themselves, and owned it outright, while we still had over twenty-five years of payments. Our home wasn't even ours, and it didn't seem worth killing hundreds of innocents just to stay on good terms with a lousy bank. So, we moved here, with a new mortgage at a much better interest rate and much more yard, which is a bonus."

"But the new homeowners will kill the hornets."

She sighed. "You're probably right. Well, now the annihilation of innocent souls will be on their hands, not mine. Everyone's just looking out for themselves these days, with no concern for others, and I agree it's a shame. The world's gone to total hell is my short summary of the situation."

I decided not to mention that the prior owners of her new home had constantly battled roaches and mice. I'm old enough to know that most of the time is the perfect time to shut up.

"Well, welcome," I said, trying to smile my most handsome smile. "If you need anything at all, just let me know."

"Thank you," she said. "Likewise."

* * *

That night, I was in bed looking at horrible nonsense on my phone with my wonderful wife snoring softly beside me, when I heard squeaks, clicks, and steps downstairs, like someone was coming in the front door.

Adrenaline blasted through me, and I remembered I hadn't locked the front door. I thought of my gun under the bed, but my wife hated my gun, and I debated which I was more scared of—unknown armed invaders or my livid wife—while I listened closely. Then the noises seemed to stop, and I thought maybe I had been imagining things.

I got out of bed and walked quietly over to look out the window. I could see light glowing from the kitchen below, and I saw long shadows moving around. My heart quaked—*intruders were in our home!*

Suddenly, a giant hornet stood in the bedroom doorway. It was more than seven feet tall with enormous, shiny black eyes, and it ducked under the doorway coming in.

"We're all very sick," the giant hornet said. "A poison killed most of us, and we're all sick, but it made some of us bigger and stronger, and now we're coming to your nests to finally get rid of you. We heard you running your big mouth today. Why are you telling people to kill us? What'd we do to you?"

"You're always stinging people," I blurted. "You're too aggressive."

"It's all perspective. Think about how we see it. You destroy our habitat— cut the trees, pave the fields, dig up the ground, and poison everything. All we want is a home."

"I don't think hornets have souls," I explained.

"I don't think humans have them," the hornet countered. "What kind of soul murders thousands of innocents?"

"Please don't hurt us," I pleaded, and I moved towards the bed, closer to the gun under it.

"Define hurt," he replied. He came closer and ran his upper leg through my sleeping wife's auburn hair. "She seems nice," he said, "when she's asleep."

"She is."

He climbed up, sat on her, and plunged his stinger deep into her midriff. She screamed out in pain, then her screams faded, and she laid there, groggily sobbing.

The hornet looked at me. "One human down, a few billion to go," he explained. "The good news is we outnumber you. And we can fly pretty fast."

I let my arm drop, positioning myself to grab my gun. The hornet got off my wife, and I made my move. I grabbed the pistol and pointed it at the hornet.

"Is that a new poison? If so, it will make our future generations even stronger. Haven't you heard of evolution?"

"It's different. This can kill every single one of you. So please leave."

Another hornet appeared in the doorway. "Hi, Steve," the first hornet said.

"Hi, Mike. What's going on?"

"I found two in here. I got that one, but this one's got some new poison."

"Screw it," Steve said. He flew at me and I fired. The bullet bounced off his thorax and his insect eyes bulged. "Ouch! That stings!" he exclaimed.

I shot him again.

"You little bastard!" he yelled.

He jumped on top of me and buzzed, "Nighty-night." He plunged his thick, barbed stinger into my belly, and I screamed in pain until I passed out.

The next afternoon, when we were finally able to barely function, we packed some things and moved to a hotel. I made sure the door was bolted, then called a realtor and she said she'd take care of everything.

"It's such a phenomenal neighborhood, very quaint, marvelous lawns, and your home will sell in a flash," she said.

"Honey, there are ants in the mini-fridge," my wonderful wife complained after I hung up. "Call the front desk."

"Baby, no. We're going to leave the ants alone," I replied.

Pet Predicaments

"Let's get a cat," Zora said. She was the youngest member of the family, very stubborn, and probably the smartest.

"Cats are boring. We're getting a dog!" Eldon insisted. He was the oldest sibling and loved being outside, adventuring in the woods and the mountains.

"No, I want a human. Cats and dogs are stupid!" Rachel pleaded. She was the middle sister, and everyone could rely on her common sense and excellent judgement.

"No pets!" Mom replied. She had long, softly curling, blondish hair and a certain smile that, when she decided to use it, could make everyone else smile. "No one's being realistic. And just guess who'll end up having to take care of a pet? Me."

"We have a predicament," Dad said. He was thin, tall, and very handsome, except for odd eyes that sometimes looked a bit too big and other times looked a bit too small. "I really think the kids deserve a pet, honey. We both had pets growing up. We'll make sure they take care of it, and it teaches them responsibility."

Mom protested, "When I was a kid, we had the cutest, cuddliest, brown and white hamster—we named her Cinnamon Roll—and she loved us all so much. Then she starved to death in her cage because everyone thought someone else was feeding her. It was horrifying and I still haven't recovered from the tragedy."

"It was character building," Dad said. "That was a valuable lesson about responsibility and the fragility of animal life, and an inspiration to appreciate our immortality. How about this? Each kid does a presentation on their recommended animal to the whole family, and we decide on one?"

"So, just one pet, you agree?"

"I tentatively agree." Dad smiled.

"You're a maniac! Let's just get herds of assorted creatures. Do you want to live in a zoo?" Mom asked, laughing, and she smiled her special smile and pulled Dad close.

"Okay, kids," Dad said, "Thursday night, give a presentation with your recommendation of the best animal to consider for our family pet. We'll decide together."

"But I have veto power," Mom declared.

"Approved, but I have super veto power," Dad replied.

"Authorized, but I have super-duper veto power," Mom said, giggling, and she grabbed Dad's hand.

Dad said, "Recommend your animal using different criteria such as companionship, cost, maintenance, intelligence, and obedience."

"And cuddliness and cuteness," Mom added.

"And we'll get a pet this weekend?" Eldon asked.

"That sounds good to me," Dad said.

"Mom?" Zora asked.

"If you promise to take care of it, that sounds good to me too," Mom answered with a smile.

"Yay! All right! Awesome! Thank you!" the kids yelled.

* * *

On Thursday night, the family gathered in the kitchen. Zora presented first. "Cats are independent and low-maintenance. They can be left alone for days at a time. They don't demand attention or need to be let out every few hours. Cats scare away rodents and bugs, and they never need to be trained."

"That's because they *can't* be trained," Eldon scoffed.

Rachel interjected, "A human can be trained to make meals, clean the house, even do laundry. But a cat can't be trained to do anything, and a dog can only sit, shake, or fetch a stupid ball. Who cares? *Boring!*"

"No interrupting," Mom said. "You guys wait your turn."

"Cats love people," Zora continued. "They are low-cost, and there are tons of them at the shelters that need a good home or else they'll be put down. Cats are more affordable than humans or dogs. They're quieter than dogs and humans, and they groom and clean themselves, while humans and dogs need frequent baths and haircuts. The cat breed I recommend is the British Shorthair. They are compact, well-balanced, and powerful, with a short coat. They are graceful animals with above-average intelligence, independence, and friendliness. Cats are the absolute best pet! Thank you."

"Well presented, Zora," Dad said. "A cat sounds like the smartest choice to me. Okay, Eldon, you're next."

Eldon said. "Dogs are known as a replicant's best friend because they've been by our side as companions and protectors since our first versions, thousands of years ago. Dogs are easier to train than cats and much more obedient than humans. We've all heard the phrase 'herding cats' because they do their own thing, not caring what you want them to do. And humans can be even worse, sometimes pretending to be loyal while secretly sabotaging you."

"That hardly ever happens," Rachel cut in.

"Let Eldon talk," said Mom.

"The most unselfish pet a replicant can have, the one that never deserts us and never proves ungrateful or treacherous, is a dog. A replicant's dog always stands by him until the last beat of its heart. When all other friends desert, a dog remains. Its wagging tail and friendly woof, will bring us joy, beneath our roof."

"Oh *brother*," Zora mumbled.

"Dogs can be taught tons of tricks and commands. Cats can't be trained, and humans can be, but most of them despise it. But dogs love having tasks and being part of a pack. Dogs will help guard our home and alert us to strangers. They love to go on hikes and adventures in the Wild. The dog breed I recommend is the poodle. They don't shed, are very intelligent and loyal, and love replicants.

"And they are so, so cute!" Mom said. "I love cuddly poodles!"

"Eldon, you're swaying the toughest constituency," Dad said. "Okay, Rachel, you're up! The best for last. Why should we consider getting a human?"

"A human is the best pet," Rachel began, "for so many reasons. It's much smarter than a dog or cat. It can be trained to take care of itself and help with tasks around the house. Humans are our ancestors; they invented the first versions of us, way back before we had features like wings, wireless transmission, and night vision—back when we needed to walk, talk, and use lights."

Rachel presented pictures, charts, graphs, and videos that showed all the benefits of a pet human. For her grand finale, she dimmed the lights and displayed a full-sized hologram of a twenty-something woman. "She can do so many things and be a great friend to all of us."

"Well, you definitely win points for the most professional presentation," Mom said.

"Humans require a hard sell," Zora proclaimed. "Razzle-dazzle to smother logic. And remember the Wilsons? They had a human, and it always stole food and talked back and tried to run away."

"That's if you don't take care of them!" Rachel protested. "Long ago, they had their own languages and many of them had families. Some of them lived with the same partner and children their whole lives, just like us. They invented the first tools and machines and computers. They were almost extinct before we made it illegal to kill them, and now the tame ones are perfect pets. Each one is unique, even within the same breed. The breed I recommend is Hispanic. They are fun-loving, loyal, and intelligent, but also laid-back and fine with just relaxing."

"Okay, it's time to vote," Mom announced. "This is a tough choice, but a dog sounds like the best pet to me. What does everyone else think?"

"Cat," said Zora.

"Human," Rachel said. "A cat also sounds good, but I think a human would be better."

"It's a tough call. You all did great, and I really love dogs, but I'm voting human," Dad said. "Eldon?"

"Dog for sure! No question," Eldon proclaimed.

"Uh-oh. We have a tie between dog and human," Mom said. "Zora, you get to break the tie. Dog or human?"

"I voted for a cat! I don't want a stupid dog or a conniving human. They both smell and are needy and take too much time and attention. If we don't get a cat, I don't want it, and I won't take care of it!"

Dad frowned. "Zora, it's a family pet. We're all taking care of it and loving it, or we won't get any pet. Nothing. Is that what you want?"

"We voted, and for *once* you're not getting your way," Rachel said. "Don't be such a pouty, spoiled brat this time! *Please!*"

"We can get a cat also! I'll do everything for it!"

"No. One pet. And it's a family pet. We all love it and take care of it," Mom said.

"Fine, whatever," Zora huffed.

"Well, honey, you need to pick one," Mom said. "We agreed to decide as a family."

"I can't decide this *exact* minute. Can we do this? Can we go to the shelter together and see what dogs and humans they have? And I'll decide when I see them. But I want an animal from the shelter instead of a breeder, to save it from being killed. So, it might not be a poodle or a Hispanic but we are saving a life."

"That's a great idea," Dad said. We can have a family outing to the shelter and decide there which animal to save. Then we can bring our new family pet home!"

"Family hug," Mom said. "Come in, everybody."

They circled in together and held onto each other for a bit.

* * *

The animal shelter smelled like wood shavings, chlorine, and urine and was filled with the sounds of animals chirping, growling, and meowing. It was easy to imagine that the animal noises had sad pleas inside them, longing cries for a good home with a loving family.

A replicant employee had her pinkish hair in a ponytail and wore a blue collared shirt with the yellow words, 'Humane Society' on it. Her name tag read:

HI, MY NAME IS
CHARLOTTE
SENIOR ASSOCIATE
ASK ME ANYTHING

Charlotte welcomed the family, gathered some information, and said she'd start by showing them a human who needed a home.

Charlotte said to the family, "This human here is very intelligent. He can think almost at the level of a newborn replicant. He's all-natural. There's not even a wireless implant, so you'll need to talk out loud to him, but that means he'll be more loyal and very obedient because there are fewer distractions."

Rick, a human in his late twenties, looked out through the bars of his cage at the elegant replicant family—a man, a woman, and three children. He wore the sleeveless t-shirt, tan trousers, and blue sneakers issued by the shelter. The replicants smiled at him, and his mind chanted a familiar mantra: *Please, God, let me get out of here. Please, God, let me get out of here.*

Do I want to be a pet? Or do I want to be euthanized? he asked himself. It was a predicament. One way or the other, he wanted out of the animal shelter. Even the horrors and chaos of the Wild was better than the shelter, he decided. Meals were consistent here, but the pellets tasted like packed dirt. The scruffy couch was smelly and too short to sleep on comfortably, and the biggest problem of all was the boredom, the insanity-creating, fluorescently-lit boredom, day in and day out. There was no intellectual stimulation and zero privacy in the cage.

The only silver lining to captivity was the medicine. He didn't know what was in the pills, but they made him feel that everything was okay. The constant craving for something he couldn't pin down left, and he felt long periods of comfortable numbness when he believed that everything was great and always would be despite the cage, cold floors, horrible food, and confinement—as long as he took the medicine. There were humans in the Wild who let themselves be captured by Animal Control just so they could get the shelter medicine, even though it meant captivity.

He just wanted a peaceful home, and maybe these replicants would pick him as their pet. If not, it was better to be euthanized than to live like this. Susan, the young woman across from him, was gone this morning, and he hadn't seen any replicants considering her, so she must have been put down—given her final shots and sent to the animal resting place in the sky. Some humans believed that animal souls lived on after death in a place called Heaven. There the animals lived forever, just like the replicants did on Earth.

Or maybe, just maybe, he'd find some way to escape the shelter and go live back in the Wild with the untamed humans who banded together in the wilderness areas. They were starving and hunted, but they were free. *Free. Free. Free.* Rick wondered if he'd gotten too old and domesticated to survive in the Wild. At this point in his life, it was best to become a pet and hope for the good chance that he'd be well taken care of.

There were laws to prevent replicants from being cruel to humans—physical and sexual abuse was illegal now, though with exceptions for product testing, leather production, and organ transplant farms. Meat consumption was almost abolished, but there were still grandfathered stockyards where humans were raised to produce delicacies for the super-wealthy replicants that enjoyed human recipes such as heart-tarts, ribs, and feet-loaf.

Just kill me, Rick thought. Shoot me and put me out of my misery. But this family seemed nice and dressed like they had money. Being their family pet might be great. Wealthy replicants were likely to feed him well, spoil him, and hopefully give him some degree of autonomy in return for loyal companionship. He knew many pets were treated lavishly, with special clothes and grooming, their own beds, and fancy food. Some got their own yards and even little pet houses. Some replicant families even took their pets with them on vacations. Maybe I'll get that lucky, he prayed. Please, God.

Replicants aren't evil anymore, he reminded himself. The wars ended long ago, and they've built a society that's kinder and more loving than anything the ancient human tribes ever accomplished. As a pet with the right replicant family, there was the possibility of living a life that was better than death or the Wild. And if he wanted to be euthanized, he could always act out until the family put him down. Studying this family, he got the strong feeling they'd be nice to him. But would he feel free? Or be a puppet slave?

Freedom, freedom, freedom. What he wanted more than anything was freedom. He remembered his dad saying, "Every freedom is its own prison," and he realized now what Dad had meant. The animal shelters were prisons that came with freedom from starvation and freezing. The Wild was total freedom, yet it imprisoned you in a constant search for food and shelter while always on the run from Animal Control.

Rick noticed the replicants looking at each other like they were messaging, hopefully about him. He put on his friendliest face and disposition. He tried to look healthy, loving, loyal, non-aggressive, authentic, obedient, intelligent, eager to please, and low-maintenance. It was a tough look to pin down, and he worried he looked like a pathetic fool, but he had to try.

Of course, he could never manipulate a replicant's heartstrings they way a dog could. Dogs had evolved to become virtuosos of the *take me home today because I love you more than anything* look. But he'd been watching the dogs closely and used what he'd observed to mimic them and give it his best shot.

Rick prayed they'd already visited the dogs and cats and were visiting the humans last. Both were tough competitors with an instinct for turning on their distinctive charms, and whoever got the last look had an advantage.

The cats had a unique angle but played it perfectly. They acted indifferent and hard to get but added a knowing look of soulfulness, and they had their performances nailed down. If aloof loyalty was what a replicant wanted, no other animal could beat the worst cat at it.

Mom smiled at her family. "Aww, this human is so, so cute!" she said.

"Yeah, Dad, can we get him?" Rachel asked

"We haven't seen the dogs yet," Eldon whined.

"Can he help with household chores?" Dad asked.

Charlotte, the Humane Society associate, said, "Of course. They can do a lot. They aren't as efficient and consistent as a robot, but they're much more versatile. Corporations still use humans to test production lines before programming expensive robots to replace them. At the factories, humans get apartments, and their tribal chiefs even get houses and families of their own, with two weeks of vacation a year."

"What about making kids?" Zora asked.

"This human's snipped; he can't reproduce. We sterilize all our animals to help with the overpopulation problem. Also, his vocal cords are ploomed to reduce loud noises, and he's been de-fingernailed. He's been trained to be cooperative and docile. He's numbered and microchipped, so if he gets lost you can easily find him. He's got all his shots and a clean bill of health from our vets. We include all that for free for shelter animals. From a breeder, those extras would cost you a lot. He's intelligent, good-mannered, and healthy. You'll love him. But just in case, we offer a thirty-day return policy if for some reason he's not a fit for your family."

"Breed?"

"He's a mutt. Animal control brought him in. We don't know anything about his actual parents. His DNA shows Asian and Caucasian, which are both intelligent breeds. The Caucasians can sometimes be aggressive and rebellious, but we haven't seen that in him."

"What happens if no one takes him home?"

"We give every animal thirty days to find a family, and then we have to put them down."

"Is it painful?"

"Not that I can tell. It's the same for all the animals—a sleep medicine, a general anesthetic, and then a poison that stops their heart and lungs. It's as peaceful as death can be."

"Daddy, do you think animals have eternal souls like we do? Even though they die?" Zora asked.

"No one knows, lollipop. The priests say animals don't have souls—that their short lives are all they have—but no one really knows for sure what happens after they die."

"I think they have souls," Mom declared. "He looks nice and loving."

"Some of them can be nice and loving," Eldon said. "But they can also be cruel and ferocious. Read history. Sometimes they were homicidal maniacs, right, Dad? Guns, bombs, drones, landmines, nukes—always inventing new weapons to kill as many people as possible."

"And chemical and biological weapons too," Dad said. "Yes, sometimes they were intelligent and loving, but they were always insane to some degree, so you could never predict when they might go crazy individually and kill one person, or crazy as a group and kill millions of people, especially people in different tribes."

"How'd their tribes work?" Zora asked.

"No one fully understands it," Dad said. "It was part of their mass insanity, but they had a lot of tribes. Just like how wild wolves live in packs. The humans divided themselves up by colored lines their leaders drew on maps, by religions some of them invented, and by the corporations they worked for. Each tribe thought they were the best, and they competed with each other."

Charlotte said, "You won't have to worry about that. We have a regimen of medication to keep them well-behaved so they can be good pets. Ritalin so they'll pay attention, Xanax so they are calm, and Prozac keeps them complacent living as a pet versus wishing for something more. They also love a little bit of alcohol as a special treat for behaving.

"They love entertainment—tubes and tunes from a few thousand years ago back when they were in charge. That stuff's public domain now, so it's free, and they really like it. Make sure you go with our curated selection; some of the stuff they made then is off-the-wall violent and pornographic, and it gives them bad ideas. We want them to believe that being a pet is the natural order of things and that being a good pet is the purpose of their existence. We'll give you sites for entertainment to keep them happy and distracted. The basics to keeping humans happy are: distraction, a purpose, medication, and a hope for something better—then they are calm, productive, and happy.

"They're very curious," Charlotte continued, "and sometimes they'll steal, even when they know it's wrong, so keep medicine, drugs, and alcohol out of sight. Only let them take vet-prescribed medication. If you get one that really loves to steal, vets recommend hiding some regular doses of prescribed medicine where you'll know they'll find it. That way they feel like they're getting away with something. Many humans enjoy thinking they are getting away with something.

"Also, they need hope to survive, so always make sure they have something to hope for, like a new toy, time outside, or a great meal. If they don't have anything to hope for, they can get mischievous and destructive. Also, if you can afford it, it's great to rent or even buy another human of the opposite sex. They fall in love like we do, and a partner gives them a lot of companionship. They like tons of drama with their partner, and it's entertaining to watch them argue and pout over silly things, then make up and love each other again."

Rick watched Charlotte, the Humane Society associate, standing with the well-dressed replicant family in front of his cage. They were almost certainly messaging amongst each other about him, and he wished he could hear what they were saying. Was it good or bad? He studied their faces and body language for any clue. *Please, family,* he thought, *please take me home.* Get me out of here, out of this cage, off the cold metal floor, and away from the always-on lights and the horrible food pellets.

Any remaining uncertainty evaporated, leaving only pure longing. Rick wanted to go home with this replicant family.

He decided to turn on more charm. He grinned and waved, trying for a vibe of love, loyalty, and fun. He made a small laughing noise, like he was happy to see them, but was careful not to overdo it and give the mistaken impression that he was mentally unstable.

"He really likes us! Please, please, please, Dad, can we get him?" Rachel begged.

"I'd like to get a human," Mom said. "I love how we can train it to take care of itself and to do lots of the chores."

"It's up to Zora," Dad said.

"He's so great," Zora said. "I like him, and I think I could be okay with a human. And I want to save his life—I don't want him to be killed. But we haven't even looked at the dogs yet. And then I want us to just look at the cats for a few minutes."

"You have to pick a human or a dog! No cats!" Eldon exclaimed.

"I know! We can just look while we're here."

"Look, if no one can agree, we'll get a hamster," Dad said.

"Or a fish," Mom said. "Those are easy to take care of."

"Even better! Genius, honey! A low-maintenance, affordable, and very loyal fish."

"Are there other humans we should look at before the dogs?" Mom asked.

"This is our only human that would be good with children. The others aren't well-behaved. But lots more come in every day," Hannah answered.

The replicant family started walking towards the dog kennels. *No!* Rick thought. He wanted to scream hysterically at them that the dogs were stupid, slobbering, hair-shedding idiots, but instead, he put a longing, despairing look on his face just in case they glanced back at him.

No, no, no, no, no! It wasn't fair! The dogs won too often. The dogs had it figured out. Even the most ferocious, killer canine was able to look loving, cuddly, and forlorn, and no human could compete with the dog's ability to capture a replicant's heart. They were known as a replicant's best friend because that's what they were. Something inside dogs, deep and evolutionary, bred into them by nature over thousands of years, truly loved and worshipped the replicants. They had earned their spot.

Rick saw the family an hour later. He stood up to get a good look at which lucky dog they had picked and was astounded. The mom carried a cat in her arms! The gray-and-white tabby was purring, her eyes partially closed and her tongue hanging out of her mouth in contented bliss.

The mom, dad, and three kids smiled with joy and love. It made Rick smile despite his disappointment. They had chosen a cat! Wow. Rick was surprised but somewhat satisfied. At least the dumb dogs hadn't won again! He was so tired of seeing a dog led out on her leash, prancing with her new owners, wagging her tail in a pathetic blur, nuzzling each family member in turns as they hugged and petted her. At least it was a cat instead of a dog. It was exhilarating to see the dogs lose occasionally.

Rick watched the happy cat snuggle with his new family. A tear rolled down his cheek as he thought of what could have been and what would be next for himself. Congratulations, Mister Cat. Enjoy your new home, he thought. Great work, animal friend.

What was next? Maybe another family would come today, but Rick worried that it was hopeless. If I was a replicant, he thought, I'd pick a dog or cat too. Humans aren't as cuddly as dogs and cats, and our intelligence and emotions make us high-maintenance. I'll never get chosen. It's the Wild or death.

Rick punched his leg repeatedly to stab his brain with pain, to jar his thoughts and reset his mind. Think positive, he told himself. No moping and feeling sorry! Put on a smile and get ready to impress the next replicant. Be optimistic! There's always hope, his dad had promised, if you never, ever give up.

Watching the World Burn

Reveries
خيالات

Colonel Omar Mahami flew his personal ship, a sparkling new Audi, to General Abdullah's villa compound in Columbus, Ohio. The general had asked him to come alone, in a non-military vehicle, without his driver and assistants, and wearing civilian clothes.

Colonel Mahami was very curious and more than a bit concerned about the special instructions, but he was glad to be alone this evening, to play civilian for a few hours, and to have a short respite from the constant burden of command, of everyone looking to him for leadership. And it was much safer to travel in a non-military vehicle. He was less likely to be ambushed.

He hadn't had any time yet to enjoy his new Audi—every day overflowed with war—and this drive gave him a chance to race his new machine, blazing low over forests and farms in the Ohio countryside.

It was early autumn. Brilliant bursts of red and orange leaves exploded out of the trees like pockets of unquenchable flame that were preparing to consume everything. Flocks of birds flew south overhead, soaring away from the coming dead winter. Apples were sweet red orbs, moments away from falling off the trees.

The corn was ripe and nine feet tall, green stalks pregnant with ears of yellow kernels and overflowing with lush ribbons of corn silk. Every stalk looked proud of itself, upright and confident that it had done its job. The corn wasn't uneasy about jihad and unbeatable Buckeye insurgents. It wasn't worried about preparing for Isa's return before the end of the world.

It was almost harvest time and Mother Nature had accomplished everything she'd set out to do in the spring. Everything sown was being reaped. It appeared that Mother Nature wasn't concerned about the war, Colonel Mahami mused. Maybe she'd seen it all before and decided that in the long run, it wasn't a big deal.

Colonel Mahami lost himself in thought while the corn blurred by, creating a green, fuzzy carpet. He stared west into the sun, it was lower now, and the bottom edges of some of the clouds were just beginning to turn dusky pink. His mind shifted back in time and he slipped into a reverie.

He was seventeen, driving with Gisele before they were married. It was summer vacation from school, and they were in his beater Toyota pickup. His truck was falling apart—the gas tank leaked when it was over half-full and the seats sagged lopsided—but the truck was his and he loved it, and Gisele was his and he loved her, and she was so beautiful beside him with her long, black hair curled across her shoulders, she'd naughtily lowered her burka and exposed them. She leaned into him, and he fell into a similar reverie back then, as the old pickup cruised along a desert road outside Kabul, almost seeming to drive itself, with no other cars or people in sight, headed towards the setting sun. Time stopped, then it disappeared, and everything became eternal—he and Gisele beside each other, driving onward forever, and the destination became driving forever towards the desert horizon, there was no hurry or concern because everything was perfect in that eternal moment.

His mind fell out of its warm trance and he realized he desperately missed Gisele and his three children who were all safe back in Kabul. He missed Gisele more than ever before. Maybe because, for the first time in his life, he worried that he would never see her again. His heart ached to see her smile. His body craved her embrace. He'd mistakenly thought the war would end quickly after he took command—that he'd only be away a few months to wrap things up before heading home. But now it seemed likely he might never see home again.

His thoughts shifted back to jihad as they always eventually did. The insurgents were stronger than ever, and if he failed, the Caliphate would relieve him of command and execute him.

Maybe General Abdullah had summoned him to execute him. Maybe this was how they did it. In that case, they would behead him tonight.

Rather than abhorring the idea, his overwhelming emotion was relief. He was instinctively scared to die, of course, but after death, he believed his life of struggle would be over and he would be in paradise or else nowhere, his soul extinguished as many of the kuffar believed. Either way, his troubled soul would finally be at peace.

Maybe the general wanted to discuss strategy and war plans. Or maybe it was just to meet as friends. His friendship with General Abdullah was a major reason he'd taken this difficult Ohio command. He loved Abdullah and wanted his respect even though he'd be executed if he failed.

He'd been so cocky, so sure that he was the officer who could lead the mujahideen to win the last battles against the ragtag Redneck and Amish rebels. The vision in his mind had been victory in a month or three, ensuring his glory and future career. In his daily prayers, he'd thanked Allah so many times for the opportunity to make history in the final push to victory. His name would be known forever.

But now he saw what he'd been blind to—all the official reports had severely understated the challenge. The pagans were too committed, there were too many of them, and they were violent and ruthless. There would be no quick victory and return home. He was stuck in Ohio until victory or death, and death increasingly seemed the more likely way out.

If he'd been smarter, he would have taken a staff officer job instead of requesting this command in the last rebel stronghold. Staff officers worked leisurely days in Washington, Riyadh, or Kabul with long breaks for prayers and meals, evenings of extravagant teas and sumptuous banquets, and weekends and holidays off. Best of all, the staff officers had the luxury of pinning all the blame for failure on field commanders like him.

I'm imprisoned, Colonel Mahami thought. He should have been more thoughtful about taking command; he should have studied the long history of failure against the Buckeye insurgents. But he'd ignorantly believed he could win. If he had known then what he knew now, he'd have chosen to be with the staff officers, far from the realities of the battlefield, drinking tea in comfortable conference rooms covered with graphs, charts, and statistics showing that victory was just around the corner—next month or next season, but no more than six months, Allah willing.

So far, Allah wasn't willing. Victory had been a month away for more than thirty years now. Colonel Mahami had always regarded the leaders on the ground as fools and cowards, thinking the mujahideen only needed firmer leadership to make a quick end of it. But now, on the ground himself, every day he saw dozens of dead men—killed in ambushes, sniper attacks, and bombings. An entire platoon had been massacred while on routine patrol that very day in an area they thought was clear of rebels.

And the Redneck rebels kept infiltrating the mujahideen. Last week, one American, a new recruit, turned his machine gun on his fellow soldiers, spraying bullets while screaming, "USA, USA, USA!" before he was shot.

The Redneck had killed sixteen men and injured ten. The injuries were worse than the deaths, as they drained resources with ongoing medical treatment and disability payments. And injured veterans weakened public support, making it tougher to recruit young Americans for jihad.

The insurgent strategy was to win a war of attrition, Colonel Mahami realized. They knew they couldn't win head-on—the Global Caliphate was too powerful—so they adopted terrorist tactics with hit-and-run ambushes, sniping, roadside bombs, and surprise attacks. Then they faded back into the population and pretended to be loyal citizens.

Thirty years, Colonel Mahami reflected. Thirty years of occupation and what have we accomplished? The Buckeyes—an alliance of Redneck Christians and Amish militants—were more entrenched than ever, made stronger by three decades of war. The mujahideen had bombed them mercilessly, so they should have been decimated, and yet for every rebel killed, two new ones rose up, hating the Caliphate. Things were going backwards.

Victory was certain eventually, Colonel Mahami knew. The world couldn't end until every land was Muslim, so eventually the Caliphate would triumph. There was no deadline and the mujahideen could be patient. Thousands of years were a moment within Allah's eternity, and all would unfold as Allah willed.

Allah was patient, but Colonel Mahami wasn't. He wanted war to end in his lifetime, under his command. Once it ended, Isa and Mahdi would return to Earth, ushering in global peace before the final judgment. He wanted to be on Earth for that.

Besides Ohio, the rest of America was firmly controlled by the Caliphate and lived under sharia—women wore the hijab or niqab, men wore beards, everyone was called to daily prayers, and alcohol, drugs, improper music, and pornography were prohibited.

Most of America had toppled easily. The cities and coasts were godless, with no principles other than selfish materialism, so it had been easy to subdue them almost bloodlessly. When people had no collective values to fight for, they were easy to conquer, and within a generation, as their children were properly educated, more and more Americans had become truly devout Muslims, not just compliant to avoid crucifixion.

In the end, no nation on Earth could oppose the mujahideen war machine. It had marched victorious across every continent and now stood on the cusp of world domination once Ohio was completely subdued.

But Ohio was a conundrum, Colonel Mahami thought, a puzzle without a solution. It was a chessboard on which the mujahideen kept arranging the pieces in their favor and yet time and time again the Buckeyes outwitted them. The Rednecks and Amish persisted.

After the Twin Towers fell at the beginning of the millennium, the Islamic Caliphate had steadily taken over the planet. The powerful USA had reacted like an insane beast, a raging animal that lashed out without thought, exposing her neck to the mujahideen blades. She overextended herself with losing wars in Iraq and Afghanistan, and after withdrawing in defeat, bankrupt and humiliated, the world was left wide open for jihad.

Now the planet was divided into emirate nations within the global Caliphate except for the last holdout, Ohio. Bordered by Lake Erie to the north, the Ohio River to the south, and the Appalachian Mountains to the east, and populated with brutal insurgents too stupid to surrender, the scrappy state kept proving impossible to finish off.

The Ohio war was going horribly, but how could he explain that to General Abdullah? The mujahideen had won almost every major battle for thirty years, yet still couldn't find a way to win the war. The Buckeyes were composed of the drunken, savage Rednecks with their loud music, bourbon, tattoos, and dope, and the militant, uneducated Amish who joined forces with them and fought on horseback with crossbows.

They should have been beaten into submission decades ago but were somehow still stubbornly fighting relentlessly. Their stupidity and fierceness combined with their fanatical Christian faith, made them tenacious enemies.

The Caliphate had the most advanced technology—missiles, planes, satellites, night vision, attack helicopters—and they outnumbered the crusaders ten to one. It was an international coalition and all the emirate nations had sent their mujahideen, weapons, and technology, leaving no logical reason why the war was still being fought. The enemy, according to every computer war simulation, should have been wiped out in an afternoon. And yet, three decades later, the insurgents persisted.

With no weapons other than rifles, homemade bombs, crossbows, and a death wish to live free or die, the Buckeyes were formidable foes. Colonel Mahami grudgingly admired them. As long as just one of them still lived in the hills, they were winning. In their minds, fighting was victory in itself, and death wasn't feared as it made them martyrs, like their saints. He was convinced they would fight for hundreds of years if that was what it took. Unlike Muslims, Christian fanatics thrived on war, not peace. Their passion was fighting an evil oppressor, and if there wasn't oppressor, they would create one.

Rebels from across America had migrated to Ohio. The state was crawling with insurgents, and attacks were constant. One never knew who was an insurgent in disguise, cooperating with a smile while waiting for the right moment to blast you in the chest with a sawed-off, double-barreled, twelve-gauge shotgun.

A man would chat politely about the weather and crops then reach under his pickup seat for a gun and blow your face off. The vast arsenal of guns and ammunition that the insurgents possessed astounded Colonel Mahami. It was as if the Buckeyes had been stockpiling guns and ammo for decades, just waiting for a future time to fight the government. And now was the time.

The surprise July Fourth offensive by the insurgents was great public relations for the rebels. They sent out a call to arms across the net—"Crack the Sky, Shake the Earth"—and many Ohioans rose up and joined the rebels in violent uprisings against the Islamic government. Substantial sections of Columbus, Cincinnati, and Cleveland were overrun by rebels and the population lost confidence in the Emirate.

The mujahideen finally retook the cities, but the fact that the insurgents could launch a powerful offensive made people across the country wary. They'd been told the ragtag insurgents were defeated, low in numbers, just loud-mouth drunks who weren't a threat. July Fourth told everyone the tough truth: there was still a long war ahead.

The Buckeyes are different from other Americans, Colonel Mahami realized. They had principles and beliefs that they would die for. Most Americans were faithless and had no center, no core purpose worth fighting for. The Buckeye holdouts, however, were different. The Amish and the Redneck Christians were worthy foes who would fight to the death for their beliefs.

He turned on the ship's audio and selected the presidential surrender speech from three decades ago. Hearing the American president surrender soothed him. It gave him confidence in eventual victory. The Islamic Caliphate was inevitable.

US President Meredith Mirohito had addressed the country the day after the mujahideen seized Washington, DC, and raised the Islamic Caliphate flag over the Capitol Building. The president announced that the United States had accepted the United Nations Kabul Declaration demanding America's unconditional surrender. Her speech referenced the terrorist nuke attacks as a reason for surrendering, although the Caliphate denied responsibility for the nukes.

"The Star-Spangled Banner" played, and President Mirohito's calm, clear voice from thirty years ago came through Colonel Mahami's ship speakers:

To the good and loyal citizens of the United States of America:

After deeply pondering the trends in the world and the conditions in our nation today, I have decided to end the war by resorting to an extraordinary measure.

I have ordered the American ambassador to communicate to the Islamic Caliphate that our nation accepts all the provisions of the United Nations Kabul Declaration and that we unconditionally surrender.

A solemn obligation has been handed down to us from our Founding Fathers and lies close to my heart—to strive for the common prosperity and happiness of all nations, including the security and well-being of the United States.

Indeed, we declared war on the Islamic Caliphate out of our sincere desire to ensure America's self-preservation and the stability of the world. We never desired to infringe upon the sovereignty of other nations or to seize territory from them.

But the war has lasted for over twenty years. Despite our best efforts—gallant combat by our American military and naval forces, and the devoted service of our eight hundred million people—the war situation has developed to our constant disadvantage, and the trends of the world have turned completely against us. We are the last remaining nation who has not surrendered to the Islamic Caliphate, and all our former Allies now fight against us.

Moreover, the mujahideen employ the cruelest tactics, the power of which to do damage is incalculable, taking the toll of many innocent lives. The horrible devastation of their terrorist nuclear bombs, years ago on calendars but yesterday in our horrified hearts, will never be forgotten. Should the war continue, not only could it result in the obliteration of our great nation, but it could lead to the total extinction of human civilization.

Such being the case, how are we to save millions of lives? Or atone ourselves before the noble spirits of our Founding Fathers? This is why I have ordered our acceptance of the United Nations Kabul Declaration and I declare our immediate and unconditional surrender.

I express the deepest regret to our former allies, the people of North America, Europe, and Asia who cooperated with the United States in fighting the Islamic Caliphate but have also surrendered for the sake of world peace.

The thought of all the men and women who have fallen in the bloody fields of battle, those who died at their posts of duty, and those who met with untimely death, as well as all their bereaved families, pains my heart night and day.

The welfare of the wounded and the war sufferers, and of those who have lost their homes and livelihood, are the objects of my profound solicitude.

The hardships and suffering that our nation will be subjected to after surrender will certainly be great. I'm keenly aware of the innermost feelings of all of you. However, it is according to the dictates of time and fate that we have resolved to pave the way for a final world peace for all the generations to come, by enduring the unendurable and suffering what is insufferable.

Having been able to safeguard and maintain our nation, I am always with you, my good and loyal citizens, relying upon your sincerity and integrity.

Beware of any outbursts of emotion or rebellion that may engender needless complications, or of any contention and strife that may create confusion, lead you astray, and cause us to lose the confidence of the Islamic Caliphate.

Let our entire nation continue as one family from generation to generation, ever firm in our faith in the imperishability of America the beautiful, from sea to shining sea. Be mindful of our heavy burden of responsibility and of the long road before us.

Unite our total strength and devote yourselves from here forward to building a strong American Emirate within the Islamic Caliphate. Cultivate the ways of rectitude, foster nobility of spirit, and work with resolution so that we may enhance the innate glory of America and keep pace with the progress of the world.

May God bless each of you and watch over us.

The six-minute speech had officially ended centuries of American empire, Colonel Mahami reflected. America had once been the most powerful nation in history, but by the time of surrender, the United States had been on the ropes for decades, fractured and on the verge of civil war, with many states declaring independence in a secessionist movement nicknamed 'No Law.'

The United States started lurching towards extinction after the twin towers fell, and the disintegration accelerated after nuke detonations by unknown terrorists in LA, New York City, and DC. The federal government was losing control of the country, and global jihad had nudged the inevitable future forward.

Many Americans blamed Islamic terrorists for the nuke blasts, but that hadn't been proven, and no group had ever accepted responsibility. It was possible domestic terrorists had detonated the nukes. He prayed that the Buckeyes never got hold of a nuclear bomb—Allah help everyone if they ever did. The maniacal Redneck contingent would definitely use nukes if they had them.

Many in the American military had been violently opposed to surrender, believing it was dishonorable, and over a thousand troops had raided the White House after President Mirohito's broadcast. The rebels were unable to find the president, who'd been hidden in a fortified basement complex, and their coup failed.

The Islamic Caliphate had quickly established the American Emirate and implemented sharia: non-Muslims converted to Islam or paid the punitive jizya tax; children attended Islamic schools; women stopped dressing inappropriately; swine, alcohol, drugs, improper music, and pornography were prohibited; and everyone was called to prayer five times a day.

The insurgents regrouped, drawn from across the country to Ohio, where gangs of heavily armed Christian fanatics, Rednecks, were resisting the Caliphate along with militant Amish, who were normally pacifist but had also taken up weapons against the mujahideen. The Rednecks learned from the Amish how to subsist completely off the grid, avoiding detection.

The Amish Ordnung rules prohibited alcohol, tobacco, and most modern technology, so there was frequent tension between the Amish and the hard-living Rednecks, but wise leaders on both sides kept the alliance strong and called the combined rebel force the Buckeyes.

America had been easy to topple except for the Rednecks and Amish, Colonel Mahami remembered. The country had decayed from the outside in, with the rot beginning on the coasts—New York and Los Angeles—then spreading. Putrid values had consumed the once-great Christian nation: atheism, materialism, corporatism, pornography, gambling, homosexuality, abortion, legalized drugs, and the worship of personal gratification. The degeneration wormed its way throughout the citizenry until the only true Christians left were in rural pockets of countryside.

The Amish and the Rednecks thrived in these isolated areas, opposites in most ways but both fanatically faithful, with enormous families who lived independent of modern life. They were brave, ruthless, and nimble. Their leaders made decisions in seconds that Caliphate committees took weeks to ponder. The Buckeyes were outnumbered and outgunned, but one of their men equaled ten mujahideen in decisiveness, courage, and conviction.

As sharia had rolled across the country, most of the converts came easily. They had no beliefs to fight for, and faced with the choice of converting, death by beheading or crucifixion, or paying the crushing jizya, they worshipped Allah enthusiastically. It was both glorious and pathetic how smoothly most of America had crumbled. Even the Jews flopped. Most were Jewish in name only, but even the orthodox Hasids—when faced with death, Islam, or a punishing tax—had chosen Islam.

The Audi's dashboard indicated that Colonel Mahami was less than ten minutes away from General Abdullah's villa. He knew the general didn't want to hear a list of problems; he wanted a strategy for victory. Colonel Mahami's predecessor had been crucified, and the colonel before him had been beheaded. General Abdullah's predecessors had also been executed, all of them decreed traitors by the caliph for being unable to conquer Ohio.

General Abdullah would press him for a plan, a new tactic or strategy that could end the war quickly. And Colonel Mahami had no easy solutions. The mujahideen had to become tougher, like the warriors of decades ago. They must train harder, fight viciously, and be willing martyrs. The general wouldn't like what he had to say.

He was almost at General Abdullah's—just a few kilometers now. Driving past a school playground, Colonel Mahami saw a swing set, the swings empty except for one girl in a yellow dress with long black hair who was swinging alone. He slowed to study her, then stopped the ship beside the schoolyard, and a clear memory from his childhood came to him—a nightmare memory that he loved revisiting—and he fell into another reverie.

He was nine or ten, and it was dusk in his village on the outskirts of Kabul. He was playing at the village playground when hundreds of American drones descended—screaming so loud it was the only sound—and he watched them drop thousands of firebombs on a neighborhood several kilometers away. The sky lit up, exploding white, so bright white that everything became a black silhouette. He looked away from the blast and saw a young girl alone on the swing set, her legs dangling out from her dress, her long black hair tied back with a bow from her beautifully sad face. She kept swinging, her banana-seat bicycle leaning on its kickstand beside the swing set, and she looked upon the distant flames, at the mass murder kilometers away, and she kept on swinging and swinging. Swinging while watching the world burn. Swinging and watching while thousands of innocent people were burned alive into dancing cinders. Time stopped, then it disappeared, and everything became eternal and the young girl was swinging forever, watching the neighborhood in flames on the desert horizon. Children burned alive while he and the girl watched from the playground, and yet there was no worry because nothing could be done to change anything, and so everything was perfect. And the little girl kept swinging while she watched the world burn.

And her swinging haunted him and fascinated him and terrified him, more than the American monsters and even more than all the innocent people burning alive.

Meeting with General Abdullah
لقاء اللواء عبدالله

Colonel Omar Mahami arrived at General Abdullah's gated compound just before seven. It sat perched on a hillside overlooking Columbus and the wandering Scioto River. The early-autumn sun hovered low above the city, preparing to set and igniting the colored foliage into magnificence. The view was miraculous, all praise be to Allah, but he wanted to be punctual, so he didn't pause to enjoy the stunning scene.

General Abdullah's home was a rambling villa well away from travel lanes, hidden behind high stone walls that were shockingly clean of the blasphemous graffiti that the insurgents plastered over everything. Heavily armed guards, elite mujahideen, stood at perimeter checkpoints. One carefully checked his identification, inspected his vehicle, and then let him through.

He'd been here before and knew the place. The general lived in Columbus, in the midst of the insurgency, to show leadership on the ground, but he also lived opulently. Inside was an open courtyard lined with blue pools, fountains, and expertly manicured gardens. There was a massive stone fireplace in the main living area and smaller ones in every room. In the kitchen was a cooking pit with room enough to grill an uncut camel. Walls throughout the villa were lined with framed maps, mounted weapons, and other mementos from General Abdullah's younger days as a victorious mujahideen officer in Australia, Canada, and Mexico.

He walked up to the entrance and rang the bell. The general's aide opened the door.

"Peace be upon you," Colonel Mahami said.

"And unto you, peace. Welcome, Colonel Mahami. I'll take your coat and you can leave your sandals on the mat. General Abdullah is in the library."

He walked down the hall, past the dining room and the kitchen, glimpsing the large banquet table underneath an elaborate chandelier and the mammoth cooking pit. The hallway walls were lined with trophies of General Abdullah's many conquests. He pushed open the library door and the general was already standing, waiting to welcome him, just like Colonel Mahami knew he would be. The walls were lined with shelves filled with military, religious, and science books.

"Omar, my dearest friend!" Abdullah said.

"General Abdullah! Peace be upon you."

"And unto you, peace."

"Please sit and let's have some tea." General Abdullah was wearing a pristine white robe and an elegantly wrapped brown turban. His beard was brushed and almost glistening. The general was near seven feet tall, and even now, in his mid-sixties, was in fighting shape.

But Colonel Mahami noticed the man's face looked lined and tired for the first time. His beard had turned from salt and pepper to almost completely gray. He's finally getting old, and he's stressed about the insurgency, maybe more than me, Colonel Mahami thought. He sat down and picked up his cup of tea.

"How are you, Omar? What's the news from home?"

"Good, sir. I'm healthy and well, thanks be to Allah. My family is doing wonderful in Kabul. Baboo is an exceptional football player! Niha is our scholar—math and physics. Tanfir loves nature, the garden, and the animals. Gisele is well. I miss them, of course. More than usual for some reason. How is your family, sir?"

"Good, good. Thank you. My children are all grown, now with their own children, and to all of them I am a myth. They are done waiting for my return. They are polite to me in messages and on the screen, but they know me more as a flicker in the news than as a father and grandfather. I always miss them terribly but then I'm home for a few days and I miss jihad more."

"Yes."

"So . . . let's talk honestly about our failure to conquer Ohio. American Emirate. These Buckeyes are tough bastards. For one thing, it's impossible to know who they are. Everyone's so friendly, devout, and patriotic when you talk to them face to face, but these Rednecks and Amish are lurking everywhere behind the woodwork, like rodents—but rodents with huge, hidden caches of weapons financed from selling illegal alcohol, dope, tobacco, and swine. Despite our overwhelming superiority, these ignorant maniacs keep stupidly fighting. Thirty years and this Ohio district still isn't under our control."

"We have Columbus, Cleveland, and Cincinnati mostly secured."

"It had appeared so. But they seized control of those cities during their July Fourth offensive, and just a few clicks outside those cities, the insurgents hold sway—going to church, displaying crucifixes, drinking alcohol, eating swine, smoking dope, and the women dress like harlots. They gamble and loan money at interest, exploiting the poor."

"Yes. I keep studying the problem. We have to learn from our mistakes and try something new to defeat them."

"Well said," General Abdullah replied. "Very well said. We must look in the mirror, examine our failures, and learn from them. I'm curious what new strategy you suggest. But first, let's watch this news report from a couple of hours ago."

Abdullah pressed his palms together and the wall screen displayed a video from Al Jazeera News. "This reporter was able to interview Buckeye fighters," General Abdullah said. "Allah only knows how she got access. Watch these kuffar and then tell me how we beat them."

On the screen, a reporter, a twentyish blonde American woman wearing a black hijab, spoke into the camera: "Thirty years ago, the Islamic Caliphate proclaimed victory in America and established the American Emirate. The Global Caliphate was almost complete except for piddling pockets of resistance in the American countryside.

"Now, three decades later, the resistance fighters, called Buckeyes, have consolidated in Ohio, where against all odds and expert predictions, they've become stronger than ever. With only guns, crossbows, homemade bombs, and unwavering commitment, they continue to wage war against legions of mujahideen equipped with advanced technology including drones, laser-guided missiles, attack helicopters, and fighter jets.

"Greatly outnumbered and outgunned, the Buckeyes have adopted terrorist tactics, using hit-and-run attacks, roadside bombs, sabotage, and snipers to constantly undermine government control while blending in with the general population.

"The Buckeyes are a hodgepodge of groups, mostly Christian Rednecks and militant Amish, who themselves have many significant differences between them. The Amish are a historically pacifist Christian sect that rejects all modern technology, alcohol, photography, and immodest dress. The Rednecks are Christian fundamentalists who love guns, intoxication, swine, and obscene music. And yet these very different groups are strongly united by the conviction that the Caliphate must leave America.

"Both groups have become entrenched throughout the state of Ohio, united in war against the mujahideen. They meet in secret hideouts and have proven time and time again to be a formidable enemy that, so far, has been impossible to defeat."

The reporter continued. "For thirty years, the mujahideen have been on the cusp of total victory in the American Emirate, yet the insurgents keep fighting. And the United Nations recently warned that the Ohio region could become a breeding ground for international terrorism by Christian extremists.

"A new commander, General Abdullah, has been appointed, with clear orders from Kabul to end the insurgency once and for all by whatever means necessary. He's already reset the leadership ranks, firing dozens of career officers and filling key posts with trusted commanders from his previous victorious campaigns—war-tested officers from the bloody but victorious jihads in Canada, Mexico, Australia, and South America.

"One of the general's key appointments is Colonel Omar Mahami, now overall commander of the mujahideen in the Ohio region. In a controversial first move, Colonel Mahami has tripled the number of mujahideen on the ground, a clear admission that despite Caliphate claims to the contrary, the American insurgency is far from defeated.

"Previous generals tried to reach some kind of prolonged truce with the insurgents, negotiating extended ceasefires and peaceful coexistence. But constant insurgent attacks in violation of the agreements, most recently a surprise offensive in July, along with the caliph's mandate that the entire Earth must be conquered for Islam, meant that the shaky ceasefires were always untenable.

"I was able to meet today with some of the Redneck insurgents. Rebels blindfolded us and escorted us to a secret location in the southeastern part of the state, outside an Appalachian cave complex. The Rednecks, reacting to the change in military leadership, have a clear message for the newly appointed General Abdullah."

The reporter was standing in the woods amidst a dozenish bearded men wearing leather or canvas jackets and olive work pants or jeans. Most of the men carried automatic weapons, some toted shotguns or rifles, and all had handguns and hunting knives holstered on their hips. They looked fierce, tired, and wary. All-terrain vehicles and dirt bikes were parked around the perimeter, and scruffy dogs roamed across the camp.

A Redneck with a red beard stood in front of the reporter. He wore a brown leather jacket over an olive-green t-shirt, and a wooden crucifix hung from his neck on a leather cord. He cradled an assault rifle in his arms like it was a lover.

The reporter said, "General Abdullah has taken command and ordered the mujahideen forces to annihilate the Buckeyes by whatever means necessary. Since your violent July Fourth attacks violated the ceasefire agreement, the Caliphate has ordered the general to win at all costs. How are the Buckeyes dealing with this situation?"

The Redneck said, "In all honesty, we didn't achieve our main objective in July, which was to spur uprisings around the country. Still, we inflicted heavy casualties on the mujahideen, and this was a big gain for us. Our advice to General Abdullah is to go back to the ceasefire his predecessor set up and then get the hell out of Ohio before we murder all of y'all. Let us have Ohio to live free. Withdraw the mujahideen completely from here. He shouldn't trouble himself anymore, and neither should the Caliphate. You dirt-lickin' dogs have lost enough blood and treasure. Y'all don't have no other options neither."

"Why fight?" the reporter asked. "Why not just pay the jizya tax and be left alone?"

"We're not payin' your jiz tax to be Christian, and we're never going to live under sharia or anyone's rules but our own. It's a lot more than just prayin' to Jesus. We like to drink beer and bourbon and smoke dope. We like smokin' and dippin'. We like bacon cheeseburgers and barbecued ribs and playin' cards. We like rockin' out. We want our kids goin' to Christian schools. We don't want our beautiful women buried under that retard burka or niqab. We want our own rules in Ohio, and after that we're takin' it all back—from sea to shinin' sea."

The reporter nodded. "But you're no longer fighting against foreign mujahideen; you're fighting against your own people. The American people surrendered unconditionally to the Caliphate over thirty years ago and are living peacefully and prosperously. The mujahideen are now your fellow Americans. You're fighting against your brothers."

"Hey, if we can live by our rules and practice our faith, live the way we want, then we don't have any problem with any government and there'll be peace. But we won't live under sharia. The solution with the Caliphate is simple. We've told them the way to peace. They want peace—leave Ohio. They want war—stay. They can decide. We want peace, but if they want war, they're gonna have it. We'll put a bullet through their heads while they walk in the park. We'll slit their throats in their sleep."

"Is that a message or a threat?" the reporter asked.

"This is both a message and a warning. If General Abdullah and Colonel Mahami and their dog-humpin' Muslim devils intensify the war, then we're ready to fight. We never get tired of war. Injuries don't sadden us. Martyrdom doesn't pain our hearts. We win even if we get martyred. If we're tired, that's success. We succeed by just being at war. We'll enter Columbus in victory, God willing, and establish it as our capital, and then we'll take back this whole country from the Caliphate. This is our way. Our glory. We're in no hurry. It might be a few hundred years from now. We're training our children to fight, and when we die, our children will be the ones who slaughter you, then our grandchildren, then our great-grandchildren. You will kill ten of us, we will kill one of you, but in the end, you will tire of it first. They can never stop us. Never!"

General Abdullah touched his thumb to his finger and the screen went dark. He stared quietly at the black glass screen for several moments before saying, "How can we defeat this? These ignorant kuffar. They're too stupid to know they can never win, and yet that's why we can't defeat them."

Colonel Mahami said, "We've gotten softer while the infidels have gotten tougher. Victory has made us lazy while they've become more ruthless. One Buckeye is worth ten mujahideen."

"Yes," General Abdullah said, still staring at the black screen, his reflection staring back at him. "They are a worthy enemy, and I've come to believe they can't be defeated until every single one of them is annihilated."

"They've learned from us," Colonel Mahami said. "They fight the way we used to fight—lean, hungry, fearless, and welcoming death. Now? Now we spend mountains of dinar on the best weapons and drones. We fight with machines—robots and missiles made of inhuman motors and circuits—while they fight us with human blood and spirit. All they have are bullets, arrows, and bourbon, and yet they keep winning."

General Abdullah turned to look at Colonel Mahami. "Yes, yes. So, how do we defeat them?"

"Buckeyes," Colonel Mahami said. "When I first heard of the word, I thought it was referencing the male deer. But I learned it's a native tree. The nut's covered in a shell of thorns, almost impenetrable. With a sharp knife, you can get one open, usually after cutting yourself, and inside is a fascinating, tough brown sphere resembling polished wood, and on it there's a creamy white circle, like an eye that's always watching you. It's poisonous. From the leaves to the bark to the nuts, the buckeye tree is poisonous. Not so poisonous that it kills you all at once, but enough to kill you slowly, over time—first weakness, then paralysis, then death."

"They are aptly named," the general said, laughing.

"What do you think of this area?"

"Ohio is impressive," General Abdullah replied. "I can see why they'd fight for it. The majestic Lake Erie to the north, the rolling Ohio River to the south, the ever-fertile farmlands, and the forest-covered Appalachian hills jammed with coal and gas. But it's not the land they're fighting for, these infidels. They're fighting for a cause they'll die for. And that spirit can't be defeated as long as one of them lives. While even one Buckeye lives, we'll always be at war."

"Yes, war is about killing people," Colonel Mahami agreed. "After we've killed enough of them, they'll stop fighting."

General Abdullah's face darkened. He spoke slowly. "I need your perspective. I want to make sure I'm not just tired and impatient, or worse, that I'm losing my mind."

Colonel Mahami was intrigued. "What is it, sir?"

"It sounds crazy to say this out loud. I'm nervous for the first time in forty years."

The general closed his eyes for a moment, then opened them and continued. "I have authority from the Caliphate to detonate atomic bombs throughout Ohio. We'll martyr everyone, and the insurgency will end. We'll finally, after all these centuries of struggle, be ready for Isa to return. We're close. So close. But to finally end this war, we must be brave."

Colonel Mahami was stunned. "Allah, help us!" he gasped. "No!"

"Consider it thoughtfully," General Abdullah said. "All true believers will enter paradise as martyrs, the kuffar will go to hell, and centuries of jihad will finally end, bringing world peace. One night of terror will finally end centuries of bloodshed."

Colonel Mahami said angrily, "I can't believe this is even being considered! The Americans always accused us of detonating the nukes in

New York, LA, and DC. Did we?"

"No. I promise that wasn't us. It was Allah's will, but we didn't do it."

"How can you know?"

"I've seen everything on it. Our intelligence discovered those bombs were detonated by a rag-tag domestic terrorist group led by a deranged American physicist named Johnny Twain, for reasons we still don't understand. I promise you that we've never used this horrible power before, thanks be to Allah. But now it appears our time has come. It appears to me, and to the Supreme Council, that Allah has willed this final step before establishing the Global Caliphate. The Supreme Council—the top sultans, emirs, kings, imams, and the caliph himself—have secretly granted me the power to make this decision."

"It hasn't been decided?"

"No. I was sent here to decide. And now I need your help and wisdom, Omar. Do we kill tens of millions in an instant tonight? Do you and I finally end the bloodshed? Or do we fight on and on and on, for countless more decades, perhaps centuries?

Colonel Mahami didn't speak. He stared at the floor, dazed.

General Abdullah said, "Talking with you earlier, looking into your eyes, I think you believe, like me, that these Rednecks and Amish can't be defeated otherwise. That as long as one Buckeye lives, we're at war, and that victory requires annihilating everyone."

"No! There are too many innocent people. Women and children!"

"We must be brave. There are times in war that call for great courage. The Americans demonstrated courage when they firebombed Dresden and Tokyo, killing tens of thousands of women and children in their sleep, burning them to death. They showed fortitude again when they dropped napalm on innocent villagers in Vietnam, burning them alive. They showed determination when they carpet-bombed peaceful countrysides in Iraq and Afghanistan. And of course, their most courageous moment of all, dropping nukes on Hiroshima and Nagasaki.

"Americans once held these same secret councils, contemplating how to defeat an enemy who would never surrender. Their famous general, Curtis LeMay, explained the decision to nuke Japan by saying, 'All war is evil and if you let that bother you, you're not a good soldier. It doesn't make a difference how you kill a man. Your choice should be which weapon gets the whole mess over with.'"

Colonel Mahami replied firmly, "Iblīs always has reasons. But we are with Allah, so we can't use nukes. Too many innocents will die. Nukes are what devils use, not us. That's how cowardly pagans fight, not mujahideen. We'll have victory when Allah wills. But we must win as mujahideen, obeying Allah's commandments. If we lose our souls, then we've lost, no matter what victory we achieve.

"You said it yourself, General. Americans are the ones who drop carpet bombs on villagers, fire artillery into marketplaces, and drop nuclear bombs, murdering tens of thousands of innocents in an instant. And now they've reaped everything they've sown."

Colonel Mahami continued. "They've been defeated because evil never wins in the long run. I share your impatience, sir. I want victory now, and I know I'll be executed soon if we're not victorious. But if we become the kuffar then we've fought for nothing. Our victory will have its time when Allah wills, and we must trust in him and obey his commandments."

"What do you say to the idea that Allah has given us the bomb? That Allah has given us this power to be victorious? That all of history has led us to this moment to end jihad once and for all?"

Colonel Mahami replied, "Sir, I must talk to you as a friend. Like when we were younger, puzzling the world together. Man to man, as equals."

"Yes, please, please, go ahead."

"I don't trust the Supreme Council. They want the easy way out. These lazy royals and imams never leave their cushy palaces and compounds. They sit back safe in Arabia and issue orders and take all the credit and place all the blame, but they've never seen war in person. They haven't fought. What matters is when you place your own life on the front line and our mujahideen see that you aren't some tea party commander, ordering them to die while you enjoy the good life.

"Morale is everything, and leaders don't build it by mingling with celebrities at banquets. Our men see this and lose their will to fight. Too many on the Supreme Council are more concerned with wealth and prestige than with fighting for the principles of Islam. Those men are political whores paid to screw the faithful. And you know what? They never lose one night's sleep over it. They never get shot at, and they never wait for the knock on the door telling them their son was killed. These men with royal titles and fancy degrees have never been in battle, yet they make decisions about killing millions.

"You know the difference between a politician and a leader?" Colonel Mahami continued. "Here's my definition: a politician is a prostitute looking for money. He's owned by the royal families and corporations, doing their bidding like a slave. A leader's allegiance is to Allah, and he always does what's right, even if it costs him his reputation and career.

"This applies to our military officers. We have too many friendly officers who can't maintain the brutal discipline needed to win. We need no-holds-barred, get-it-done warriors who push the men and always expect better results. The easygoing leader may be liked, but the hard-nosed bastard will have their attention, and if he fights alongside them, he'll have their respect.

"Respect and integrity are critical, but we've lost them, and we'll lose them forever if we use nukes. Other than this last pocket of resistance, we've defeated America. The country is under our control, and if we fight harder, with integrity, we'll win soon."

"Win soon?" General Abdullah laughed. "Omar, are you teasing me? You sound like a member of the Supreme Council yourself! We've been fighting this last pocket of resistance for thirty years now, always believing we're a season away from total victory, and yet the insurgents keep fighting. For every man we kill, two more Buckeyes rise up in rage against us. Has it occurred to you that these people will never be civilized? That they will never live under sharia? That's what they keep saying, and when will we finally believe them? They want alcohol and drugs, and women's bodies exposed like whores, and tattoos, and blasphemous music, and little children eating filthy swine. The pagans have an animalistic way of life so ingrained that we can't change it."

"Are you saying we can never win?" Colonel Mahami asked.

"I'm saying what you said—that so far, we haven't had the will to win. We can end the war tonight if we have the will."

Colonel Mahami objected. "Winning with nukes, killing millions of innocents, is worse than losing. We need to make tougher mujahideen. We used to live in caves, wet and hungry. We used to move through the forests and mountains like the Buckeyes, like panthers stalking prey. We once lived on cold tea and stale bread. We once lusted for battle and martyrdom.

"But now our soldiers are soft, like their leaders—marshmallow men living in barracks with every amenity, with soft beds, fancy restaurants, and cinemas. We're scared to die, so we send drones and machines to fight for us. We're cowards! We must revive the spirit of the mujahideen from long ago and fight like men again. Then we'll have victory, and then we'll have earned it."

General Abdullah protested. "That will take years, and it's no guarantee! The Americans dropped nukes on the Japanese because that's what it took to win. Why shouldn't we do the same? The Buckeyes will never stop. They will never surrender. They want to be martyrs, so let's give them what they want."

He continued. "I'm reading American history, trying to understand their warrior mentality. They were masters of total war, surpassing the Nazis. An American senator once said to General LeMay, 'General, you told us six thousand nuclear weapons could reduce the entire Soviet Union to cinders. Why is the military asking for ten thousand?' And Lemay replied, 'Senator, I want to see the cinders dance.' Ahhh, a brilliant answer. Genius.

"Nukes are what it took for America to defeat Japan, and that's what it will take for us to defeat the Buckeyes. We can be courageous and decide now, or we can leave the tough decision to future leaders. We can end jihad tonight, or we can keep fighting until others are brave enough to make the tough choice. I argue that nuking Ohio is less evil than a never-ending war."

"You're mad! The council is mad! The caliph is mad! Everyone's too impatient and has gone insane. Evil has taken hold to the point that you can't see it!"

"'Cinders dance,' my friend," General Abdullah replied. "Let us reason together and hear the brilliant clarity in those two simple words. If cinders dance, there will be peace, and sharia will rule the world. It's the moral thing to do. All we need is the courage to make the cinders dance. Do we have the fortitude to turn Ohio into dancing cinders and rebuild it in our image? Do we end jihad tonight? We can bring the Global Caliphate to completion and welcome Isa. The final decision is in our hands."

"It's wrong," Colonel Mahami insisted.

"You sound so certain. How can you be so certain?"

"I trust in Allah. He makes me certain."

"Your certainty proclaims your ignorance! As a colonel, you should know better. Certainty is a luxury for women, children, the faithful, and soldiers. Leaders never have the luxury of certainty. Know that. Know that no matter what I decide, no one except Allah will know if I made the right decision."

"I believe in the teachings of Allah, the Qur'an, and the Hadith. I've fought for Islam my entire life, General, like you. And I believe that killing millions of innocent people with atomic weapons is evil."

"War is evil, and we have the power to end it tonight."

"I've shared my advice, sir. I don't have anything else to say without repeating myself. I just pray with all my heart that you hear me and that Allah guides you in making the right decision."

In the distance, they heard a man's voice singing, haunting and enticing. It was the call to prayer from a nearby mosque. The song carried across the early autumn evening into the room.

"So," General Abdullah said, "the sun has set and a new day has begun. Come, let's say the sunset prayer together. Follow me."

General Abdullah stood up and Colonel Mahami followed him outside to the musalla, a gold-tiled dome held aloft by pillars that were covered in intricate, multicolored mosaic designs. The men stood beside each other under the dome on an elaborately patterned Persian rug, facing Mecca. They raised their palms in the air, crossed their arms over their chests, and prepared to say the Maghrib sunset prayer.

Colonel Mahami closed his eyes and made his intentions from the heart, trying to clear his mind, trying to calm his thoughts, and trying to focus on praying the sunset prayer sincerely. Both men clasped their hands over their hearts.

General Abdullah began to sing in Arabic, his voice low and melodic:

Allah is the Greatest
In the name of Allah,

Most Gracious, Most Merciful

All praise is due to Allah,
Lord of all that exists
The Most Gracious, The Most Merciful

Master of the Day of Judgement
You alone we worship,
and You alone we ask for help

Guide us to the Straight Way
The way of those on whom
you have bestowed Your Grace

Not the way of those
who earned Your Anger,
nor of those who went astray

Amen

The men moved into different positions during the prayer—bowing, raising their arms, prostrating themselves on the floor with their foreheads touching the ground, then standing, always facing Mecca, never looking left or right. Their bodies knew the ceremonial movements and poses by instinct—more than instinct because they had practiced the recitations and positions five times a day since they were children.

In the name of Allah,
Most Gracious, Most Merciful
Verily, man is at a loss

Except those that believe
and do righteous good deeds,
and recommend one another to the truth

Allah is the Greatest
Glory be to my Lord, the Most Great
Glory be to my Lord, the Most Great
Glory be to my Lord, the Most Great

Allah hears those who praise Him
Praise is due to our Lord
Allah is the Greatest

Glory be to my Lord, the Most High
Glory be to my Lord, the Most High
Glory be to my Lord, the Most High
Allah is the Greatest

My Lord, forgive me

The prayer continued with the general's solemn singing carrying through the Ohio night, quieting the crickets who seemed to stop and listen. Lightning bugs winked yellow lights around them and Colonel Mahami imagined the insects were the *jinn*, supernatural spirits gathering to listen to the sunset prayer.

Did the jinn know what would happen tonight? Many suspected they could see the future. The decision was completely in the general's hands, Colonel Mahami realized, and he didn't envy his superior. He felt a moment of hesitant comfort that it wasn't his responsibility, and he was proud of himself for giving honest advice, for not giving in to the temptation to tell General Abdullah what he wanted to hear.

The prayer ended and General Abdullah sat quietly, not moving, his eyes closed. Colonel Mahami didn't want to interrupt the general's meditation, so he stayed still and listened to the night. The crickets resumed chirping and their rhythmic squawk pushed through the dark like a simple question asked over and over, a question that should have an easy answer, but didn't.

After a few more minutes, Colonel Mahami quietly left the general and walked back to the study. The study was dark except for a fire in the fireplace that a servant must have lit while they were praying. The flickering light cast shadows across the dark room, turning everything into black silhouettes.

General Abdullah came in less than ten minutes later. He sat down on the sofa, leaned back, closed his eyes, and spoke with them still closed. "It's done. I've given the order. I was unsure of my decision before you came. But our conversation convinced me to choose the courageous path. We're warriors, charged by Allah to win the jihad. I heard your counsel and prayed for wisdom. I prayed harder than I've ever prayed in my life."

He paused and opened his eyes. "I notified the Supreme Council that tonight nuclear warheads will fall across Ohio, wiping out everything. It's done."

Colonel Mahami couldn't believe his ears. "But we need to evacuate our men! All our people!"

"No. We will all be martyrs. The rebels have spies everywhere. They may already know we're contemplating this, and they will certainly know if we try even the smallest evacuation. They'd evacuate also and regroup to carry on.

"You and I are the only ones on this continent who know my decision, and I'm saying goodbye to you, my dear friend. I'll stay here and perish in the flame, joining the martyrs. I'm old. I've seen everything I wanted to see, and too many things that no man should. I pray I will be in Jannah tonight; may Allah have mercy on my soul.

"Now, I order you to evacuate. Missiles will land on Ohio in about an hour, and each warhead has a blast radius of thirty kilometers. Leave immediately. Follow Interstate Seventy, straight east, max speed, on autopilot. You'll make it to Claysville, Pennsylvania, two hundred twenty-five kilometers from here, just outside the reach of the thermal radiation. You can pull over there and watch the cinders dance. You'll get hot and probably have cancer in a few years, but you'll survive. Stay away from buildings and glass. Leave now and you'll make it."

"No! I'll stay and perish beside you and my men."

"No. You need to survive and lead our mujahideen in the new world, when our entire earth will be Islamic and we're ready to welcome Isa. You're promoted to general. I informed the Council that I've ordered you to evacuate and promoted you to lead the rebuilding."

"Sir, I don't know what to say. I don't agree with these decisions, but if that is your order, I will follow it. I will do the best I can for you. I promise."

"You're the best man for it and we're lucky to have you. And you will be able to see your family after this is over."

Colonel Mahami felt reluctant joy flood his heart, rolling over the terror. Yes, he would see beautiful Gisele and his children again. Thank you, Allah. He wouldn't be crucified for losing the war. He would be a general, leading after victory. *Perhaps this is Allah's will,* he reflected. General Abdullah, the Supreme Council, and the caliph were all united in their decision. Maybe, just maybe, everything was happening exactly as Allah willed it.

Redneck Interlude

المتخلف الفاصل

Rodney, the evening guard commander, said, "I'm sorry to bother you, sir, but an informant's here. It's that blues guy, Sylvester, and he says it's urgent."

"Who's here? What? Ugh." Major Dusty Talbott had been lost in thought, thinking he shouldn't have drank so much. When in the hell would he ever get smart enough to just have one or two?

But the guitars came out after dinner and they started singing gospel, then Johnny Cash, and then Tom Petty. He couldn't help getting all riled up and the next thing you know, three of them had almost polished off a handle of bourbon. Idiot. Well, he'd pay for it the next two days, starting now apparently.

"What is it? What's he saying?"

"He says he has to talk to you in person, sir."

Raejean was nearby, looking at Dusty through her brown bangs. "What's goin' on? Are the kids okay?"

"It's all good, honey. Work stuff."

"Is everythin' okay?"

"Yeah."

"Kay," she said and came closer. "You smell like a still." She kissed him on the forehead and walked away.

Dusty turned back to Rodney, the guard. "Okay, okay. Hold on. Let me clear my head and I'll be out there."

He picked up his belt from the wall hook, his gun and hunting knife holstered on it. He checked that the nine-millimeter was loaded, flipped off the safety, and put it back in the holster. He looked at himself in the mirror—his eyes looked like raw meat and he really needed a shave and a haircut. *I'm getting to look as ragged as one of the dog humpers*, he chuckled to himself. *I just need a turban. But first things first. Let's see what's going on.*

He went into the family room where several men were standing around, Redneck guards with their guns out, surrounding a short, obese turncoat with jet-black hair who called himself Sylvester, one of their best spies.

Sylvester kept giving them solid intel, and in return they kept feeding him money, booze, pot, and blues. The guy had swallowed the hook on blues. Tough monkey, since his towel-head bosses would crucify him when he was found out. And blues-heads always slipped eventually. In the meantime, the guy was feeding them so much good info, it was like Allah himself was texting what would happen next.

A guard handed Dusty a cup of coffee and an already lit home-rolled cigarette.

"Thanks," Dusty said. He took a gulp of coffee, dragged on the cigarette, and felt the caffeine and nicotine blast through his brain, clearing away the bourbon fatigue.

He looked at the spy. "Okay, Sylvester. What's so hot to trot that we gotta talk tonight? Can't you ever bother those Amish bastards instead? They don't got your pills, do they? So, what's up? Some big surprise attack? Or you just need an emergency fix?"

Sylvester said, "Major, I have news about an attack tonight. From the butler at General A's. They're planning big attacks tonight across the entire state. First, can your guy help me? I'm so nervous I can't think."

Dusty nodded at a guard, who brought the man a shot glass of moonshine, a baggie with a dozen dark-blue capsules, and a stack of gold dinar coins. Sylvester put the coins in his pocket, took out two of the pills, swallowed them down with half the booze, then said, "Their plan is to nuke the whole state, destroy everything. He believes missiles are inbound tonight, that there's only a few hours before they land."

"That's crazy. Nukes? They'd never do that! Why would they do that?"

"To finally win."

"They'd kill themselves, you idiot. They'd kill themselves and a lot of innocent people, and the whole country will revolt. They aren't that stupid. They didn't conquer the entire world without having some sense. And they never used nukes when facing tougher bastards than us. Hell, they beat the Russians and the United States with just tea and Kalashnikovs. You think they're gonna nuke us? Nah, that General Abdullah's too smart. He knows he's got turncoats in the pipes and he's shoveling a lot of rotten manure into them. They're onto you, don't you realize that? Your head's so clogged up with blue dope, you ain't thinkin' straight. The general knows they got big leaks, so he's feeding people a bunch of stinking manure and then sittin' back, sniffin' to see where the crap oozes out. I betcha they followed you here, stupid."

Sylvester said earnestly, "Sir, the Supreme Council and the caliph himself authorized these attacks, and they are tonight! Nukes across the whole state to end jihad once and for all!"

Dusty replied, "Yeah, right. Maybe they'll put saddles on the missiles so Isa and Mahdi can ride 'em like broncos. The judgement day posse is ridin' into town!"

The Redneck men laughed.

Dusty said, "Okay, well, what else you got?"

"That's it. That's it."

"Okay, well, it's nothing. You ripped us off again. Take what we gave you and go."

"Fine, Major. But I'm leaving the state. I'm getting out of here because I want to live. Can I take a bottle too? If you all stay here, you're never going to see me again."

"Okay, sure. Hook him up," Dusty said to a guard, who went into the pantry and came back with a bottle of corn whiskey. The spy took it and left.

Dusty looked at Rodney. "What do you think?"

"He's been right every time. And he don't seem to be lyin'. But it's tough to believe they'd kill themselves to kill us. Maybe they are tryin' to catch him, like you said. Or trick us. But maybe somethin's up."

"Possibly. They'd never use nukes, no way, right? But I agree somethin' could be up. They're tryin' to throw us off. Alert everyone; get all the teams up, on watch and in position. Send Griz's company south, out of state, with some women and kids, just in case. Right now, head over to Moses Yoder's yourself and tell him in person what we heard. Make sure his guys know what's up and get his thoughts on the whole thing. Tell him exactly what Sylvester said and what we think so he's in the loop. Ask the Amish to go on alert with us for the next twenty-four hours while we keep an eye on what the mujahideen are up to."

"Yes, sir."

"I'm going to radio HQ and let 'em know what's up. And the next time I pour a third glass of bourbon, please remind me I'm an idiot."

Rodney laughed. "Yes, sir."

Watching the World Burn
مشاهدة العالم يحترق

Colonel Omar Mahami's new Audi ship raced east, across the Ohio countryside towards Pennsylvania at more than two-hundred-fifty kilometers per hour. The dashboard clock showed the time, counting forward until the Ohio doomsday. He was on schedule to escape the blast radius if he maintained this speed.

His terrified euphoria from earlier was subsiding and turning into something different. A placid feeling settled through him and made him feel detached from everything. Soon, in less than an hour, everything around him would be gone. He was the only part of everything around him that would still exist, and he was the only part of everything around him that knew that.

He needed to think. He needed to study the countryside and remember it because soon it would all be poisonous ashes. He had several minutes to spare and decided to risk it and stop for a few moments.

He pressed a button and the ship slowed, pulled over, and stopped on a hillside. He got out and stood, looking out over the cornfields with stalks ripe for harvest and the hayfields with fat bales rolled up, ready for the barns.

He was in Buckeye territory for sure, surrounded by Amish farms and dirt roads. He was wide open to attack, but it didn't matter anymore, did it? All the fighting for all time was about to end. He left his body armor and helmet in the ship. Everything was Allah's will now. Everything.

The sun was below the purple horizon, lighting up the dusk in a golden hour of twilight. He listened to the birds saying their goodnights, he studied the brilliant autumn leaves, and he checked the time. Soon. This world would end soon. So soon.

A thought came to him. Maybe he shouldn't run to Pennsylvania. Maybe he should stay here, watch the apocalypse, and die in the fire. Maybe he should join the millions of martyrs.

He remembered that girl on the swing from his childhood in Afghanistan. Was there a young American girl somewhere on a swing right now? His mind's eye imagined her on a playground in western Pennsylvania, close enough to see the destruction but far enough away to survive, swinging and looking west.

She was swinging gently, looking right now into the Midwestern sunset, her banana-seat bicycle parked close by. Soon she'd become a pitch-black silhouette in the apocalyptic flash and watch millions of people burn alive in a bright moment.

He hoped so. He prayed to Allah that somewhere a young girl would watch this world burn, and swing and swing and keep swinging, watching and still swinging because none of it really mattered. Innocent children would become dancing cinders while she watched from the playground, and yet there was no worry on her face because nothing could be done to change anything, and so everything was perfect.

When it was over, she'd get back on her banana-seat bicycle and go home to eat dinner with her family. And tomorrow would be a brand-new day. The first day of world peace under the Global Islamic Caliphate.

Colonel Mahami decided he would die here, watching. He would watch Ohio end and he would end with it. As he perished in the fire, a reign of love and peace would begin, and soon Isa would return.

He leaned against the ship and watched the twilight horizon, entranced, and a while later he saw streaks in the sky, like hundreds of comets descending, then bright white and silver flashes, and then cataclysmic booms.

White light was everywhere, and he saw clouds racing for the sky, launching faster than rockets. The clouds burst into the sky and raced outward at the top, turning into rocketing mushrooms that grew and grew. A warm wind blew on his face—warmer, then hot, then hotter.

Horrendous flashes scratched apart the sky; a tremendous blast wave slammed him into his ship, making him stumble and he couldn't stand up, he couldn't get his balance, as if the world was jerking out of orbit. Stupendous balls of fire rose from the earth, belching forth enormous pillars of white smoke inside orange fire, thousands of kilometers high, shooting skyward with accelerating speed.

He saw the pillars shoot upward, erupting out of the earth, becoming more alive as they climbed skyward through the white clouds. The pillars became living things, a new species born right before his incredulous eyes.

The pillars began to look like totem poles, kilometers wide and higher than the clouds. They were alive, their fire and smoke carved with grotesque faces and creatures that laughed and screamed, grimacing down at the earth, like monsters in the act of breaking any bonds that held them down. They freed themselves and flew upward with tremendous speed, their momentum carrying them closer to the stratosphere.

Then, like demons growing new heads, new mushroom clouds shot out of the tops of the totem poles. The mushroom tops were even more alive than their totem pillars, seething and boiling in a white fury of creamy foam, sizzling upwards and then descending earthward, a million geysers rolled into one.

Now red and orange exploded in an unquenchable flame, consuming the world in an instant. Everything stopped, then disappeared. The trees, corn, birds, apples, hay bales, animals, and farmhouses were gone. Everything sown for centuries was reaped in a moment.

Mother Nature vanished for a time, taking a respite, resting before the rebuilding to come. Time stopped, then it disappeared, and everything became eternal.

As soon as the fire came towards him, hundreds of stories high, it was all around him. The road lit on fire first, and then everything was on fire.

Colonel Mahami screamed.

The war for Ohio is over, he thought. We won. We won. We won. Now the Islamic Caliphate will rule the entire earth. Now Isa will return. And soon I will be in paradise.

Colonel Omar Mahami's final terrified thought was that he was almost certain.

السلام عليكم

or Victory

Air raid sirens, roaring planes
overture before the flames
Bombs descend from the iron sky
blessed are the first to die
Then children burn and mothers scream
paradise in a demon dream

Wonder if there is somehow
murder that God won't allow
Or maybe it's supposed to be
humanity or victory

Politicians write the script
we each play our part in it
Monsters frolic in corporate suits
insisting we support the troops
Preaching peace is constant war
means kill until there are no more

Wonder if there is somehow
horror that we won't allow
Or maybe it's supposed to be
humanity or victory

Victory is annihilation
Satan struts, God vacations
Love is nowhere on the path
of triumph planned with war room math
Tallied corpses score the match
dead children counted one by batch

Wonder if there is somehow
anything that I won't allow
Or maybe it's supposed to be
humanity or victory

ACKNOWLEDGEMENTS

Thanks so much to first readers and editors for their valuable suggestions including Morgan Macedo from Glasswing Editing, Megan Blackmore, and Hannah Skaggs. Thanks to Milan Jiram for sharing his amazing artwork.

ABOUT THE AUTHOR

Benjamin L. Owen lives in New England. He is the author of *Quantumnition* and *Last Way West*. His favorite writers include Mark Twain, Phillip K. Dick, and J.D. Salinger. He can be contacted at benl.owen@yahoo.com

ABOUT THE AUTHOR

Made in United States
North Haven, CT
13 August 2022

22687961R00150